At the mental hospital, I saw a boy slumped in a chair. He wore hospital scrubs and a white robe with slippers. And when I got close enough, I took off my sunglasses and knelt in front of him—crying.

It was White Bird.

His keen dark eyes were glazed over and empty. *Dead.* With his arms limp, he stared into a world only he could see.

And it broke my heart to see him so lost.

"Oh, my God. What have they done to you?" I whispered, not recognizing my own voice. "What have I done?"

* * *

Praise for *USA TODAY* bestselling author JORDAN DANE

"*In the Arms of Stone Angels* is eerie, dark and rich with unforgettable characters. A page-turning suspense story that will haunt you long after you finish it. Jordan Dane is a fresh new voice in young adult paranormal fiction."
—P.C. Cast, *New York Times* bestselling author of the House of Night series

"Deliciously dark! Gritty and suspenseful, *In the Arms of Stone Angels* is a new take on the paranormal. One of the most compelling and honest voices in young adult fiction!"
—Sophie Jordan, *New York Times* bestselling author of *Firelight*

in the arms of stone angels

Jordan Dane

HARLEQUIN® TEEN

HARLEQUIN® TEEN

Recycling programs for this product may not exist in your area.

ISBN-13: 978-0-373-21029-9

IN THE ARMS OF STONE ANGELS

This edition published by arrangement with Harlequin Books S.A.

For questions and comments about the quality of this book please contact us at Customer_eCare@Harlequin.ca.

www.HarlequinTEEN.com

Printed in U.S.A.

To my niece, Dana—a kindred spirit
(and lab rat when you thought I wasn't looking).

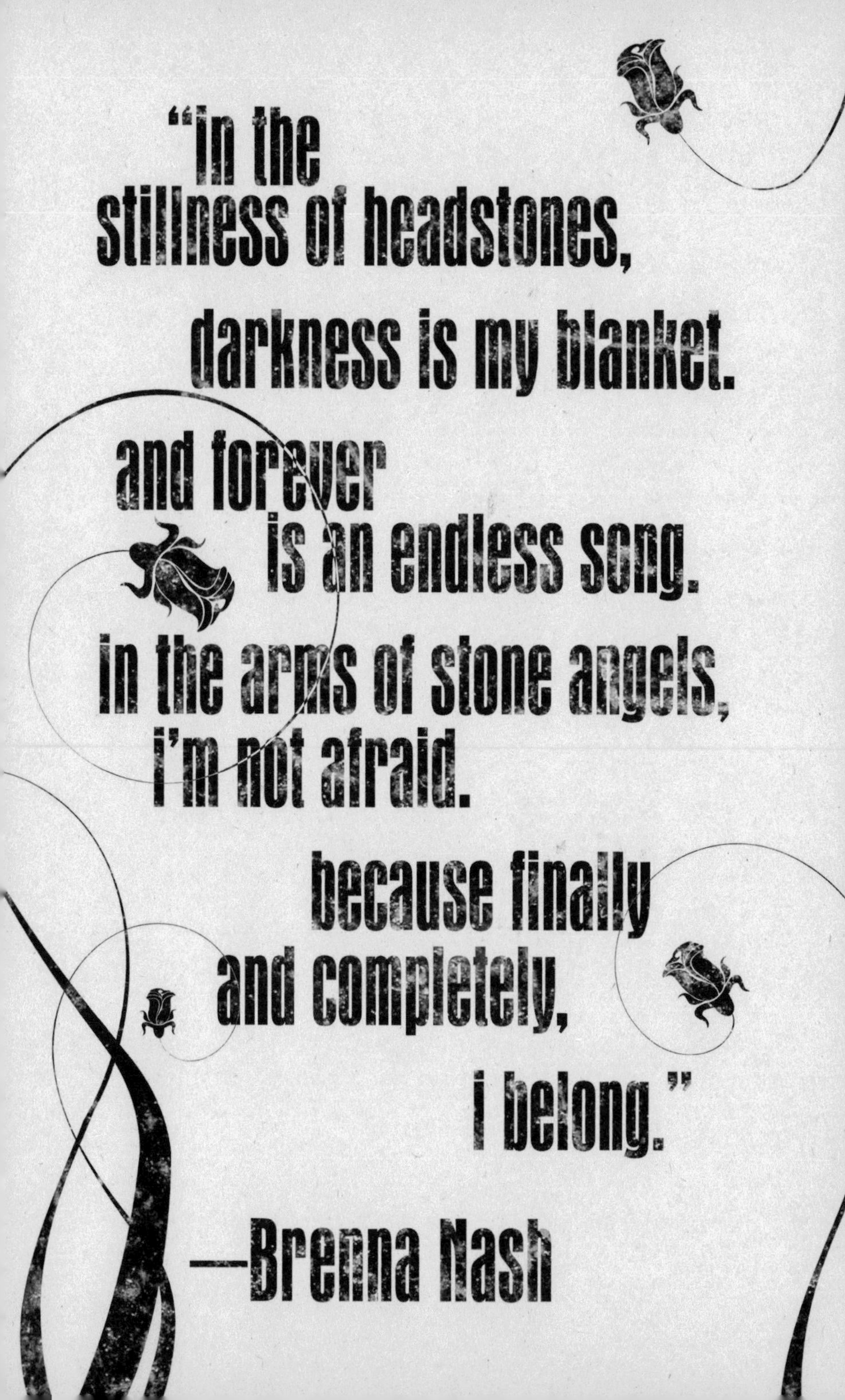
"in the
stillness of headstones,
darkness is my blanket.
and forever
is an endless song.
in the arms of stone angels,
i'm not afraid.
because finally
and completely,
i belong."
—Brenna Nash

prologue

I sleep with the dead.

I don't remember the first time I did it and I try not to think about why. It's just something I do. My fascination with the dead has become part of me, like the way my middle toes jut out. They make my feet look like they're shooting the finger 24/7. My "screw you" toes are my best feature, but that doesn't mean I brag about them. Those babies are kept under wraps—just for my entertainment—the same way I keep my habit of sleeping in cemeteries a secret from anyone. Not even my mother knows I sneak out at night to curl up with the headstones...and the stillness. Some things are best left unsaid.

In the arms of stone angels, I'm not afraid.

I wish I had remembered the part about not telling secrets when I came across my friend White Bird under the bridge at Cry Baby Creek. A woman's spirit cries for her dead baby and haunts that old rusted steel-and-wood plank footbridge. I'd seen her plenty of times, I swear to God. She never talked to me. The dead never do. She only cried and clutched the limp body of her baby to her chest.

Back then I didn't fully understand how fragile the barrier was between my world and another existence where the dead grieved over their babies forever. And I had no idea that a change was coming. Someone would alter how I saw the thin veil between my reality and the vast world beyond it.

And that someone was my friend, White Bird.

When I saw him crying in the shadows of that dry creek bed, just like the ghost of that woman, the sight of him sent chills over my skin. I should have paid attention to what my body was telling me back then—to stay away and leave him alone—but I didn't.

He was rocking in the shadows and muttering words I didn't understand. When I got closer, I saw he wasn't alone, but I couldn't see the girl's face. And tears were running down his cheeks. They glistened in the gray of morning, at the razor's edge of dawn. I wish I had stayed where I was that day—hiding in the dark—but my curiosity grabbed me and wouldn't let go.

Like an omen, the buzz of flies should have warned me. And thinking back, I wish that I had paid more attention to the sound. Even now, a single housefly can trigger that dark memory. And on nights when the dead can't comfort me to sleep, I still hear the unending noise of those flies and I think of him. Our paths had crossed that day for a reason, as if it was always meant to be, and both of us were powerless to stop it.

I remember that morning like it was yesterday and I can't get him out of my head.

White Bird was the first boy I ever loved. He was a half-breed, part Euchee Indian and part whatever. He was an outcast like me, only I couldn't claim anything cool like being Indian. Because he was half-breed and without parents, the Euchee didn't officially claim him, but that didn't matter to White Bird. In his heart he belonged to the *Dala,* the bear clan of the tribe, because the bear represented the power of Mother Earth. And the strong animal was a totem sign of the healer. The way I saw it, he had picked his clan well.

In school, the teachers called him by his white name, Isaac Henry. But when it was just the two of us, he preferred I call him by his Indian name and that made me feel real special. He was different from the other boys. I was convinced he had an ancient soul. He was quiet and didn't speak much, even to me. But when he did open his mouth, the other kids listened and so did I.

Some people were scared of him because he was taller and bigger than most of the boys and he kept to himself. Sometimes he would get into fights. But after he got his tribal band tattoos, the fights stopped and everyone left him alone, including his teachers. His tattoos made him look like a man. And that was fine by me.

He wore his dark hair long to his shoulders and his eye color had flecks of gold and green that reminded me of a field of wheat blowing easy in the Oklahoma wind. And his skin made me think of a golden swirl of sweet caramel. That's how I thought of him before the nightmare happened. He dominated my mind like a tune I couldn't get out of my head, something memorable and special.

White Bird was my first crush.

And in a perfect world, my first crush should have been unforgettable and magic. But when mine turned out to be the worst nightmare of my pathetic excuse for a life, I knew I'd never deserve to be happy and that magic was overrated.

And as for White Bird being unforgettable, the day I saw him under that bridge covered in blood and ranting like a crazed meth head over a girl's corpse with a knife in his hand, I knew that image would be burned into my brain forever.

It was highly unlikely that I'd forget him and I made sure he'd never forget me. I was the one who turned him in to the sheriff.

chapter one

Charlotte, North Carolina

Two nights before Mom kidnapped me and screwed up my summer, she told me I was going with her. I didn't want to go back to Oklahoma, but she said I was too young to stay home alone. The real truth was that she didn't trust me. I'd given her plenty of reasons to feel that way. And I had the razor scars to prove it. After she told me, I screamed into her face until I shook all over.

"You never listen. When are you gonna stop blaming me for what happened?" I wanted to throw something. *Anything!* Instead I turned my back on her and headed for my room.

"You come back here, Brenna. We're not done." My mom yelled after me, but I knew she wouldn't follow.

Not this time.

My heart was pounding and my face felt swollen and hot. I had been out of control and couldn't stop my rage. And when I got in my mother's face, I had seen myself yelling like I was outside my body. From behind my eyes—in the heat of the moment—I usually don't remember much. But this time I was outside looking down. And I saw my mom's disappointment.

I knew she was afraid of me—and for me. And I still couldn't stop.

I'm a freak. I'm toxic. I don't know how to change and I'm not sure I want to. When I got to my room, I slammed my door so hard that a framed photo of my dead grandmother fell off a wall in the hallway. The glass shattered into a million pieces.

I didn't clean it up.

I wouldn't.

In my bathroom, I puked until I had nothing left but dry heaves. Whenever I felt like everything was out of control—that my life wasn't my own—that's when I usually hurled. I knew getting sick wasn't normal, but I didn't care. I refused to let Mom in on my little self-inflicted wound. I didn't want the attention.

When I went to bed that night, I wanted to be alone, but I felt my mom in the house. Hiding in the dark of my bedroom wasn't enough. And when the tears came, I couldn't stand being inside anymore. I slipped out my window in my boxers and tank top, like I usually do, and ran into the open field behind my house toward the old cemetery.

I didn't make it to the stone angels.

I ran, screaming, until my throat hurt. I knew no one would come and no one could hear me, but I wasn't sure anyone would care if I kept running. When I finally dropped to my knees, I collapsed onto my back and stared up into the stars. My chest was heaving and sweat poured off my body, making the cuts on my bare legs sting. Brambles and weeds had torn up my skin, but the pain wasn't enough.

It was never enough.

My mom had given me no choice. In two days, we'd drive back to Shawano, a town in Oklahoma that I couldn't leave fast enough when I was fourteen.

Just thinking about going back—even after two years—made me sick. I couldn't catch my breath, no matter how hard I tried. I was dizzy and my chest hurt real bad. And when I thought I would die, I was surprised at how hard I fought to breathe. I had to think about something else, to stop from getting sick again.

That's when my thoughts turned to White Bird and I pictured his face the way I remembered him from before. Seeing him in my mind calmed me even though being involved with him back then had gotten me into trouble. People in Shawano already saw both of us as losers. And my turning him in to Sheriff Logan didn't change that.

In fact, it made things worse. The sheriff connected the dots and interrogated me as an accomplice. He just didn't understand how wrong he was.

Reporting the murder had torn me apart. I couldn't believe White Bird, a boy I trusted with everything that I was, could do such a thing. Seeing him that day made me question everything I believed about him. And I'd never seen a dead body before. The sight had terrified me. I had to tell what I saw. I couldn't just walk away and pretend it didn't happen. But in the seconds it took me to call 911—trying to do the right thing—my life would change forever. And there was no way for me to know how bad it would get.

After the sheriff cleared me, I was released and never

charged, but that didn't mean I was innocent in the eyes of everyone in town. And it didn't mean my mom wouldn't feel the pain of guilt by association. Her real estate business dried up and I knew she blamed me.

I never liked that boy. Now look what you've done.

I heard her words over and over in my head. And I can still see the look in my grandmother's eyes the day we left Oklahoma and moved to North Carolina. I talked to my grandmother on the phone plenty, but I heard it in her voice. Even Grams had lost faith and she died not believing in me. Not even the stone angels gave me comfort the day she left this world behind. And when I didn't go to her funeral—because I believed Grams wouldn't want me there—I think my mother was relieved.

Now my mom had to settle my grandmother's estate and get her old house ready to sell. At least that's what she gave me as the reason we had to drive back. I'm not sure I believed her. I was more convinced that she wanted to torture me for what I had done to her life, too.

Lying on my back in the field, I stared into the universe and its gazillion winks of light and made a pact that I would never lie to the stars or make promises I wouldn't keep. Whatever I promised under the night sky should be honest and true because stars were ancient beings that watched over the planet. They wouldn't judge me. Every star was a soul who had died and broken free after they'd learned the lesson they had been born to master.

Me? I was in remedial class. I had more than a lifetime to go. Plus I had a feeling some Supreme Being had me in detention, too. So, speaking the truth, I had to admit that a part of me wanted to go back and see what had happened to White Bird.

But a darker, scarier part wished I'd been the one he had killed under that bridge. And that was the honest to God truth.

Three Days Later on I-40—Morning

"You hungry? There's a truck stop ahead. We can get some breakfast."

My mother's voice jarred me. On day two of our trip, I'd been staring out the car window watching nothing but fence posts, scrub brush and billboards fade into early-morning oblivion. Not even my fascination with friggin' roadkill had brought me out of my waking coma. And I hadn't spoken much to Mom since she'd told me about this road trip to hell.

"Whatever." I mumbled so she'd have to ask me what I'd said.

She never did.

Mom filled up the tank of our Subaru and pulled in front of a small truck stop café. Inside, the place smelled like cigarette smoke and old grease. And as I expected, everyone stared at me. I was used to it. I wasn't your average Abercrombie girl. I didn't wear advertising brand names on my body.

It was a life choice. *A religion.*

I got my clothes from Dumpster diving and Goodwill, anything I could stitch together that would make my own statement. Today I wore a torn jean jacket over a sundress with leggings that I'd cut holes into. And I had a plaid scarf draped around my neck with a cap pulled down on my head. My "screw you" toes were socked away in unlaced army boots. And I hid behind a huge pair of dark aviator sunglasses, a signature accessory and only one in a weird collection I carried with me. I liked the anonymity of me seeing out when no one saw in.

The overall impact was that I looked like an aspiring bag lady. A girl's got to have goals.

In short, I didn't give a shit about fitting in with the masses and it showed. I'd given up the idea of fitting in long ago. The herd mentality wasn't for me. And since I made things up as I went, people staring came with the territory. Mom picked a spot by a window and I shuffled my boots behind her and slid into the booth.

I grabbed a menu on the table and pretended to look at it while I played with my split ends.

"Do you have to do that here?"

"Do what?"

Neither one of us expected an answer.

I seriously hated my hair. It was long, thin and stringy, like me. A washed-out blond color that bordered on red. In the frickin' sun I looked like my damned head was on fire.

"You ready to order?" The waitress didn't even pretend to smile.

I asked for nachos with chili and my mom ordered a salad and coffee. Neither of us had a firm grasp of the term *breakfast.* It was one of the few things we had in common. While we waited for our food, Mom opened a valve to her stream of consciousness. Guess the quiet drive made her feel entitled to cut loose. And her talkative mood didn't change after we got our order. She jumped from one topic to another with her one-sided conversation, spewing words into the void like people do on Twitter.

Me? I scribbled in a spiral notebook while she talked. I always had a notepad stuffed in my knapsack and a collection of old notes piled in my closet back in North Carolina. Whenever

I got an idea for clothes I wanted to make or a line of poetry or a lyric that got stuck in my head and wouldn't come out until I wrote it down, that's what usually went on paper. All I was working on now was a layered hoodie skirt thingee that was beginning to look an awful lot like a Snuggie. It looked like crap, but I probably wasn't drawing it right. Maybe Dana would wear it.

My only real friend in NC was Dana Biggers, who'd been texting me. She was okay, tolerable even. I hadn't written her back. She was asking too many questions about my trip and I didn't want to explain it, thinking I might tell her too much. I'd worked hard at keeping my old life in Oklahoma a mystery. I had wanted to reinvent myself and start over. Texting her back might ruin that, so I didn't. She'd get over it.

Dana was Wiccan and she practiced magic 24/7. Because of her, I got a B- in biology this term. It was the only class we shared, so I figured she had the goods if she could deliver one shining moment in a lifetime of my underachievement. We both needed extra credit, so after we dissected our frog, we took the teacher's challenge and removed the brain whole. I used a blade, but Dana got her Wiccan mojo on and chanted her part. The frog's brain squished out in one piece. The teacher shook his head, but gave us the credit anyway.

Dana swears that I was a witch in another life. Who am I to argue with that? I know she's full of shit, but she lets me make clothes for her and she doesn't laugh when I read her my old poems. Like I said, she was okay. Kind of cool, actually.

Since I'd left Oklahoma, I hadn't written anything. I missed it, but I had a hole in me that I couldn't fill with poetry or music or making clothes. And unlike Mom and what she was doing now, words didn't come easy for me, not after what had happened two years ago.

Although I couldn't be certain, I figured Mom's talking was her way of making an effort to bond. And I had to give her props for timing. I was captive in a moving vehicle for two days. And if she didn't give me a brain bleed from the ritual, she had a pretty good shot at nabbing my attention once in a while. Picking at my nachos, I'd only heard every six and a half words as I scribbled until she finally got my full attention.

"You know…I heard that boy is still locked away in a mental hospital outside Shawano." Mom kept her face down and shoveled her fork like she was being timed. And her talking about White Bird, and referring to him as "that boy," had forced me to listen, especially when she said, "They say he never came out of it."

I stopped scribbling. Cold.

Parents always had "they" to back them up. And "they" were always right. Kids had squat. It was hard to compete with "they." I wanted to roll my eyes because I knew that would piss her off, but I got to thinking about White Bird and what "still" meant.

"Still? You mean he's been there since…" I couldn't finish. All this time, after I had moved away and taken my miserable butt to North Carolina, White Bird had been locked away. Knowing that twisted my gut into a knot. I felt worse than I ever did before.

And that was saying something.

"Yes. That's why you were never asked to testify. His case never went to trial because of his…condition," Mom explained.

I had been so wrapped in my own misery that I had missed the obvious. Mom was right. And I'd never asked about going to court, to say what had happened. I should have known.

I should have thought about what that meant for him, but I never did.

"Why didn't you…" *Tell me! Tell me! Tell me!* I wanted to scream, but instead I turned to look out at the parking lot and said, "Never mind."

All I wanted to do was lash out at Mom and blame her for my frustration. I knew it wasn't fair, but I also knew she'd let me get away with it.

White Bird had never gotten his day in court. Where had he gone? Was he still inside his head, unable to find his way out of a dark maze? Or had he clicked off like a light switch, never to return? What had happened that night to cause such trauma?

"He never says anything. That boy just sits and stares at nothing." Mom looked up from her salad, making sure I got the point. "Maybe next time you'll listen to me when I tell you some kid isn't right in the head."

Mom always knew how to throw cold water on me. Plus her timing sucked. And although she didn't come right out and say it, her eyes were filled with the message "I told you so." I resented her smugness, her certainty that being an adult always made her right, but I didn't have much going for my side of the argument. With White Bird branded as a crazed lunatic, that was one point for Mom.

Zip for me.

"I'm not afraid of him," I said as I chewed my thumbnail and stared out the window into the bright sunlight from behind my shades. If it were dark and the stars were out, I'd never let me get away with lying.

"Well, you should be, young lady."

White Bird had given me plenty of reason to be afraid. And what had happened two years ago would always be with me.

I still had trouble sleeping through the night. In many of my dreams, I was the one he stabbed. I watched him do it, over and over. And each time I felt the pain like it was real. I tried to get away, but I couldn't move. Everything slowed to a crawl like I was sinking into quicksand and heavy mud oozed down my throat so I couldn't scream.

I'd never told my mom about my nightmares. I had screwed up so much already, guess I never wanted her to know that I couldn't handle it. And since I was sneaking out of the house at night, she never heard me cry in my sleep. But every time I had those bad dreams, I thought about White Bird and how we first met.

It calmed me to remember a time when things were simpler, but inside I ached with regret for not being a better friend to him.

It was hard for me to imagine being thirteen after everything that had happened, but that was how old I was when I'd first met White Bird three years ago. I used to spend hours away from home, mostly walking through old graveyards and reading headstones or playing along the creek that backed up to our house in Shawano. I only tolerated Facebook and wasn't into the latest video on YouTube or chatting up virtual strangers. I loved being outdoors, even though most kids made fun of me. To them I was a skinny weird geek who hung out with dead people.

The town kids laughed at me. And I pretended not to care.

One afternoon I found a bird with a broken wing by the creek. It was flopping on the ground near the water and chirping, struggling to get away from a calico cat that was stalking it. The cat was flicking its tail and was ready to pounce. One second later and that bird would have been dead meat. And I would have witnessed a bent version of the circle of life, with me having a ringside seat to something I didn't want to see.

"Git!" I yelled. "Leave it alone."

I waved my hands to scare the cat away. It hissed at me and eyed the bird one more time before it took off into the bushes. I was left with a hurt bird and had to catch it to bring it home.

I bent over to scoop it in my hands—trying not to hurt it more than it already was—but the scared little thing thrashed around until I thought it would die. The bird was frantic and I was afraid it would keel over from shock. In that bird's eyes, I was scarier than the cat and way bigger.

But a husky voice stopped me.

"Don't chase it. Make it come to you."

I turned and let out a scream. I'm sure I looked like a lunatic, all wide-eyed and frightened like that panting little bird.

"Back off…or I'll scream. And I'll kick you in the nuts. I swear to God, I'll do it." I threatened him and tried to look as if I knew where his nuts were, with my heart pounding out of control.

"Thanks for the warning." He grinned.

I had to remind myself to breathe. Sure I was still scared, but something about this boy tickled a feeling deep in my belly. My stomach was doing flip-flops like hitting the peak of the roller coaster and barreling down the track out of control. And I wanted to hold on to the feeling, but I made the mistake of glancing down.

I was trapped inside the body of a thirteen-year-old girl dressed in neon blue shorts with matching shoes and a floral top that looked like I'd barfed bright yellow daisies down my flat chest. And to make things worse, I smelled like creek water and I had deliberately wiped my muddy hands all over my lame outfit—the only retaliation I had against my mother's taste. At the time I thought coming home caked in mud would be funny, but at that very moment…not so much.

The boy at the creek wasn't much older than I was, but his low voice made him sound mature. He wore his straight dark hair long to his shoulders and his appearance made him stand out from anyone else I knew. Most of the boys at my school had a burr cut that looked like they wore a bowl on their heads.

He had on worn jeans cinched with a woven leather belt that was beaded, something handmade. And he had on an unusual shirt—nothing off the rack—a gray-and-white print shirt with pale blue ribbons sewn into a crisscross pattern over his chest. Strands of satin hung down, blowing in the faint breeze. I'd seen a Native American Ribbon shirt before, but not close up. The shirt matched the bead colors threaded into his leather moccasins.

And the boy's skin was dark as if he spent time in the sun. I liked that. My skin was tanned, too. He also moved with a confidence that I hadn't seen before. Boys my age roughhoused too much, but this boy wasn't afraid to be gentle. And when he kept his distance, I knew it was because he was waiting for me to get used to him being there.

"I won't hurt you." His voice was calm.

That was the first time I had seen White Bird. I found out later that he liked coming to the creek, too.

"Will you let me help?" he asked. After I nodded, he said, "Then back away and give me room."

I did as he told me. And when I was far enough away, I watched him ease near the injured bird. He had such patience and even though his hands were bigger, they weren't as clumsy as mine. He spoke to it in a language I didn't understand with his voice low. It was comforting, even to me. The bird didn't move. It stayed put—mesmerized like me—and cocked its head toward him. Eventually that little bird came to him and I'd never seen anything like it. He cradled it in his hands with such gentleness.

"You want to see it?" he said quietly.

Seeing the way he was with that small creature, I knew I didn't need to be afraid of this boy. I nodded and stepped closer to take a peek. The hurt bird had nuzzled into his hand. It was too weak to move, but it trusted him enough to close its eyes and rest.

"I'll fix its wing. You want to help?"

I grinned and nodded. A little voice in my head—mostly Mom's voice—warned me against going with him. I'd heard how perverts lured kids with missing kitties and puppies. But when I looked into this boy's eyes, I was like that bird with a busted wing and I knew he'd never hurt me.

"Hi. My name's Brenna. What's yours?" I whispered and looked up at him. He was taller than the boys I knew at school.

"In town, they call me Isaac Henry, but my Euchee name is White Bird."

"Which do you like better?"

"No one's ever asked me that." When he smiled, I did, too.

At that moment, I remember hoping he'd be my friend—a *real* friend. But if I had known then what I did now, I never would have let him near me. I would have run and not looked back.

For his sake.

* * *

"You didn't eat your nachos." Mom's voice jerked me from my daydream. *Harsh, real harsh.* I was back at that lousy truck stop and sucked into my life, having faux breakfast with my mother.

"What?"

"I said, you didn't eat much." Mom looked at me like she knew I'd been somewhere else. And she was on the verge of asking me about it, but she must have changed her mind. She scarfed cold nachos off my plate instead. "We'll be there before the sun goes down."

Was that supposed to make me feel good? She gave her ETA like it was a good thing. I felt my jaw tense and I shoved the cold nachos away. Mom had a jacked-up way of commiserating. We were both heading to a place that would have burned us at the stake in another century. And all she could do was remind me that I had until nightfall before I became the human equivalent to a S'more.

Way to go, Mom!

Shawano, Oklahoma

We turned off the interstate at dusk and I had forgotten how intense the sunsets could be here. The sun was a molten orange ball on the horizon. Even behind my sunglasses, the light made me squint and I had to raise a hand to block the glare below my visor.

Mom hadn't said much in the past hour. Either my nerves were contagious or she was dealing with her own demons. I wished her silence meant she understood, but I didn't ask. She could have been quiet because she was tired. And if I had made a big deal about her mood, she would have blown me off and refused to let me in. I was only a kid in her eyes.

"Let's stop at the grocery store. We'll need a few things before we head to Grams's," Mom said as she turned onto the main drag of Shawano.

It surprised me that she still referred to the house as belonging to my grandmother as if she was still alive and would be waiting for us to arrive. That made me ache inside and I missed my phone calls to Grams, but when I didn't say anything, Mom raised her voice.

"Did you hear me?"

"Yeah, I'm right here, duh." I rolled my eyes and grimaced out of pure reflex. I could have spared Mom the attitude after she'd driven all day, but attitude was all I had left.

The town was how I remembered it, only way smaller. Most places on Main Street looked dirty and bleached by the sun. And graffiti was the new black. Any fond memories I had were tainted by the ugliness of why I left. I had no real purpose for coming back—except to deal with my past.

I guess Mom had her reason and I had mine. And maybe we both had something to prove.

We stopped at Homeland on the way into town to pick up groceries. The few things I wanted, I tossed them in our cart and I let Mom do the rest while I headed back toward the entrance. I had seen a pay phone at the front. And where there was a pay phone, there'd be a phone book. Yes, an ancient phone book, complete with Yellow Pages.

Mom had bought me a basic phone without the bells and whistles most kids had. Guess that was another way she punished me, so I resorted to desperate measures. When I found what I wanted, I looked over my shoulder and waited until I knew I wouldn't be caught tearing a sheet out of the damned phone book. I folded the paper and slipped it into a pocket of my jean jacket.

I couldn't stay the whole night at Grams's, not when it was my first night here. I had too many things on my mind. And sleep had become a waste of time.

"Honey? You ready to go?" Mom's voice made me jump. "What were you doing?"

I turned and kept everything off my face as I helped her with the groceries.

"Nothing. I was flipping through the phone book, looking for a few friends."

"Did you find anyone you know?"

I had to give Mom credit for effort. She knew I didn't have many friends two years ago—and certainly none who had stuck by me through the worst of it—but she'd given me the benefit of the doubt. Or maybe it made her feel like a better mother if she thought she hadn't raised such a complete loser.

All I said was, "No."

In his open garage under a dim light, Derek Bast sat on his weight bench working on biceps curls when his cell phone signaled he had a text message. It was the third one he had ignored. He took his workout seriously and jumping up every time he got a call or message wasn't something he did during the off-season. His grades were only marginal. And the only way he'd get a college education was through football.

"Dude. Spot me, will ya?" His buddy Justin was setting up for the bench press and needed him to stand behind him, ready to help if he got into trouble with the larger weight.

But when another text message came within seconds of the last one, curiosity got the better of him. He hoisted up his sweatpants when he stood and wiped the sweat off his face and arms with a towel before he went looking for his phone.

"Hold on. I gotta check this." Derek glanced down at his cell to see what all the fuss was about.

911 brenna nash was at homeland tonight
why is she back???????
meet me at usual place...NOW!!!!!!

Derek grimaced and clenched his jaw when he saw the messages.

"You gotta go, Justin. Go on, beat it."

"What? I was just..."

"I said beat it, shithead!" He glared and threw his sweaty towel at the guy's face. "I got things to do."

Justin backed down and didn't argue. He wouldn't dare. He put his damned tail between his legs—like a whipped dog—and headed out without saying another word. Derek knew he had a reputation for losing his temper and it worked to his advantage. He got off on knowing people called him "Alpha Dawg" for a reason.

After Justin took off, Derek shut the garage door and headed for his bedroom to shower and change. If Brenna Nash was back in town, that bitch had the potential of screwing with his life.

And he couldn't let that happen.

By the time Mom and I got to Grams's it was almost too dark to see, but the old Victorian home was easy to spot at the end of the street. It was the biggest house on the block and not quite how I remembered it. In the past few years, Grams had let the place go. The yard and flower beds were overgrown with weeds and the house needed painting. Brick steps that led to the front door needed repair, the wraparound porch railing could use paint and the bay windows and gabled roof looked scary at night without lights on. The place was real creepy and reminded me of a slasher movie.

Very cool. I could totally shoot a video here. But I had a bad feeling the inside would need work if Mom expected to sell it.

"Wait by the car till I get in and turn on the lights." Mom had parked in the driveway and was fumbling through her purse for house keys as I got out. "No telling what it's gonna look like in there."

"Come on, Mom. What if it's gross? There could be—"

She didn't let me finish.

"If it's bad, we'll find a motel until we can do a little cleaning." She pretended to be cheery. "Where's your sense of adventure?"

"In North Carolina. I forgot to pack it." I crossed my arms and slumped against the car.

"Stay put. I'll need your help with the groceries if we stay tonight," Mom yelled over her shoulder as she headed toward the front door.

I heaved a sigh and stared up at the old Victorian after my mom left me alone on the driveway. I wasn't afraid of the dark since cemeteries were my thing, but living in small town suburbia scared the crap out of me.

Hours Later—Near Midnight

After we ate and made up our beds—at least good enough for one night—I lay in the dark listening to the creaks and groans of the old house. And I swear to God that I heard my grandmother's footsteps walk down the hall and stop by my door. That would have disturbed most people, but feeling

Grams in the house gave me comfort. It felt natural and I welcomed her spirit.

And I would have done anything to feel her brush the hair out of my eyes or tell me a story about when she was young. In the dark, I heard her laugh again and could picture her rocking like a big bowl of gelatin. *Green, my favorite flavor and the color of Grams's eyes.* In my memory and in my heart, she was alive.

But I knew I'd never see her again. She was a star in the night sky. I was sure of it.

When the house was quiet enough, I knew Mom was asleep. I crept out of my room and slipped outside. I hadn't changed my clothes, except to ditch the scarf and sunglasses and trade my old army boots for vintage Keds high-top sneakers. And I brought my trusty cell phone, like I usually did, just in case I got into trouble. Walking in the dark and breathing in the warm muggy air felt liberating compared to the old house. I picked up my pace until I was running through the streets of Shawano, heading to a place I knew well.

Pioneer Cemetery on Fifteenth Street. It didn't take me long to get there.

A wrought-iron gate marked the main entrance with the name of the cemetery on a sign overhead. And the barrier around the grounds was made of a dark mottled stone that looked like it was bleeding rust down the mortar. I wedged my foot into the stone, hoisted my leg over the wall and dropped on the other side.

The cemetery hadn't changed much.

I loved really old cemeteries, not the new kind that had no soul. Really old graveyards were like outdoor museums. And after getting familiar with where everyone was buried, a cemetery became familiar and comforting to me. And the headstones were like…family. I would read the names and wonder who they'd been or how they died. Or I made up stories about them. Being at the Pioneer Cemetery again was like coming home.

With a small flashlight that I'd taken from Mom's car, I shined a light onto the headstones in a newer section of the grounds, looking for a name. When I found it, I took a deep breath and knelt beside the grave.

I ran my fingers over the name on the marker and remembered her face, but when I tried to imagine her alive, I couldn't do it.

"I'm…sorry," I whispered. I didn't know what else to say.

I took out the page I had ripped from the phone book at Homeland and shined the light on it. The only mental hospital near Shawano was on the outskirts of town. And tomorrow I would find a way to go there. I wanted to see if what Mom had told me was true, that White Bird was in that hospital and sitting like a dead stump with vacant eyes.

I prayed my mother was wrong.

In my mind, I wished to God that I could see him again at that creek with the little bird in his hand, that tall boy barely older than me. And I tried to picture his gentle smile and soft brown eyes, but the image of him under the bridge at Cry Baby Creek—rocking back and forth and mumbling in his Euchee language—was burned into my brain.

To imagine his world frozen in that moment scared the hell out of me, but then again, I wasn't much better off than he was. My life had stopped that day, same as his. I couldn't move forward and I couldn't go back. I had to know why he did it. That was the reason I had to come to the cemetery tonight, to connect with someone else who had been there.

I curled up on the grave of Heather Madsen—the dead girl White Bird had killed.

Heather and I had our differences in the past when we were freshmen in high school, but no one deserved to be killed the way she was. Her dead body…all that dark oozing blood… and her filmy white eyes flashed in my head as I knelt on her grave. I couldn't shake the grotesque visions I had of her and I didn't deserve to be let off that hook. Imagining her in the ground now made my stomach hurt.

Guilt and regret had forced me to come here. I had no choice.

I put my ear to the ground and listened to the sounds of the cemetery in the dark. I heard the crickets in the grass and the breeze through the pine trees as I stared up at the stone angel on the next grave. Heather didn't have her own guardian angel, but she was in good company. She had one close by.

And in the bluish haze of the moonlight, I saw that the angel's nose was chipped and dark streaks lined her face like tears. But the angel's eyes looked so real, I could imagine them opening and seeing me. And her spread arms and faint smile made me feel safe as the graveyard stillness closed in.

Until the night air sent me a message that I wasn't alone.

A wave of electricity swept over me, causing the hair on my arms and the back of my neck to stand on end. And static pops swirled around and through me. I knew what it meant and I turned, peering through the dark.

A door had opened to the other side. I'd felt it before.

And a gust of cold blew through my hair and made me squint. Movement near the stone angel grabbed my attention. Fingers crept out from behind the angel's shoulder—a slow and deliberate move like the silent stealth of a tarantula—and a small hand slid down the stone arm.

Sometimes the dead had a weird sense of what was funny.

Heather Madsen peered out from behind the statue—more timid and frail than I remembered her—and dressed in the clothes she had been buried in. *Her mother's choice.* Heather wouldn't have been caught dead in that dress. So I knew her coming had to be important. In life Heather had never smiled at me, but tonight she did for the first time. And it made her look sad.

The dead never speak. I don't know why. So I didn't expect that to change with Heather. For whatever reason the drop-dead gorgeous brunette with fierce green eyes had come, she'd let me know in her own sweet time. Without a word, I waved a hand to say "Hi" and stretched out on the grass over her grave.

I knew I wouldn't sleep, but I hoped that Heather would rest easier knowing she wasn't alone…even if she only had me.

Pioneer Cemetery

Heather wasn't alone. And neither was I anymore.

While I was lying on her grave, I heard the crunch of grass behind me. Someone was coming and they were searching for something…or someone. *What the hell?* No matter how I figured it, this wasn't good news for me. A beam from a flashlight swept over my head onto the branches of the pine trees. And when the light hit the chipped face of the stone angel, I looked for Heather, but she was gone.

The dead always knew when to leave. And I suddenly wished I had her exit strategy.

I stayed low and rolled onto my belly, looking back over my shoulder. The dark shadow of a man moved between the trees and through the old headstones. I held my breath and watched the beam move. It helped me track him.

I had to keep my cool. I couldn't get caught on my first night back. *Damn it!*

When the light moved away from where I was hiding, I crawled toward the trees. And when it felt safe, I got to my feet and ran the other way. All I needed was a head start. If I could make it to the rock wall, I could use it for cover, but I ran from hiding too soon.

"Stop!" A man yelled. "Stop right there."

The flashlight pointed at me and nailed my back in its light, but I didn't stop. I couldn't.

"Shit!" I cursed under my breath.

Now the man was running after me, yelling something I couldn't hear. As he closed in, I felt my heart pounding and my lungs were on fire. If only I could make the stone wall, I'd know where to hide, but the man's footsteps grew louder.

And I knew I'd never make it.

chapter two

My chances of getting away were blown apart by the man chasing me. He was too fast. When I knew I wouldn't make the stone wall of the cemetery, images flashed through my head. I pictured getting raped or killed, but I wasn't going down like some crying, scared little girl. I stopped and turned, clutching the flashlight in my hands and bracing my body for a fight. And when I flicked on the light, I pointed it at him and clenched my right fist, ready to punch him.

Putting on a show—of courage I didn't have—was my only defense.

"Stop. Don't come any closer," I demanded. I sounded angry, but I was mostly scared. "Why are you chasing me?" My voice cracked.

The light blinded him. He stopped dead in his tracks and raised a hand to block the glare. I kept the light steady on his face, but I saw how much bigger he was than me. And I saw one other thing.

The guy wore a uniform and he carried a gun. I'd been running from a cop. *Great, just great!*

"I didn't know you were..." I choked. And I was seriously out of breath. "You...scared me."

"I identified myself back there, but you kept running." With all the yelling he'd done, the stuff I never heard, the cop probably did try to identify himself. Now he was winded from chasing me and he took charge. "I need to see ID."

"You first. Show me your badge." I had my rights. And even though I wasn't sure if I'd broken any laws being in a graveyard after hours, I figured it never hurt to stall. After all, I'd lived my life procrastinating. And that wouldn't change anytime soon, not if I could put it off.

But my biggest reason to stall was that I left home without ID. *What the hell? Who knew?*

In the pale glow of my flashlight, I got a look at the badge of Deputy Will Tate. He wasn't ancient like Sheriff Logan. This guy was much younger. If I had to guess, I would say he was in his mid to late twenties. And he definitely tipped the scale toward cute. He had short brown hair and kind blue eyes with a faint dimple on his right cheek when he talked. The deputy hadn't been around two years ago when I had my troubles. If he had, I would have remembered him.

The way I figured it, I had a slim shot at talking my way out of being hauled in for trespassing by this deputy, except for one obstacle.

Talking. I hated talking, especially in sentences.

It wasn't my thing, but I had to give it a shot. I sure as hell didn't want Mom to find out I'd gotten busted on my first night in Shawano. And when I thought of facing Sheriff Logan again, I would have preferred eating glass to spending more time in his jail.

Talking. I had to talk. *Shit!*

"How did you know I was here?" I asked. A girl had to know where she went wrong.

"I saw you scale the wall." He didn't look happy. "What were you doing in the cemetery at this hour?"

It didn't take me long to come up with an answer.

"My grandmother died and I came to see her. To talk to her." I had plans to visit Grams before I left the graveyard. I hadn't completely lied. "I missed her funeral and my mom and I just got back to town. I had to see Grams. We were close, real close."

I nodded and shoved my hands into my jean jacket, avoiding his eyes. I never knew what to do with my hands. And even though I was laying it on thick, what I'd told him hadn't all been lies.

"By now you're probably figuring out that I left home without ID. I didn't figure I'd get carded at the cemetery. My name's Brenna Nash. My mom and I just got in to Oklahoma from North Carolina today." I reached in my pocket and pulled out my cell phone. Using my thumbs, I keyed up the ID on my phone. "See? That's the 411 on me. And my cell number has the area code for North Carolina. I live in Charlotte."

He eyeballed me sideways, like he still wasn't sure.

"Where are you staying here?" he asked.

"My grandmother's house. I'm helping my mom fix it up to sell." I gave him Grams's address and told him about my mom being a Realtor, like he cared. "Like I said, we just got to town and I couldn't sleep. I had to see Grams."

I chewed on the corner of my lip, hoping to God that he didn't ask me to show him where Grams was buried. If he knew I was blowing smoke, he'd bust me for sure. Deputy

Tate narrowed his eyes and focused them on me. I knew he was sizing me up.

I suddenly wished that I hadn't lied to him. He had the kind of eyes that made me want to tell the truth—like lying under the stars—but when it came to self-preservation and avoiding a night in jail, all bets were off.

He handed back my phone and said, "I'm driving you home. Come on."

"But here's the thing, Deputy Tate." I winced. "Mom doesn't know I'm here. And if I come home in a patrol car on my first night, she'd freak and ground me for life. I wasn't doing anything wrong. I was only visiting the grave of my dead grandmother."

Playing the dead grandmother card was getting old, even for me.

"Is there any way you could cut me some slack," I asked. "You know, as a welcome-home gesture?"

"I'm not the welcoming committee, Ms. Nash."

"I know, but you're a young guy. You know what it's like, right?"

I didn't do cute. And I had another problem. I wrung my hands and shuffled my feet. On top of everything I had against me—now I had to pee.

"I'd appreciate a lift, but can you just watch me until I get inside Grams's house?" I worked hard to control the whine in my voice. "My mom will kill me if I wake her. She had a long day of driving."

I held up the key to Grams's house and dangled it in the light. "See? Here's my key. To my dead grandmother's house." I pictured Grams shaking her head.

Sometimes—*like now*—I wished I didn't have to hear me talk.

"I promise." I crossed my heart. "You won't catch me doing this again. I swear to God."

I hoped he hadn't noticed my subtle wording that he wouldn't "catch me doing this again." I would definitely have to be more careful next time.

Deputy Tate heaved a sigh and pointed a finger at me. "If I ever have to chase you down again for something..."

I didn't let him finish.

"You won't. I promise." I forced a grin. Smiling made my face hurt. "And thanks for the lift. I owe you one."

"Yeah, you do."

I followed him to his squad car and kept my mouth shut, something I wished I had done earlier. But I'd been serious about owing Deputy Tate. A guy in uniform, who knew how to bend the rules for a kid like me, was a good guy in my book and a real exception to the rule in this town.

For some reason, I seriously didn't want to let Will Tate down—not unless it became really, really...*really* necessary.

Next Day—Noon

I was dragging. And I was too stubborn to admit that pulling an all-nighter had anything to do with it. The brutal Oklahoma sun beat down on me as I pulled weeds and long strands of Bermuda grass from Grams's flower beds. And no matter where I worked, the heat made me miserable. I wiped the sweat off my forehead with the back of my hand and took a gulp of lukewarm water from a bottle.

I went against my natural instincts as a teenager and didn't complain. I figured the heat and sweat were my penance for Deputy Tate taking pity on me last night. All things considered, I should have felt lucky, except White Bird was on my mind.

Today was the day I would see him again.

A part of me desperately wanted to be with him and talk like we used to. Even being with him in our comfortable silences would have been great. I wondered how much he had changed or if he would notice that I had grown up, too. I wasn't that thirteen-year-old awkward girl at the creek anymore. I was a sixteen-year-old awkward girl. But a huge part of me dreaded seeing him in that place—a mental hospital—knowing I had something to do with why he was there.

I hadn't actually seen him kill Heather and I didn't know anything about why he'd done it. But walking away from a boy I had grown to love—and betraying our relationship by siding with the sheriff and turning him in without talking to him—hadn't felt right, either. I was confused and completely unsure if I had done the right thing. And I knew my mom would have never understood that.

No one would.

"Bren? It's pretty hot out here. You okay?" My mom's voice came from behind me. She was coming off the porch, heading toward me.

I sat back on my haunches to stretch my back and said, "I'm good."

"Yeah, you are. You've done a lot, honey." She smiled and handed me a fresh bottle of cold water. "All these beds were really overgrown. This whole front yard used to be nothing but flowers. Do you remember that?"

I nodded and shrugged before I sucked down the cold water.

"Looks like we have an audience." Mom stared across the street and caught the movement of miniblinds in a front window. I'd been seeing it all morning. We were the new scandal to entertain the neighborhood. And I had no doubt that we were the subject of countless phone calls. If anyone hadn't found out that we were back in town, they'd know after today. Bad news spread like an Oklahoma wildfire in Shawano.

"Yeah, it's been like that all morning." I grimaced and got back to work.

"People used to be friendly in this town."

Yeah, but friends dry up when your daughter is linked to a murder. I didn't have to say it. I knew what she was thinking.

"I don't want you working through the heat of the day, hon." She handed me her car keys, a piece of paper and cash. "I need more cleaning supplies and a few things from the hardware store. I wrote it all down."

"You mean—? Ah…yeah, sure." I almost smiled when I heard she wanted me to drive. I may have had a restricted driver's license, but that didn't mean I had a restricted spirit. Driving the car on my own was still exciting for me. After I looked at the list, I said, "Yeah, I can pick these up. No problem."

"Good. And I found your old bicycle in the garage. It's not in bad shape. You could put air in the tires when you fill up my car with gas."

"A bicycle?" I scrunched my face as an image of Pee-wee Herman flashed in my head.

"Oh, come on. You'll have it when I've got the car. Don't worry. You'll get plenty of driving time."

Mom didn't give me a chance to argue. And I got over the bicycle thing in a hurry. Only one question remained. Could I run her errands and visit White Bird without Mom knowing it? Having wheels would make a big difference. This was too good to be true and I had to take advantage of my stroke of good luck.

I'd see White Bird today, whether I was ready to or not.

Derek Bast had driven around the block more than a few times in his black Ford F-150 truck with heavily tinted windows. He didn't want the neighbors to notice his interest in Brenna Nash, so he'd parked down the block. And she'd made it easy for him by working in the front yard of her grandmother's house.

"How did you know she was stayin' here?" Justin asked and took a sip of his Sonic Blue Slush. "This is an old neighborhood. I would've expected her to be at some motel, man."

"Word spread fast when that Indian-lovin' skank came back to town. Like I said, she ain't wanted here. That's all you got to know." He grimaced at Justin through the rearview mirror. "And you gotta quit ordering those blue faggot drinks. Man up, asshole."

Jeff and Garrett laughed. He knew he'd get a rise out of them. Justin was the guy everyone picked on and it was way too easy. The only reason he let the guy hang with him and his crew was because Justin did everything he was told.

"Hey, looks like something's happening." Justin pointed. "She's goin' somewhere."

When her mom talked to her in the yard, she handed over keys and some other stuff. And Brenna had gone back into the house.

"Let's wait awhile, see what she does." Derek sent a text message and waited. It didn't take long for a reply to come back. His cell phone signaled that he had a text.

"Is that her again?" Justin asked, leaning forward to check

out his cell from the back seat. "She's been texting you all morning, man."

"Shut your pie hole. You're giving me a headache." Derek glared at blue-slush boy. "You're like some nosy little girl, dude. Mind your own business and grow a dick."

Derek would have thumped Justin in the head, but movement down the street caught his eye. Like he figured, the bitch came out of her house again after she'd changed clothes. She was heading for her mom's car—and that made him smile.

"She's on the move. And so are we." Derek started his engine.

He'd have to follow her at a safe distance until he picked the right time and place to clue her in. She wasn't welcome here. Before he pulled from the curb to follow her, he sent a quick text message on his cell.

Heather Madsen had friends in Shawano. He wasn't the only one who hated Brenna Nash's guts. That bitch would have to watch her back. Today would be a warning.

Next time would be…way more.

Nearly Two Hours Later

After hitting two stores, I had every item on Mom's list checked off in record time. As I came out of Home Depot carrying my bags and heading for my car, I glanced down at my watch. Visiting hours at the hospital had already started. I could be there in thirty minutes. It would have been tight for me to visit White Bird, but I'd called Mom from the hardware aisle and told her I was hungry and had a craving for Chick-fil-A.

That wasn't total bullshit.

But my being hungry wouldn't get in the way of the real reason I was taking a side trip. Red Cliffs Hospital was an examination and detention center, according to what I'd read in the phone book. And I had called the facility earlier to find out about visiting hours. I wasn't sure how tight security would be in a detention center. Maybe I was fooling myself to think I could walk in and see him, but I had to take a chance.

I owed him that much.

But as I was putting the last of my shopping bags into the trunk of the Subaru, a truck barreled up to my car and screeched its tires behind me. My heart jumped and so did I. When I turned, the chrome grill of the truck was only a couple of feet from my legs.

And a familiar face was smirking at me through the windshield—Derek Bast. He wasn't alone. Bullies like Derek traveled in herds. They dressed alike. And looked alike. No-neck bubbas in muscle shirts who wore sweats that reminded everyone they were jocks—like "duh," anyone could forget. But Derek's brain-dead crew was meaner than most.

They were clones of Derek, a semihuman version of a junkyard dog. And to make matters worse, Derek was the nephew of Sheriff Logan. That had always bought him special treatment in town, but his status as a football jock had apparently earned him even more star power. I'd read about him and some of the other kids in Shawano on Facebook after I'd left the state.

I knew they wouldn't "friend" me if they recognized my name and photo so I made up an online name, "Rolo Girl." I was addicted to chocolate and had the zits to prove it, but the chewy caramel center in a Rolo had reminded me of the color of White Bird's skin, so I was hooked. And for my Facebook photo, I took a pic of my "screw you" toes and posted it. That worked for me, so I became one of the two thousand plus friends Jade DeLuca had on Facebook. And with her being the apparent heir to Heather's vacant throne, Derek was always on her page, the idiot.

Whenever he got out of control, everyone in this town knew how to turn the other way and Derek had always known how to take advantage of that.

Mr. Teflon scared me plenty.

"Well, look who's back, guys." Derek got out of his truck and his boys followed. Four of his buddies slipped beside him and blocked me in. I couldn't run, even if I wanted to. "Guess you didn't get it through your thick skull the first time. Your pal, Tonto, killed a white girl. And he's gonna pay for that. He can't hide forever, pretending to be a retard."

Derek backed me against my car and I could barely breathe. And when I didn't say anything, he wouldn't let it go. From the corner of my eye, I saw shoppers coming out of Home Depot. Most of them rushed by and didn't make eye contact. No one was going to help me…until one woman grabbed her cell and made a call. I hoped she dialed 911, but I couldn't be sure.

"That damned Indian killed Heather. Ain't you got nothin' to say?" He stared down at me. "He's gonna pay when they stick a needle in his arm." I felt his bully friends close in and the heat mixed with the stink of sweat and body odor. It was so bad that I had to hold my breath, but Derek's words were even more torture.

I imagined White Bird strapped to a table in an execution room and it scared the hell out of me—like I needed something else to keep me up nights.

"He hasn't been convicted. His case never went to court." I swallowed hard and raised my chin, digging deep for a little defiance.

Being related to the sheriff, Derek wasn't stupid enough to

beat me up in broad daylight, not when there'd be witnesses. But what scared me was what I knew would come. This redneck was only getting started. I had to curb my inner smart-ass and keep my mouth shut or I'd pay later when the jerk could corner me without witnesses. If I pissed him off now, that's what would happen for sure. I had to play it right and let him think he'd won this round.

"Oh, but he's guilty. And we all know it." Derek got in my face, close enough for me to smell his bad breath and get a zoom on his zits. One on his chin was ripe. The dude seriously needed to harvest.

"If you're so sure, why are you hassling me?" It was the only comeback I could think of. *Lame, I know.* I had no business arguing with a guy who could break me like a twig. And I didn't want to die in the parking lot of Home Depot, especially on an empty stomach.

"You were screwing him, weren't you?" he said.

With guys like Derek, it always came back to sex. *What a tool!* He couldn't see a guy being friends with a girl. Correct that, friendship between a white girl and a Native American boy was off-limits in his pea brain. Guys like Derek shouldn't be allowed to breed.

When I opened my mouth to speak—completely unsure what I'd say—I saw a police patrol car coming and I breathed a sigh of relief when Derek saw it, too. He backed off and leaned against his truck, crossing his beefy arms and acting all innocent. *The jerk!*

"Is everything okay here? Derek, is that you?" A deputy I didn't recognize took in the scene. "What's going on?"

He was older than Will Tate, the cop who had found me at the cemetery. But this guy saw I had shopping bags in my trunk and that Derek and his buddies had blocked my car.

I glared at Derek and made him sweat more than he already was. I could have narked him out, but I knew it wouldn't end with me filing a complaint for the sheriff's office to deal with. Derek was the kind of guy who hated losing, especially to a girl.

"Nothing, Deputy. I was heading home. My mom had me running errands, but she's expecting me. I gotta bounce." I avoided looking at Derek when I slammed my trunk. He was a guy who had worked hard on his body, but anything above his shoulders needed a serious "do over." All I wanted to do was get out in one piece.

"Then you better back up your rig, son. Let the little lady out. You're in her way."

The deputy stepped between us and got Derek to back off my bumper. And in my rearview mirror as I drove away, I saw that the deputy wasn't done with the beef boy squad. He kept Derek talking while I drove off the lot. Hell, they were even laughing like it was a damned frat party. Although the cop had given me a head start, I wasn't dumb enough to believe it was over between me and Derek and his no-neck buddies. Guys like him never let anything go, but I had better things to do.

And all I had on my mind now was seeing White Bird.

Red Cliffs Hospital

Wearing torn jeans and a striped tee with a long scarf, I slipped through the automatic double doors of the hospital and pulled my cap down. With large dark sunglasses, my face would be hidden. I had no idea if anyone would know me at this place, but keeping a low profile wouldn't hurt.

I pretended to know where I was going. And when it looked as if no one was watching me, I followed signs down a corridor that led me to a reception area for visitors wanting to see patients held in detention. Picking an inconspicuous place to sit, I flipped through magazines and looked bored while I watched the guard and nurse at a desk located outside a locked door. I sat long enough to look like a permanent fixture. Even my butt had gone numb.

There was enough activity so that my loitering didn't stand out. I kept my head down and sunglasses on, even inside the hospital. Eventually, no one looked at me twice. People came and went, signing a register on the desk. And they showed ID. I got a feel for what was normal and listened to conversations. I even talked to a girl my age that I had followed into the bathroom. She told me what to expect inside after I said this was my first time visiting my old man. I told her it was his birthday and my mother made me come. She bought my story and helped me figure stuff out.

Eventually I got the guts to make a move when the security guard took a break and left the nurse alone at the desk. I signed in using my name because I knew they would ask for ID. I scribbled my name so bad, I knew they wouldn't be able to read it later. And on the register, under the column for patient name, I listed someone I had seen on the log from an earlier visitor. I kept my head down and acted like I'd done this a hundred times.

The nurse buzzed me through the locked door. Once I got inside, I followed the signs to a large room where visitors met with patients. I didn't see White Bird anywhere. I looked up and down the hallways beyond the visitor area, too. Nothing. Beyond the locked door, I had limited places to go that I wouldn't get noticed. I hadn't counted on that. I thought that once I got past the closed door, I could roam down the halls looking for White Bird's room, but that wouldn't happen now.

My trip to the hospital had been a stupid idea.

I didn't know what I was doing. And if I got caught now, there'd be no explaining it. I'd get busted and Mom would know exactly what I'd been up to. *Shit!* I had almost given up until I saw a patient in blue pajamas and a matching robe being wheeled down the corridor by a nurse. I noticed they were heading toward a glass door that led outside. And I had nothing to lose, so I raced toward the door and opened it for the nurse.

"Thanks, honey. You visiting someone?" the black woman in uniform asked. She had a big friendly smile, so I grinned back.

"Yeah, they told me my dad was out here. I came to look." Most days I barely got two words out of my mouth, but for some reason, lying came easy. It was an aptitude I didn't want to think about. And talking about my dad—the sperm donor I'd never met—felt strange, too. He was more of a concept than a real person to me.

"Well, if you don't find him, go back to reception and they'll help you." She smiled again and wheeled her patient toward a patio. "Take care now."

"Thanks." I waved, even though the nurse had turned her back.

Outside the hospital was a fenced-in area that surrounded a garden with walkways and a series of covered patios for patients to sit. It was beautiful and peaceful. And if someone could forget they were locked up in a boot camp for loonies, surrounded by razor wire and security guards, the grounds weren't half-bad.

But I hadn't come for the scenery.

Looking for White Bird, I walked through the gardens, deathly afraid I wouldn't recognize him even if I found him. I hadn't seen him in two years. And two years was a lifetime, considering what I remembered of the last time I saw him at the creek on that horrible morning.

A flash of dark memories raced through my mind and made me sick with worry. I pictured him caught somewhere between the innocence of the boy I had first met at the creek—the one with the gentleness to heal a small bird—and the crazed killer capable of murdering a young girl nearly his own age.

Someone like…me.

I had walked the last of the patios and hadn't seen anyone as young as White Bird. My heart sank as a wave of nausea hit me. When I thought about turning around and heading home, giving up on all I had hoped would happen today, that's when I saw a guy in a wheelchair under some trees near the high fence. He was alone and his back was to me.

My heart crammed in my throat as I walked toward him. And I had trouble breathing. I desperately wanted it to be him. It *had* to be him. And when tears filled my eyes, I fought the lump in my throat and clenched my hands into fists.

"Please, God. Let it be White Bird," I whispered as a tear slid down my cheek.

I wasn't sure God would listen to me. He never had before.

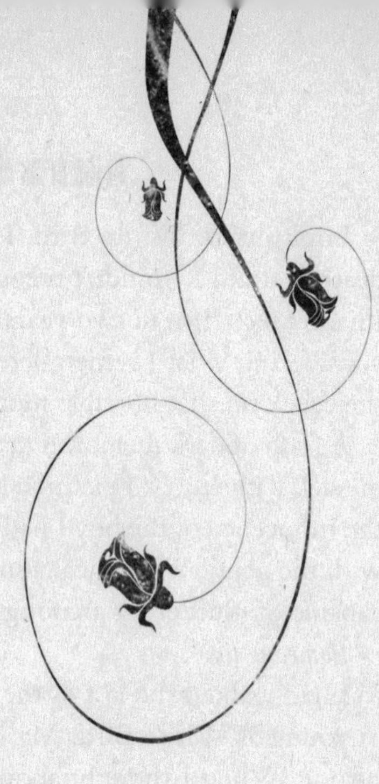

chapter three

Red Cliffs Hospital

As I walked toward the guy in the wheelchair, my stomach twisted into knots. I couldn't catch my breath, but I kept walking anyway, unable to take my eyes off him. The sun, the trees and the people on the grounds of the mental hospital, they faded to nothing. All I saw was that boy slumped in the chair with his head too heavy to lift. He wore pale blue hospital scrubs and a white robe with slippers on his feet. And when I got close enough, I took off my sunglasses and knelt in front of him—crying.

It was White Bird.

He looked thinner, not like the strong boy I remembered. His golden skin that once looked like sweet caramel had turned pale. And someone had cut his long black hair to make him conform to what they thought he should be. If White Bird knew what they'd done, he would have fought them. And I would have given anything to see the fire in his eyes again.

But in his condition, he had no fight left. His keen, dark eyes were glazed over and empty. *Dead.* With his arms limp in his lap, he stared into a world only he could see.

And it broke my heart to see him so lost.

"Oh, my God. What have they done to you?" I whispered, not recognizing my own voice. "What have I done?"

I reached out a trembling hand and pulled it back. I wanted to touch him, but I didn't deserve to be comforted by that touch. I had played a part in putting him here. And if he could truly see, I knew he would glare in anger at my betrayal. Every time I looked in the mirror, I stared back at myself with the same blame.

"White Bird." I said his name and lowered my head to meet his gaze. "It's me, Brenna. Brenna Nash. Remember me?"

The words stuck in my throat. *How the hell could he forget me? You're an idiot, Bren!* Tears stung my eyes. And I had no idea what to say.

Over the past two years, any suffering I had done wasn't enough, not compared to what had happened to him. The life had drained from him. His body was nothing but an empty shell where my friend used to be. I clutched my hands tight on the armrests to his wheelchair until my fingers ached. And bile rose hot in my belly.

None of this was right!

"Please…look at me. I have to—" I stopped.

What did I have to do? I wanted to know what had happened. Why had this gentle boy killed Heather? It made no sense. And yet I couldn't shake the images I saw that morning from my head. The reality of what I had seen blocked everything out.

"I have to know what happened. Why did you…?" I swallowed, hard. I couldn't bring myself to ask why he'd killed

Heather. Saying it aloud made it real. Saying it aloud meant I had accepted it.

But why did I have to know what happened? Did my reason have more to do with letting me off the guilt hook? I hated myself for even wondering that. If he were guilty of murder, that would justify what I had done by turning him in. But guilty or innocent, I should have stood by my friend. Why hadn't I done that? Why had I skulked out of town with my tail between my legs like a damned coward? He was my friend and I abandoned him to a town full of strangers. He had no parents or anyone who believed in him. Not even the tribe he loved had lifted a finger. All anyone saw was a cold-blooded killer, a half-breed Native boy who was different.

I choked on my sobs and wiped away tears, but when I looked at him again, White Bird had lifted his head and stared straight into my eyes.

"White Bird? Can you see me?"

I touched his hand to make a connection after the years we'd been apart. But when I did, something strange happened.

In the blink of an eye, everything turned black and I lost sight of him. I couldn't feel his hand in mine. Hell, I couldn't feel anything. Even the ground under me had dropped away and left me floating weightless in a murky void as if I had spiraled into a dark bottomless pit.

My stomach pitched and rolled. And with a haunting thunder rumbling in the distance, streaks of lightning flashed in violent fury, casting images in a glimmer of bright light. A large bear erupted out of the darkness and gnashed its teeth at me, barely missing my arm. I screamed and the fierce animal roared so loud that the sound blocked out the thunder. When I tried to run from it, I only grasped at air, unable to move in the thick, inky black.

Between the bolts of lightning, I couldn't see at all. And I had no way to stop it.

"Oh, my God. What is this?" I choked.

That's when a strange memory rushed into my mind. The wounded bird that White Bird had healed when we first met flew into my line of sight. It came at me fast and scared me when its wings hit my face. I gasped as the tiny bird thrashed through the void in sheer panic with its beak gaping open.

"White Bird? Where are you?" I called out to him, but he didn't answer.

At first, the memory of the wounded bird had been a comfort. It reminded me of White Bird, as if he'd sent a messenger to me so I wouldn't be afraid. But when I reached for the little thing, to clutch it to my chest, I tumbled forward and the terrified bird got swallowed in the darkness. And a sound from my imagination that I couldn't shake—from countless nightmares—smothered its frantic chirping.

A girl's screams gripped my heart.

I couldn't see her as I spun out of control, but I heard a torturous thud as she cried out in pain—the meaty sound of a knife striking her body. Warm blood splattered my face and I flinched. I could smell it. Taste it. And all I wanted to do was run. I careened through the blackness and toppled end over end, flailing my arms. Everything jumbled together—the bear, the knife, the blood and the gut-wrenching screams that usually invaded my own nightmares. Images and sounds pummeled me from every direction.

"Heather?" I called to her. I knew she was there. I felt her.

But when I yelled, White Bird finally cried out from far away. I heard him. I recognized his voice, but I didn't understand what he said. I only knew—with dead certainty—that he was afraid. Did he know I was with him? Did he care?

His cry was the last thing I heard.

I was sucked out of the waking nightmare and thrust into the bright sunlight. Still gripping White Bird's hand, I came to with a gasp. I shielded my eyes from the glare and squinted around me until I remembered where I was—the damned mental hospital.

"Shit! What the hell—" I muttered, panting out of control. "What's happening to me?"

My heart was like a battering ram slamming against my ribs. And I was shaking all over. When I looked at White Bird again, he was slumped back into his wheelchair the way I had found him. It was as if I had never come. Seeing him like that made me deathly afraid that I had imagined the whole thing. Touching him had triggered everything, but maybe that dark nightmarish world had been inside of me. *Me!*

Maybe I was the one who deserved to be locked away in a straitjacket.

"I'm sorry. I gotta…get out of here."

Like the coward that I was, I ran and didn't look back. If I had, I never would have left him alone.

Minutes Later

"Did you see that girl?" Winded, Dr. Sam Ridgeway grabbed the arm of a startled nurse as he rushed from the ward into the outside courtyard. "She was with that patient over there. Isaac Henry." He pointed to the boy in a wheelchair sitting under trees near the fence.

The nurse turned to where he pointed and shook her head, "No, Doctor. I didn't see anyone with him. As far as I know, that boy doesn't get visitors. The sheriff's office calls to get his condition from time to time, but that's it. Why?"

"Someone was with him, just now. I saw it from my office window upstairs. She left before I got down here."

"I'll check with visitor's registration. If he had a visitor, they would have a name."

"Yes, please do that. And let me know as soon as you can," he called after the nurse as she headed inside.

Ridgeway raked a hand through his thinning blond hair and heaved a sigh as he stood on the main patio. He searched the faces of the visitors in the garden, but he didn't see the strange girl with long reddish hair dressed in a scarf and hat. In the heat of Oklahoma, the girl had stood out in the way she dressed, but something much more had grabbed his attention.

What forced him to race outside was that the girl had gotten a reaction from the catatonic boy—something electroshock treatments and high doses of benzodiazepines hadn't achieved since Isaac Henry had been admitted two years ago. Every line of treatment had been exhausted and every external stimulus had been tried, but nothing would bring the boy out of his constant, mute stupor. But with the girl in the courtyard, Isaac had raised his head and looked at her, a reaction the doctor had seen with his own eyes and found extraordinary, given the boy's circumstances.

Isaac Henry's case had been very puzzling from the start. And he'd begun to think that something more was at play—something he didn't understand about the Native boy.

But for the first time since he'd taken over the case, he had seen another human being touch Isaac deeply enough for him to lift his head and make real eye contact. Given his condition, that was amazing. Ridgeway kept his focus on the boy as he headed toward him. When he stood beside him, he looked down and saw no change in Isaac, except something dark was on the ground next to his wheelchair.

A pair of sunglasses.

Ridgeway's conviction that he had seen the girl was confirmed; she'd left something behind. He bent down to pick up the glasses and stared into the vacant eyes of the Native boy.

"Who's your friend, Isaac?" he whispered, not expecting an answer. "You really looked at her, didn't you?"

When the boy didn't respond, the doctor pulled out his cell phone and made a call to the private number of Sheriff Matt Logan. When the call rolled into voice mail, he left a message.

"Hey, Matt, this is Sam. We had a break in the Isaac Henry case. I thought you'd want to know. Call me."

Ridgeway had been a close family friend of the sheriff of Shawano since they were in high school together. And he had personally taken on the Native boy's case at the request of Matt Logan. As he saw it, his first duty was to his patient and he had to be careful walking the fine line between being a friend to the sheriff and being the doctor in charge of Isaac's case.

But, since the boy had been unfit to stand trial and had been sent to the hospital detention unit for allegedly killing a local girl, that line had blurred in his mind. What would be good for the patient could serve the needs of the town. That's how he reconciled his involvement in a case he would have assigned to another staff member.

Locating the girl who had visited Isaac might put an end to his interminable balancing act.

If he finally broke through the kid's catatonia, he'd do the right thing for his patient. And if that earned him favor with Sheriff Logan—so he could bring the kid's case to trial and finally render justice for the grieving parents of the dead girl—then he'd reap those benefits, too. Some might even think he was a hero. Of course, the kid would have to pay the price for what he'd done, but at least he'd be fully cognizant of what was happening to him. It wasn't a merciful conclusion, but it was one the kid probably deserved.

Only one thing stood in the way of justice now. With the help of the sheriff, he'd find the girl and convince her to cooperate with him for the good of the town.

How difficult would that be?

I can't remember the first time I actually saw a dead person. I've thought about that tons of times, too. When I was a kid, they came to me as strangers, nothing more than faces crowding my sleep. At least, that's how I figured it out later when I accidently read the obituaries and saw a familiar face staring back. And after I went to the library, I found more faces in the newspaper archives. They'd been with me for as long as I could remember and I didn't even know it.

Hell, I thought I had imagined them, until I saw Frank Sullivan when I was ten. It was the first time I realized something wasn't right—*with me.*

Mr. Sullivan used to work at the hardware store. He helped Mom whenever she needed to fix things at our house. She always said what a nice guy he was, but one day she quit saying that. Mr. Sullivan had died in a terrible car crash, she'd told me. Guess after he was drunk, he tried to beat a train to the railroad crossing and lost. After Mom told me all about how drinking can get anyone into trouble, even nice guys at hardware stores, we went to his church service.

But months after he'd died, I saw Mr. Sullivan again in broad daylight.

He was dressed only in blue boxer shorts and black socks and was using his severed arm to organize nuts and bolts at the hardware store. I'd thought it was his idea of casual Friday until I remembered hearing the town rumors about the scandal. Apparently Mr. Sullivan died without many clothes on. How he got that way, no one really knew, but plenty of folks had got off on the gossip.

Sure, I acted like seeing him didn't bother me much now, but back then, I nearly peed in my pants. It was scary enough to see an old guy in his underwear, but the whole arm thing really got to me. I pinched myself until I was blue, but I wasn't asleep. And when Mr. Sullivan saw me watching him from down the aisle, he followed me through the store, peeking at me between the shelves. The dead really get off on having an audience, especially when they get caught wearing nothing but underpants.

I stayed close to Mom and after we paid for our stuff, Mr. Sullivan followed us toward the exit. He kept his distance but stopped at the electronic doors and waved his bloody stump at me as we drove away.

I wanted to ask Mom if she'd seen him, but that seemed way too strange, even for me. And I might have to explain my fascination with the obituaries, something Mom had laughed about plenty of times. I quickly found out that nothing is too weird for the internet and the folks who posted stuff online didn't make fun of me.

The day I saw Mr. Sullivan made me realize something more might be wrong with me, something not as harmless as dreaming about dead people. After that I Googled my way into a deep depression. The internet fed my paranoia until I broke down and admitted that seeing the dead had become part of me. I made the decision that it wasn't a bad thing. It wasn't good. It simply was. But as I drove home now, I couldn't stop thinking about what had happened today. And I dredged up a horrifying question that I could no longer ignore.

Was I schizophrenic?

Had my obsession with graveyards and the dead spiraled into or masked something far worse? Schizophrenics were psychotics who saw their bent version of reality and deciphered the world through different filters. They had enhanced perceptions of sounds, colors and their environment, making their existence a puzzle with moving parts they couldn't grasp. And they heard voices and saw things that weren't real. Every day they walked a tightrope with meds as their only lifeline. But if they went untreated, they gradually withdrew into their delusions. That's what I thought had happened to me. I'd taken the first step into becoming a full-on, certifiable whack job.

What had happened at the mental hospital—when I touched White Bird and my world erupted into a waking hallucination—had me terrified.

I wanted Mom to fix it. I wanted to be a kid and have my mother hold me and tell me everything would be okay. But I'd learned that my mother couldn't protect me from everything. And if I were losing it like White Bird, my mom's life would be easier if I was locked away. At least then she wouldn't have to deal with the unleashed me. She'd been through too much already by having to move and rebuild her real estate business from scratch in a new town. How could I make things worse for her by tacking on a life sentence of caring for a defective kid?

At that moment, I'd never felt so alone.

And I couldn't imagine what White Bird was going through. Maybe his being locked in his head and not knowing what was happening had been a good thing. I wanted to believe this, but if that were so, why did I feel physically sick with worry for him?

When I hit the outskirts of Shawano, I seriously needed an injection of happy. And while I looked for a gas station, my mind immediately shifted to my favorite time with White Bird, even though it made me ache to remember it.

It always made me happy to picture the little fort he had made near the creek. I thought of it as our special place even though he'd built it before he'd met me. It was a shelter made of tree branches that he had woven together. And on a bright day, the sun dappled light through the green leaves, a picture I still carry in my head.

From the outside, no one even knew his shelter was there, except for the medicine wheel he had made of stones, placed on the ground in a nearby clearing. The medicine wheel had a large center boulder with four rock spokes branching off from it, surrounded by a circle of stones. White Bird had told me the wheel was sacred and had the power to bring good medicine to his shelter.

He'd done a good job of making his fort look like part of the forest we both loved. And the ground inside his hut was soft, better than the mattress on my bed. Decaying leaves and tree limbs had made the ground spongy. And the rich smell of the earth and the trickling sound of the nearby creek made his hideaway my favorite place.

That's where he kept the bird with the broken wing.

He'd made a simple cage for her out of branches that he'd carved with a small knife. Those days, when I'd come to see the bird, had always held a special place in my heart. Yes, I had marveled at the way the little bird improved. I thought for sure she would have died from shock, but White Bird had been so gentle with her that she grew stronger every day. And she no longer was afraid of us.

But the real reason I looked forward to coming was to see him, even though our days together would be numbered.

When he'd told me that the bird was healed, I had to admit that I was sad. The next day, we'd release her. He'd given me a day to get used to the idea and he wanted to make a ceremony of it. I had grown attached to the little thing. But the main reason I hated the idea of releasing her was that it meant I had no more reason to visit him every day.

"You should be happy. She'll be free of her cage tomorrow." Inside the hut, White Bird looked at me and smiled, lying stretched out near me. He expected me to be happy, but I wasn't.

"Yeah, but I'll miss her." Sitting cross-legged, I scrunched my face into a pout as I stroked the cage he'd built for her. "Couldn't we keep her? I'd help you take care of her."

He shook his head and said, "It's better to die free than live life in a cage. She must be free to fulfill her destiny. And thanks to you, she has one."

He always reminded me of my part in rescuing the bird. Repairing her wing had been all him, but he always made me out to be the real hero. And I loved him for it.

"Then tomorrow it is. At dawn. I'll be here." I took a deep breath. "She should have a full day of freedom."

"That's the spirit." He grinned and tapped my nose with his finger, a gesture I'd grown fond of.

The next day I showed up at his hideaway at dawn, as I had promised. And I tried to look happy, for his sake. He'd come earlier and had started a small fire in a stone pit in the clearing outside his shelter. He was hunched over the flames now and the burning wood smelled good. It made my stomach growl.

Not even the big wad of chewing gum I had in my mouth stopped my hunger.

When he looked up from the fire, he smiled.

"Come here. You've got something in your hair."

When I sat next to him, he leaned closer and pulled a small twig from my hair. I had brushed against a low tree limb on my hike in. But instead of throwing the twig away, White Bird put it into his pocket and grinned again.

Something sad and wonderful struck me. I remembered thinking that I wished I could freeze us both in that moment. And even though it made me sad to know I couldn't, that didn't stop me from wishing I could remember him like this forever. His smile always made me feel that way, like every moment of our being together was precious and important… and fragile.

I knelt beside him near the fire without saying a word. The crackling flame felt good against my clothes even though the drifting smoke stung my eyes.

"You ready to do this?" he asked.

"Yep. What do you need me to do?"

White Bird asked me to get the bird. I went into his hut and brought out the cage. He had removed her bandages and she looked as good as new. When I came out from the shelter, he stopped me to grab a small feather that had gotten stuck in a branch of the cage. He made a point to stuff it into a beaded leather pouch that had a drawstring—a part of the ritual he had planned—but that wasn't the only thing he put into the bag. He took the twig from his pocket, the one he had taken from my hair minutes before, and placed it into the pouch, too.

"What's that…that bag?"

"It's my medicine bag." He blushed and slid the pouch into his pocket. "I made it…myself."

I could understand why he'd taken the feather, but the twig he'd taken from my hair was another story. I grinned.

"What do you keep in it?" I don't know what I expected him to say, but when he looked into my eyes with a serious expression on his cute face, I stopped smiling.

"I keep things that are…special to me."

Both of us blushed, but before I said anything else, White Bird pointed to a spot away from the fire.

"Set the cage over there, away from the smoke."

I did what he told me, finding it hard to fight a grin. When I turned back, White Bird was on his knees, chanting words in Euchee with his eyes closed. The fire had mesmerized me until he chanted in his Native language. The words were foreign sounding and magical. And in English, he translated for me.

"The universe whispers to all of us, from the realm of the Great Creator, *Gohantaney*. Messages of wisdom are carried on the wind if we are open to hear them, even in the sweet song of a morning bird." He opened his eyes to look at me. "Are you open to hear the Great Creator, Brenna?"

I blinked twice, surprised he'd used my name in his ceremony.

"Yes. I mean, I hope so. I'll try."

I rolled my eyes at how stupid I sounded. His words were so beautiful, but I acted like a moron. I should have swallowed my gum, but that would have been gross.

"She is healed and ready to fly free," he said in English. "And the next time you hear a morning bird, you will remember her and be happy."

His ritual had been for me, so I wouldn't be sad to see the

bird go. After he finished his chanting, he picked up the cage and held it out for me to open the door. At first, the bird stayed inside, scared to fly away. But eventually she perched at the open cage door and cocked her head at us before she flew away.

"Oh, my God. Look. She's flying," I whispered as he set down the cage.

We watched the bird fly into the glowing pink of early morning with the warmth of the sun on our faces. And when he quietly slipped his hand in mine, my heart nearly stopped. I couldn't look at him. I was sure my eyes welled with tears and I wanted to cry. The moment was perfect and I didn't want to spoil it. I was afraid that if I peeked at him, I would see he only thought of me as a friend.

If I didn't look, I could imagine he loved me.

I didn't think I could feel any better than I did in that instant we held hands, until he looked down at me with his dark eyes and stroked a strand of hair off my face. And I knew he wanted more.

"Can I kiss you?" he asked.

My eyes opened wide and my breath caught in my throat. I nearly choked.

"Ah, no." My mouth said it before my brain knew what was happening.

"No?" He smiled and cocked his head.

I looked down at my watch. "In two minutes, okay?"

When he grinned and looked down at his watch to count down the time, I turned my head and spit out my gum. It shot out of my mouth like a pink cannonball.

I remembered my body was shaking all over. I was terrified and completely happy at the same time. I'd never kissed a boy before. What if I screwed it up? When was I supposed to close my eyes? What was I supposed to do with my tongue? Should I have spit on my lips or should they be dry? All my insecurities came rushing to the surface and my knees almost buckled.

When my two minutes were up, he lowered his lips to mine and kissed me for the first time.

In the pale light of morning, he pulled me into his arms with the same gentleness that had healed the bird with the broken wing. I felt his hand on my face and his lips were perfect on mine. It was as if we'd done this a hundred times, maybe in another lifetime. Kissing him sent a rush of emotions through me. I was no longer a little girl. I had crossed a line that made me feel different. And I wondered if it would show on my face.

When he pulled away, I opened my eyes to see him looking down at me. He grinned and didn't say a word. He hugged me without an ounce of selfishness. And as we both gazed into the morning sun, I buried my head into his chest and found it hard to fight the smile on my face. And I wondered if he was smiling, too.

When I think of the single most important moment of my life, I always remember kissing White Bird. Even now I can feel his touch on my skin and the way his lips felt. That memory should have made me happy on a day like today, but it didn't. All I could think about were the words he'd said about the bird.

"It's better to die free than live life in a cage."

A tear rolled down my cheek when I thought about him locked up, without knowing whether he'd ever be free again. What I had with him was gone now. And I had been the one who had killed it.

I had no one to blame except me.

★ ★ ★

By the time I pulled into the driveway at Grams's house, I was feeling pretty low. And if Mom wanted to make a big deal about me taking my sweet time to run her errands, then she'd better be prepared for a fight. I was in no mood to play nice.

But when I saw a car parked on the curb in front of our walkway—a shiny red-and-white Mini-Cooper—I had a feeling my tardiness would take a back seat. I quickly unloaded my old bike and put it in the garage. And with shopping bags in hand, I opened the front door.

I found my mom sitting in the living room with Chloe Seaver.

"Hey, Brenna. I was hoping to catch you." The thin blonde stood and smiled.

Like I remembered her, she had huge blue eyes smeared with smoky dark makeup. Her eyes always reminded me of those orphaned cat pictures that made you want to adopt every stray at the kennel, even if you were allergic.

Chloe had the same frail-looking face. Pale skin, a narrow chin and thin lips shining with pink gloss. It was like she was a little girl playing dress up. She wore her straggling blond hair with bangs these days, razor cut in layers to fall beneath her chin. When I realized that she looked like a pixie elf, I gazed down at her shoes and was disappointed not to see her wearing curly satin slippers with bells on her toes.

"You remember Chloe Seaver, don't you, honey? You used to be good friends." When my mom smiled, my mind lurched into conspiracy mode. Had Chloe come on her own or had Mom orchestrated the *chance* meeting? I set the shopping bags down near the door and went into the living room.

"Yeah, Mom. I remember. What's up, Chloe?" I stuffed my hands in my jeans.

What's up? I greeted her like nothing bad had ever happened between us. Like Chloe's best friend hadn't been brutally murdered and like I had nothing to do with the boy who had killed her.

In my screwed-up world, very little surprised me anymore. Chloe Seaver showing up on my doorstep was one more piece of crap piled on my WTF day. And since I was already under a heaping pile, what was one more smelly glob?

But there was something I had to know. Did my mom put Chloe up to this visit, or had she come for another reason?

chapter four

Chloe Seaver standing in Grams's living room was a sight I never thought I'd see again. We used to be friends before she became a part of Heather Madsen's crew of popular kids, the "it" girls that every boy in school had fantasized about and every girl envied—every girl except me.

Call me strange, but I always felt sorry for all of them, especially Heather. She demanded attention like a drug addict needed that next fix and that made her high maintenance. And she got a perverse kick out of preying on outsiders and loners, the weak ones in "the herd." The less someone had, the more she wanted to take. I guess that made her feel superior.

Being envied for having it all was the air that she breathed.

"Your mom says you're here for the summer, to fix up your grandmother's house." Chloe smiled again, but it didn't cover up her shaky voice.

"Yeah, we just got here. How did you know I was back… and here at Grams's?"

"Oh, guess a little birdie told me."

Vultures, more like it. Either the rumor mill in Shawano was in fine form or my mom had something to do with Chloe's visit. Either way wasn't good for me.

It was ironic that Chloe had talked about a little birdie telling her I was back. White Bird had told me once that she reminded him of the little bird with the busted wing. She thrashed around, all wounded, not realizing what she was doing to herself. Guess he felt sorry for her, too.

That image of her was perfect. Because we'd been friends, I felt sorry for the person she could have been if she had the guts to find her own way.

"Well, I'll leave you two alone to talk." Mom grinned and gave an awkward hug to the Hobbit Princess. "It was good to see you again, Chloe."

"Yes, ma'am. Thanks for letting me wait for Brenna."

Once it was just the two of us, the normal thing to do would have been to sit, but I didn't do that. Being alone with Chloe didn't feel natural to me anymore. And I could tell she felt the same. In another lifetime, we'd been friends, but after she'd fallen so easily under Heather's spell, I'd lost my respect for her.

And she hadn't changed much. Chloe chewed her nails, even though she hid it with black nail polish. And she had a nervous edginess that had made me want to protect her, until Heather came into her life and sucked the personality out of her. Chloe became a devoted follower to her much more intimidating BFF. And since every diva had the blind obedience of her faithful inner circle, that made me wonder about the real purpose of Chloe's visit.

Either the Queen of Hearts had sent an emissary through the rabbit hole to entice me to Wonderland or someone else was pulling the strings of the pixie drone with Heather gone. Jade Deluca was a likely candidate since she had been number two in line for Heather's throne. At least, that's what her Facebook page had declared.

"Why are you here, Chloe? It's just the two of us. Talk to me." I crossed my arms and waited for what she'd say. "Who sent you?"

Chloe slumped into the chair behind her and looked at me with her baby blues.

"I heard you were in town." She shrugged. "And I wanted to see for myself, that's all."

Okay, that *so* wasn't the truth. The girl had more on her mind and I wouldn't let her off the hook. I decided to make her squirm, with silence being my weapon of choice. And apparently, honesty was now a real showstopper in Chloe's world.

She clammed up and wrung her hands like I'd asked her to scoop cat shit with her bare fingers. I was afraid she'd break one of the "little bird" bones in her hands. I knew it wasn't nice to think so little of someone as fragile as Chloe, but the girl had inflicted the damage on herself. She didn't have the strength to stand on her own two feet and "safety in numbers" determined her self-worth.

Like I said, I felt sorry for all of them. And my cynicism showed.

But the biggest difference between someone from Heather's crowd and me was that I never shared my opinions. Heather and her peeps thrived on passing rumors as if hurting people somehow inflated their status. And if they didn't have anything real, they made shit up. That was why I kept my damned opinions to myself. I carried on whole conversations in my head, like I was doing now, but my thoughts rarely saw the light of day. They were strictly for my own amusement, like my "screw you" toes.

And who the hell would I talk to anyway?

"Actually, I'm having a party at my house tonight, the first one this summer. I was hoping you'd come." She looked at me, trying to appear casual. When I cocked my head and glared, she added, "You'll know some of the kids. I swear. It'll be… nice."

Nice? I'd rather have a pinecone shoved up my nose.

"Look, Chloe—"

She didn't let me finish.

"I think this whole town is wrong about you. And maybe if they see you now, things will blow over."

I hadn't expected her to say that and she looked as if she meant it. I wanted Chloe to be right, but I didn't need anyone to like me.

Or accept me.

Or tolerate me.

I shook my head and without hesitation, I said, "I've gotta help Mom. Sorry. We just got to town, like I said, and—"

"Brenna, I think you should go, honey." Mom had been eavesdropping and hadn't seen the harm in stabbing me in the back. "It'll be good for you to reconnect with old friends. In fact, I insist that you go. You'll thank me later."

I sure thought about showing her my appreciation now. A well-placed two-by-four to the head would do the trick.

"But, Mom, you had me buy like a hundred things of SaniWipes. I thought you'd need me. Those things dry out if you don't use them in like…three hours or something. I think I read that in the fine print while I was in line at the checkout."

I couldn't believe I was arguing in favor of doing chores,

but seeing the look in my mom's eyes, I knew she'd give me no choice. I hated it when she thought she knew best about every aspect of my life, including my taste in friends. So much for democracy and free will.

And apparently my mom didn't think twice about spying on me. No civil liberties violation there. She didn't give a flip about me deciding what I wanted to do with my time. Mom had decreed that Chloe's invitation was a good thing and that would be that. Any argument against the idea was based on me not respecting Chloe and the people she hung out with, but I knew debating the point with my mother wouldn't be worth it.

She wouldn't take me seriously. And forget about her take on my judgment. Mom always saw me as strange for not having hordes of friends, like a good head count on a Facebook page of two thousand virtual strangers would solve all my problems. She had no idea that Chloe Seaver was only a Trojan horse for the rest of dead-Heather's posse. Any problems I had, coming back to Shawano, had only just begun.

And Mom would drive me to the slaughter. *Good times....*

Hours Later

Mom had pulled into the Seavers' driveway and let the engine idle as I sat there staring at Chloe's house. Cars were parked down the street on both sides and I heard music thumping through my closed car window. A strobe light made everyone look as if they were moving in super slow-mo under eerie-colored lights. And kids were still arriving. A party with one of the "it" girls was the place to be seen.

All the hype made me want to puke. I had no business being here. All I wanted to do was shrink into the darkness of the cemetery with the stone angels, but that wasn't going to happen. Mom would get her way again. And I knew less than nothing.

"That place is packed. She won't miss me if I don't show."

I expected Mom to argue, but instead she surprised me by grabbing my hand.

"I want you to be happy, Bren. You're a great kid and you should have friends. Maybe Chloe can help you with that. I just wish—"

She didn't finish. A part of me didn't care what she wished for me, but I had to admit that a small fragment wanted her to blurt it out and mean it. I squeezed her hand and looked her in the eye. It was strange how our roles got reversed sometimes, like she needed the reassurance more than I did.

"I wish I could be happy, too, but there are things I've got to deal with first…on my own."

Mom picked a fine time to have a heart-to-heart; parked outside the party she had coerced me to attend for my own good. Treating me like a child, she had trumped my objections with her parent card and made the decision without any input from me. And now she expected me to open up?

Well, it doesn't work that way, Mom.

Sitting in that car with her, I couldn't help but think about the morning my world crashed down on my head—when I knew my mother couldn't protect me. At fourteen, I didn't think much about my future. I blindly accepted stuff and I assumed my mother was in control and that nothing bad would happen.

I was wrong. *Dead wrong.*

My mother had been as helpless as I was when Sheriff Logan questioned me for hours. And that scared the hell out of me. She told me later that she thought I'd be in and out, and that she believed he'd only ask me about finding the body. That's why she gave him permission to do what he did to me, but Sheriff Logan had lied to her and she bought it. She'd waived my rights to have anyone present during my interrogation. Not a lawyer—not even her. When he got me alone, he accused me of being a part of Heather's murder and I freaked, but I had no one to help me. And my mom had let it happen. A kid didn't forget stuff like that.

I never forgave her. I'm not sure I ever will.

So her reaching out to me now felt fake and way too easy. Sometimes her being nice made me feel like shit, but not bad enough to trust her again. And forcing me across the country—to face the aftermath of the worst days of my life—wasn't the way to earn my trust back. As far as I was concerned, I only had me. And I'd gotten used to that.

"Being a mom, it's hard to know when to let go, but I feel like you left me a long time ago. I see you drifting away and I'm scared for you, Bren."

"I know you are, Mom." I nodded. In truth I was scared, too, but admitting that would only make her feel worse. I leaned over and kissed her cheek instead. And when I pulled back, her eyes were watering. "I'll call you to pick me up… probably by the time you get back home."

She'd given me a curfew, but I knew I wouldn't need it. I'd make an appearance at Chloe's, long enough to satisfy Mom, before I'd split. I got out of the car and slammed the door, not looking back. I knew Mom was watching me, but I pretended not to notice.

Why is it that the people who are supposed to love us most can hurt us so bad? I had a terrible feeling about coming here. It didn't feel right. And I really wanted my mother to see that. I wanted her to realize she'd been wrong and to stop me before I went inside. I wanted her to foresee the future and warn me.

But that didn't happen.

I took a deep breath and headed for the front door. I didn't need a psychic and a crystal ball to know I would hate this.

"Brenna Nash just walked in." Derek Bast sneered and took a gulp of beer as he slumped against a wall in the game room. "What do you want me to do?"

"Get her a drink. A strong one." Jade DeLuca didn't hesitate. She knew what she wanted. "And keep 'em coming." When he turned his back on her, she called out to him, "I want her messed up."

"Wait a minute. What are you doing?" Chloe questioned. "I don't want any trouble at my house."

With Chloe's parents gone for the weekend, Jade had twisted the girl's arm to throw a party, the first bash of the summer. Even though Chloe cringed at having to clean up before her parents got back, she didn't say no. She wouldn't dare.

But having Brenna at the party was an unexpected bonus Jade couldn't resist. That's why she had insisted Chloe invite her. Brenna Nash wouldn't have accepted the invitation from anyone else. And Chloe was the only one who could have pulled the invite off with a straight face.

"There won't be any trouble. Not really. And even if there was, we've got Derek. His uncle is the sheriff. You don't get any more bulletproof than that. Relax and have another drink on my dear old dad."

Jade had used her dad's credit card to pay for the booze and munchies. And Derek's fake ID did the rest. The old man would never notice the charge. She'd done it before. And even if he did find out, she knew he wouldn't make a big deal about it. He was a divorced dad trying to be a "friend" to his only daughter. Being a parent was something he had gotten good at faking.

"I gotta see her. Where is she?" Jade craned her neck to peer over the crowd to catch a glimpse of Brenna Nash. "Oh. My. God." She dropped her jaw and exchanged looks with Chloe. "What has she got on? I swear I've seen homeless people look better than she does. I hope she took a bath, at least. If she reeks, I'm gonna tell her, to her face and in front of everyone."

Brenna had on a red gingham sundress with a tattered jean jacket over it. Strands of long blond hair covered her face and hung down from a straw hat where she'd stuffed the rest of her hair. A ratty black scarf was tied around her neck and hung below her knees. And she wore bizarre white leggings, torn in several places, with clunky unlaced boots.

In Europe, she might have pulled the look off, but this was America, damn it. The girl had no appreciation for designer labels.

Chloe batted her blue eyes and didn't give an opinion on Brenna's party clothes. And that pissed Jade off. The idiot had her eyes on Lucas Quinn, who sat across the room with an acoustic guitar in his lap. The boy was in his own world, ignoring the music Chloe had playing. Lady Gaga and Buckcherry were bands too commercial for Lucas. He had his own gig going.

"You should do the guy and get it over with already." Jade rolled her eyes at Chloe.

Lucas was Chloe's obsession and everyone knew it, but she was too pathetic to take what she wanted.

"He's been watching me. I see him looking over here." Chloe smiled and took a hit off a joint, sucking in her breath and blinking her eyes when the spiral of smoke trailed into her face. Jade knew the weed was from a private stash Chloe kept hidden in her bedroom.

When Jade looked back at Lucas, the boy was chatting up a blonde sitting next to him as he hunched over his guitar, strumming chords. Chloe was clearly delusional. He had no clue she even inhabited the same planet.

"That's 'cause he knows you're stalking him, along with half the girls in school." She grabbed Chloe by the shoulders and shook her. "Screw him and get it over with. You're boring me."

Lucas was definitely cool. He was a musician, a high school boy who played guitar with a local band of college guys. He was that good. And cute, too. He had dark hair that looked like he'd just gotten out of bed. His hair made a girl want to run her fingers through it. He was tall with dark, soulful eyes. And he had a pierced ear and wore a Celtic cross around his neck. Everything about the guy made him seem older.

Lucas was real fantasy material, mainly because he never said much. Most guys opened their mouths and ruined everything. Not Lucas. He had an air of mystery to him, as if he were above it all. And since he didn't say much, a girl could make up anything about him and it would fit. His quiet self-confidence meant that he didn't just talk about doing stuff. He actually did it and didn't have to brag about it later.

If Chloe hadn't drooled on him first, Jade would have rocked his world. Who knows? She might still step in and save Lucas from boring Chloe, if the boy was still worthy by the end of the party. And doing it in Chloe's bedroom, right under her nose, would be a stunt worthy of Heather herself.

Jade grinned at the idea and took off to find Brenna. The real fun was about to start.

* * *

Mom's idea of a good time for me was a house filled with enough secondhand smoke to give me a tumor, cheap booze and grass to get me busted and several hundred losers I didn't want to know. And for a real laugh riot, someone had barfed on the stairs, the kind with chunks. I got out of smell range of blown chow and wandered through the house looking for Chloe. Once I made an appearance, I could split. The way they had the music blasting, the neighbors were bound to complain about the noise anyway.

Since the party had been Mom's idea, I didn't get the usual twenty questions like, "Will her parents be there?" As I walked through the chaos, I didn't see anyone older than twenty. That meant I'd stay sober in case I had to ditch if cops raided the place. And all I wanted was to smell fresh air again, stare into the night sky and save my eardrums from bleeding.

When I turned to go, I ran into a wall of pectorals.

"I didn't figure you'd show. Come to apologize?" Derek grinned down at me.

I had enough that kept me up nights. The last thing I needed was a parting shot of Derek Bast's face—God's best endorsement for birth control.

"Apologize for what?" Before he answered, I raised my hand and yelled loud enough for him to hear me. "Forget I asked. I don't want to know."

I don't friggin' care, was more like it. Before I pushed by him, he handed me a glass. Even in the dim lights I saw the drink was mostly alcohol. I could've smelled it at twenty paces.

"No, thanks. This was a mistake." When I shoved by him, he dumped the whole glass down the front of my dress and pretended it had been an accident. I gasped and stood there in shock—dripping wet—with everyone laughing at me. I saw some of their faces through the darkness.

But one face stood out from the rest—*Jade DeLuca.*

She glared at me with her arms crossed. Backlit in an aura of pale light, her reddish hair made her look as if she glowed red-hot, like she had superpowers. Maybe girls like Jade did. She wore a low-cut tank top and skinny jeans that showed off a body that she knew how to use. Her face was cast in shadow, but I remembered she had cold gray eyes that changed color with her moods.

And I wasn't the least bit curious what color they were now.

"You reek. And where'd you get that outfit? Some pizza joint is missing a tablecloth." Jade took the hat off my head and tossed it across the room. My hair fell in a tumble onto my shoulders. "Oh, nice. When was the last time you washed your hair…or took a bath, for that matter?"

My hair was still wet from the shower, but none of that would matter now that Jade had everyone's attention. Conversations died and someone had killed the music. All eyes were on me.

I'd become the new entertainment.

"You actually thought you could come to our party? Oh, you did, didn't you?" Jade faked a condescending show of sympathy like she felt sorry for me, but that didn't last long. "How utterly pathetic."

"Chloe invited me this afternoon, personally." I sounded lame.

All I wanted to do was crawl away and hide, especially when I caught a glimpse of Chloe standing in the crowd. She looked mortified. And she couldn't look me in the eye, but when she pushed through the crowd, I thought she'd speak up for me.

"Jade, don't do this. I told you before, I don't want any trouble." Chloe didn't sound convincing. And she looked scared.

"Shut up, Chloe. And stay out of this. I'll handle it." Jade dismissed her and focused on me. Whatever she was doing, Chloe hadn't known it was coming. And not all the kids in the room knew what was going on, but that didn't make Jade's torment any easier for me to take.

"We wanted to see how stupid you were. And from the looks of it, I'd say you're the village idiot." Jade walked around me, looking up and down. And behind my back, I knew she was mocking me even more because the crowd snickered when she did.

"What makes you think we'd actually want you here?" she asked. "That druggie half-breed killed Heather. And just because the sheriff didn't arrest you, doesn't mean any of us think you're innocent. You're a loser, Brenna. And your boyfriend is a damned killer. He murdered my best friend and you actually have the nerve to come to our party. I'd say you're one deranged bitch."

A part of me wanted to defend myself, but another part knew that would be a waste of time. I was in a no-win situation, like playing Russian Roulette with a fully loaded gun.

"You're right," I agreed. "This was a bad idea. I'm out of here."

When I pushed by her, she grabbed my arm and Derek blocked my way.

"Oh, you're not walking out of here. At least not without a special send-off from us." Jade spit in my face. And when I tried to wipe it off, Derek held my arms. "Heather was our friend. And anyone who had anything to do with her murder should get exactly what's coming to her. Right, guys?"

The crowd howled and closed in. And someone had turned up the music, to cover up what they'd do to me.

I squirmed to break free of Derek's grip, but more hands latched on. Some groped my body and I felt them lift me off the floor. They carried me across the room and I couldn't stop them. I struggled to get free and felt blood rush to my face. And when I cried for help, tears drained down my cheeks as I screamed. Sharp pinpoints of light spiraled in front of my eyes and everything blurred into a nightmare of faces and sounds… and humiliation.

They'd taken everything from me and from White Bird. What more did they want?

Mob mentality had taken over. And no one would lift a finger to help me. Jade DeLuca had stepped into Heather's shoes and was calling the shots now. And I didn't know how far she'd go to punish me.

This was gonna be bad. Real bad.

chapter five

Hours Later

Looking down from a second-floor window of the Seaver home, Derek was the first to spot her. Brenna's mother had pulled into the driveway and screeched to a stop. She threw the Subaru into Park with the engine running and the headlights on. And when she got out of the vehicle, she left the driver door open. He got a good look at her face when she crossed in front of the headlights. And she looked pissed.

"Oh, shit." He pushed his way through the people on the landing and the stairs. "Make a hole. Get out of my way." By the time the doorbell rang, he was there to answer it.

"Hey there, Mrs—" Before he finished, Mrs. Nash shoved by him.

"Where's Brenna? She was supposed to call me to pick her up. She's past her curfew." The woman searched the faces of the stragglers in the living room. The party was winding down.

"Brenna? I saw her leave two hours ago. She hitched a ride with some motorcycle dude."

"A biker? How did a biker know about this party?" The woman looked shocked.

"You know how it is. Those guys come off Route 66. When they hit town, they're looking for a good time. The word gets out. I'm sure they weren't invited."

"What did this guy look like?"

"I never paid much attention until they took off. I really think him and a buddy crashed the party. That's what I heard after Brenna left with them." He shrugged, knowing he had her full attention. "I'd seen them when they first walked in, but those biker dudes got a little rowdy later on. One of the girls at the party asked me to get rid of them, but by the time I got there, the jerks had split. That's when I saw Brenna take off with them."

"No, that's not right. Why would she do that?" The woman shook her head, but he could tell she had doubts about her daughter when her voice cracked. "We had an arrangement. I was supposed to pick her up. She was going to call me."

"I don't know anything about that, ma'am. Maybe she forgot. She was pretty hammered."

When she turned to him in shock, he kept his eyes on hers.

"She was drinking?" she asked. "Where'd she get the alcohol?"

"I don't know. Maybe from those guys," he said. "You need me to do anything? I'd help you look, but my parents are expecting me home."

Brenna's mom ran a hand through her hair and heaved a sigh. "I don't know where to look. And she doesn't answer her phone." She looked like she was about to cry. "Are Chloe's parents here? I need to talk to them."

"They're not here. They're in Texas somewhere. On business, I think."

"You mean there wasn't an adult here?"

"No, ma'am, but nothing happened. A few kids, like Brenna, were blowing off steam with summer bein' here, but I swear the party was pretty low-key." Derek got in front of her and touched her shoulder. "You're not gonna get Chloe in trouble, are you? She was trying to do Brenna a solid by inviting her to the party. If it'll help, I can call my uncle and we'll all look for your daughter. Just say the word."

At the mention of his uncle, Sheriff Logan, Mrs. Nash got real quiet, like he figured she would.

"No, that won't be necessary." And when she turned to leave, she said, "At least I hope not."

Brenna's mother left in a hurry and didn't look back. Derek stood on the doorstep and watched her drive away. And as she gunned it down the street, he cut loose with a smile and went looking for Jade.

With the party winding down, boredom had taken over and Jade went looking for someone to mess with, the way Heather used to do with her. And knowing Chloe, that chick had more than weed stashed in her room. The girl was quiet, but she had her secrets. And ever since Brenna Nash had come back to town, she'd been unconcerned and distant. Jade needed something new to hold over her head to keep her in line.

She'd slipped into Chloe's bedroom and closed the door behind her so she could take time rummaging through her drawers and under her bed. Most of what she'd found didn't add up to much, until she got to the armoire.

One deep drawer was locked.

"What the hell—" She grimaced and went looking for the key in Chloe's jewelry box on the dresser. When she didn't find it there, she tried a few more places and came up empty. But when Jade ran her fingers along the back of the armoire, she found a small key hanging on a hook near the base. She would have missed it if she hadn't lost her balance. Her hand brushed against the key by accident.

"Nice." She smiled.

After she'd unlocked the drawer, she was disappointed to see that was where Chloe kept her stash of weed, mixed in with more lingerie. Jade had hoped for something really juicy.

"Damn it. What's the big deal, Chloe? You're such a friggin' tease."

In frustration, she slammed the drawer shut, but something didn't feel right. The drawer felt heavier than it should have been, if it only held lingerie, a few rolled joints and a lighter in a Baggie.

"Hold on. What's up with that?"

When Jade looked at the dimensions of the drawer, they were off, too. It should have been deeper than it was.

"Oh, clever girl." Jade grinned.

Whatever Chloe had hidden beneath her stash had to be good. It took her a moment to figure out that the whole top drawer lifted out. And when Jade set the fake drawer aside, she knew she had hit the mother lode of Chloe's secrets.

"Holy shit!" She gasped and covered her mouth. "Oh. My. God."

The whole drawer glittered with Lucas Quinn. His face was everywhere.

Chloe had promo flyers where Lucas's band had played, tickets where she had probably attended the performance without talking to the guy and scraps of crumpled paper with his handwriting on it. From the looks of it, the paper had ideas for a song that he probably wrote and trashed. Chloe had obviously taken his notes from the garbage. She'd scrapbooked other mementos with glitter, like some lovesick puppy.

"You are really sick," she whispered. "A terminal case of pitiful."

Chloe had gone far past rational. She had photos of Lucas. Real candid stuff that meant she'd been following him, day and night. She'd even used Photoshop to splice digitals of them together. How weird was that? The girl had gone way beyond crushing on the poor bastard. She was seriously stalking him, for real.

Chloe even had bags of Lucas's hair. She must have scarfed it off the stylist's floor. The date, time and all sorts of details were labeled and tied onto the strand. Four Baggies in total. And one plastic bag had brown goop that held the hair together. That one had a sticker on it that read, *4 LUCAS,* in caps.

She must have been collecting his hair for years and numbered what she kept. Jade shook her head as she tossed back the Baggie. It would take her days to look at everything Chloe had stashed in her secret drawer.

But one thing caught her eye.

Buried under tons of sappy memorabilia meant as a tribute to Lucas Quinn was a hardcover book. It had a photo of his face smiling back on the cover, with glitter and lace in a heart shape around it.

"Oh, come to Mama." Jade pulled out the book and flipped through the pages. When she recognized Chloe's handwriting and read a few entries, she knew she'd found the best secret of all.

Chloe was keeping a journal.

When she found Lucas's name on a random page, Jade read a few lines that caught her eye.

Today is the first day of the rest of my life… The day when I first saw Lucas Quinn… The look on my face must've been priceless. But I knew in that moment, we had connected on a higher level. Even as I'm writing this, I keep repeating his name… I just love the way it rolls off my tongue… Lucas Quinn… Lucas Quinn. I can't wait to see him tomorrow.

"Oh, brother." Jade rolled her eyes and ran her fingers down the page. "Utterly hopeless."

But a loud noise behind her made her heart leap. "Oh, shit!" She clutched the book to her chest.

"Jade, you in there?" A deep voice bellowed from the hallway.

It took her a moment to realize she'd remembered to close the door. No one had barged in on her, but the damage had been done. And she didn't want Chloe to know she'd been prying—not before she got a better look at the journal.

"Damn it! Friggin' asshole." She cursed under her breath before she called out, "Just a minute."

Jade scrambled to put everything back the way she'd found it, including the journal, even though she'd given serious thought to "borrowing" it. She had to know what was in it, but now wasn't the time, not with Derek yelling her name outside the door. *Damn him.* Jade locked the drawer to the armoire and put back the key before she glanced around the room one more time. Everything was like she'd found it.

When she yanked open the bedroom door, she glared at Derek.

"What? Don't you know what a closed door means?" She pulled him inside the room and gave a quick look down the hall, to make sure Chloe hadn't seen them, before she closed the door again.

"It could mean a lot of things." He smirked. "In your case, I'd say you were hiding something."

With her arms crossed, she did her best to ignore his dead-on insinuation. "What's so important?" she demanded.

"Brenna's mom came here…just now."

"What? Really?" She pretended to be concerned, but couldn't hide her amusement. "What did you say?"

"I told her what we talked about. And she bought it, just like you said she would."

"And did you do that other thing I asked you to do?" She grinned and wrapped a strand of her hair around her finger, flirting with him.

"Yeah, I did. I'd say we have nothing to worry about from that Indian lover." He smiled. "And I've done everything you asked, right?"

She didn't bother to answer him. He pulled her to his chest and took what he usually got in return. And Jade gritted her teeth, hoping he'd get it over with quick like he usually did. Even young as she was, before her death, Heather had controlled Derek the same way.

And to think that crazy bitch used to brag about it.

On the Outskirts of Shawano—1:50 a.m.

Dispatch had received an anonymous cell phone call to 911 that couldn't be traced back to the caller. The technology was improving, but from time to time, they got calls like this and it drove dispatch crazy. Deputy Will Tate had been on duty and had responded to the emergency, but he hadn't been alone.

Sheriff Matt Logan got a personal call, telling him all about it. He'd rushed to the scene, listening for any updates on his radio as he drove.

By the time he got there, he hadn't missed much.

In a wash of spiraling cop lights, he saw Brenna Nash on the side of the road. He'd arrived in time to see Deputy Tate wrap a blanket around her shoulders. She'd been found wandering down a farm road on the outskirts of town—without a stitch of clothes on. She looked drunk. And from what he could tell, she might have even resisted arrest, too.

When he got close enough, he smelled alcohol. The kid was really messed up, in more ways than one.

"What happened to your face?" he asked her. The sheriff knew his deputy had nothing to do with how she looked, but someone had beaten her. Or maybe she'd done it herself. He wouldn't put that past a kid like Brenna Nash.

She stood there and didn't answer him, clinging to the blanket around her shoulders with her lips quivering. Her reaction had come from her fear of getting caught rather than any real likelihood of her being cold. The heat lingered this time of year in Oklahoma, even in the early morning. The girl looked like a deranged lunatic and she could barely stand without leaning on something. It didn't take a rocket scientist to figure out she was really drunk.

He pulled his deputy aside and spoke only loud enough for him to hear. "You give her a Breathalyzer yet?"

"No, not yet. I only got here a little before you did."

"Get that done before you take her in. And I don't care if she refuses to take it. Do whatever it takes, you hear me?"

"Yes, sir."

"And did she resist arrest in any way?"

Deputy Tate shrugged. "Not really. She tried to run, but

that didn't last long. She was more scared than anything else."

"In my book, that's resisting, Tate. We need to take a firm hand with this kid. She's real trouble. You weren't here two years ago when she was involved in that killing. You don't know her like I do." He shook his head. "You gotta trust me on this one."

"But, sir..."

"Why are you arguing with me, Deputy, when I know what I'm talking about?"

He knew his deputy was trying to do the right thing, but he didn't know Brenna Nash.

"Because that kid is scared," Tate argued. "You didn't see her when I first drove up. I'd bet money she's a victim. And I don't think it's right that we make things worse for her."

His nephew's call to his cell had triggered a reaction in him, especially after he'd found out that the Nash girl was involved. And Derek had told him plenty. Matt had made up his mind what he wanted to do before he even got to the scene.

"But there's something you don't know. I got a reliable tip that she brought this on herself. She took two deadbeats to a party with her and they had booze." He saw he was persuading the deputy when Tate couldn't look him in the eye. "I'm telling you, this kid is messed up. Even cold sober, her judgment is impaired. And we need to teach her a lesson."

"Lesson? What are you talking about?"

"When you get back to the station, book her like she was under arrest and toss her in jail. She needs to know that she was breaking the law. Cooling her heels in a jail cell for public intoxication and disturbing the peace might get her attention. And her useless mother will have to pay to get her out. Trust me, Will. For God's sake, trust me, boy."

The deputy quit arguing and got back to business. By the time the sheriff saw her again, the Nash kid was leaning against Tate's patrol car and she was crying. She looked a wreck. He had a boy and a girl of his own in college, but thank the good Lord neither of them had turned out like this.

"What's up with your hair? That some new punk style?" He didn't keep up with what kids did these days, but her hair had been hacked to shreds. And she still didn't say anything or look him in the eye.

Taking a special interest in the 911 complaint, Sheriff Logan hadn't been exactly surprised to find this girl in the thick of it. His nephew had called him personally to warn him that she had made trouble at Chloe Seaver's and left with two bikers who'd crashed the party. And that she probably would try to drag other kids into her mess.

His nephew had no reason to lie.

"Brenna Nash. So this is your encore?" He shook his head and clenched his jaw. "You've only been here a couple of days and you can't stay out of trouble. You might get away with behavior like this in the big city, but not here." He shifted his gaze to his deputy. "Arrest her and lock her up."

"I'll take her statement," Deputy Tate said.

"No, I'll do it. Just do like I told you. And I want her handcuffed, too. She's not getting a free ride, not in my town. And make sure you get a photo of all of this." He waggled a finger at her with a look of disgust on his face. "I don't want her sayin' we did this."

He'd seen too many kids like the Nash girl, a product of neglect from a mother who couldn't handle her. And if she had sneaked into Red Cliffs mental hospital to visit that damned Indian kid—like he suspected after he'd gotten the call from Dr. Sam Ridgeway and heard his description of the visitor—maybe he'd been wrong to dismiss the girl's involvement in the murder of Heather Madsen. He still had questions about that and she wouldn't get a slap on the wrist for what she'd done tonight, not if he had anything to say about it.

His nephew had been right to call him. Derek had been worried for the Nash girl. And making that call couldn't have been easy for him.

"I want her locked up and off my streets," he said to his deputy. "And get her mother down to the jail now. She doesn't get to sleep in while her kid is terrorizing the town and tying up law enforcement. Who the hell does she think she is, coming back to Shawano like this?"

He wanted to look Kate Nash in the eye to tell her that he hadn't been wrong about her kid being trouble.

Not then.

Not now.

chapter six

The Shawano jail was ten times scarier than I had remembered it. Or maybe being back here—like a three-sixty déjà vu—made it worse. The cell stank like piss and the walls were smeared with black. My little box had a dirty stainless steel sink and a toilet that hung on the wall in the open. I'd have to be totally desperate to use it. Another prisoner at the end of the row was snoring real loud, making a gross throaty noise that sounded like he'd stop breathing any second, if I could only be so lucky.

I sat in the dark on my bunk, dressed in an orange jumpsuit that was so big on me that I had to roll up the sleeves and pant legs. And when the bars closed in on me, my sudden claustrophobia was the icing on my pity cake. I felt sick. And from the stares I had gotten from the cops in booking, I must have looked like shit.

Jade and Derek had totally screwed me over—and I'd never seen it coming.

"Yeah, Chloe. Nice party."

I didn't want to cry, but I did.

The only good thing about how I'd been found was that Deputy Tate had been the first cop on the scene. He didn't say much. And he'd been quick to cover me with a blanket, but I couldn't look him in the eye. After he'd cut me a break at the cemetery on my first night in Shawano, I felt like I'd let him down. And with me riding in the back of his patrol car, in my own little cage, he kept eyeing the rearview mirror. It was hard to miss the worry in his eyes, but he never said anything. Guess that was okay. I didn't feel like talking anyway.

Jade and Derek and the others were counting on me being humiliated, so I'd keep my mouth shut. And I had to admit that telling the truth would be way worse. I would have been better off making up something less degrading that didn't make me sound so frickin' stupid. Everything they'd done had been intended to intimidate me. And it had worked.

Even if I wanted to report what really happened, no one would believe me. I'd look like the whack job that came to town looking for a fight. And I had picked up where I'd left off. A real loser. Not even my own mother would believe me after Jade and Derek lined up witnesses to back any story they wanted. I'd be outnumbered.

"So what else is new?" I mumbled as I wiped tears off my cheeks.

What happened came at me in cruel flashes that I'd never forget. Derek's buddies hauled me off to a bedroom and poured liquor down my throat until I threw up. And when they stripped off my clothes, I was terrified. I'd never been so scared in my life. I thought they would take turns raping me, but that didn't happen. Once they saw the razor scars I'd cut into my arms and thighs, that gave Jade an idea. When she came back into the room, she had a razor and asked Derek to hold me down. I screamed and struggled to get free, but I wasn't strong enough.

Jade cut off my hair. She hacked at it until it was shredded. After she'd done her worst, Derek punched me in the face. I didn't remember much after that, except the laughter as they paraded me through the party. After that, some guys shoved me into a truck and dumped me in the middle of nowhere—without any clothes—their idea of a joke.

Until tonight, only my mom had ever seen me naked.

I ran my trembling fingers through what was left of my hair and I cried harder. I was so royally screwed. And I had a bad feeling that I hadn't seen the worst. I shut my eyes and leaned my head against the cinder block wall. The darkness swallowed me whole and I welcomed it. I desperately wanted to turn the clock back, but since I couldn't do that, I pictured one of the last times I felt safe and at peace.

Thinking about White Bird had become a Band-Aid to my soul.

Being down by the creek was always special, but after the sun went down, that was when magic took over. White Bird felt it, too. I saw it in his dark eyes.

Nightfall was special for both of us.

The moon shed its luster and dappled the swirling creek water with pure glitter. And the sound of the water trickling over stones became music to my ears. I saw the world with different eyes back then. And I felt absolutely everything. The cool night air blew through my hair and the darkness was a welcoming embrace that I'd grown to love.

And White Bird had opened my eyes to all of it.

One memory in particular took shape in my mind. His voice had come to me first, as if he'd whispered in my ear to get me to remember it. It made my ear tickle and I smiled. I should have felt the cut on my lip, but I didn't.

White Bird had wanted so desperately to belong to the Euchee that he'd listened to the elders of the tribe and read everything he could at the library on his people. But when he discovered how important the language of signs was to them, he devoured anything he could on the subject. He felt a mystical connection to the earth and to the universe and to the tribal ancestors who had come before.

The study of signs had become like a religion to him. And one night he shared his thoughts with me after we'd hiked a trail along the creek and we sat staring up at the full moon. There wasn't a cloud in the sky and the moon looked huge. And everything was dusted in a powdery blue, including us.

We sat on a large boulder, back-to-back, staring up into the starry heavens. The warmth of his skin came through his shirt and I swear I felt his heart beating in time with mine. And his voice resonated through his chest and into me like an undeniable charge of electricity.

Pure magic.

"The ancient tribes used to read signs in everything," he told me. "But man became a great skeptic. And science and technology demanded proof. Having faith wasn't good enough anymore. And reading signs became nothing but superstition."

I loved listening to him talk. His voice had become a melody I couldn't shake, but that night he sounded more serious. He wanted me to understand something very important to him.

"But, Brenna, I believe there is only a thin veil that separates the mystical world from the reality we think we see. We only have to open our minds to the possibility. If we accept that dreams can be interpreted for signs to guide us, why would our waking hours be so different?"

"What are you saying?" I asked and turned toward him. "You sound like a fortune cookie."

He smiled and brushed a strand of hair from my eyes. And when he did, a sprinkle of the moon reflected in his eyes and glistened off his long dark hair. The moon's bluish haze colored his hair like the sheen on a raven's wing.

"I'm serious, Brenna. The universe is whispering to us. And we gotta keep our hearts and minds open to hear it." He touched my cheek. "I feel this connection most when I'm here with you, especially in this place. I want to know if you feel it, too."

Looking into his eyes, I could believe anything. And I wanted to believe as he believed—as deeply as he felt it—but I wasn't sure that I had it in me. I didn't feel smart enough. And why would the universe speak to me? I was just a kid.

Being at the creek with him had made me different. I knew it and felt it in my heart, but how much of that was me being a girl in love?

"Yes. Being here with you, it's special for me, too." I hadn't exactly lied. And my answer made him smile. That was all that mattered to me.

"This may sound weird coming from a kid without a family, but I want..." He struggled to find the right words. "I want you to be part of my tribe, Brenna. There's a connection between us that I never want to lose. It would mean a lot to me if you'd...think about it."

It took a moment for what he said to sink in. But once it did, I remembered how I felt. I wanted to cry. He had such a simple way of talking. And nobody had ever touched my heart the way he did. He had no idea how much his simple request had moved me.

Me? He wanted me to be a part of his adopted family. Me, the weird kid who never fit anywhere.

"Think about it? I'd be—" I struggled for my own words "—honored."

His smile broke my heart. I knew how much family and being connected to another human being meant to him. He wanted to belong. And I knew exactly how he felt.

"I never told you before, but on the day we met, I knew you were coming," he said. "A raven came to me in a dream and told me. I had been waiting that day…for you."

I melted when he told me that. I pictured him waiting for me like we were two lovers destined to meet and it made me feel even more special. But later—after I had learned that in Celtic, my name meant "Little Raven"—his words always gave me goose bumps.

White Bird slipped his hand into mine and said, "When my parents died, I was so angry. I got into fights all the time. Guess I was mad that they left me without anyone to take care of me, but I just didn't understand."

"Understand what?"

A rumble of thunder sounded in the distance. Something wasn't right. In my memory of what happened between us that night, I hadn't remembered a storm coming, but now I heard it distinctly.

A sudden headache gripped me. I didn't remember that happening, either. My memory of White Bird rolled on in my head. The same yet different. And he pretended not to notice the sound of the storm. That wasn't like him.

"After someone dies, they become connected to all living things," he explained. "Because the past merges with the present. Wouldn't that be amazing if that could happen? Many religions have this concept of the all-knowing soul. Do you believe this is possible?"

I remembered thinking that maybe he was hinting that he knew about dead people, too, but I wanted to hear what he'd say first before I blurted out the weird shit I'd seen. I had been working my way up to telling him about all of it, but a part of me was afraid he'd think I was an idiot.

I felt my headache getting worse as I played my part in the memory, telling him the same thing I did that night. I was straddling a line with one foot in the present and the other… only God knew where.

"Well, yeah. I'd like to think that when I die, that something of me will live on." Like a strange out-of-body experience, I forced the same grin I had that night. I saw myself doing it. I was there…and yet not. "And I sure would like to be smarter if that happens. Know stuff, you know?"

"Exactly." He laughed. "But I think if we open our minds to the universe showing us signs, we don't have to die to awaken that part of our soul. Why wait to get smarter? Why not open our minds to the possibility now?"

He didn't expect an answer. It was like he was exploring the idea for himself and using me as his sounding board. And he never pressured me to believe what he did. White Bird put his arm around me and kissed me in the moonlight. In my true memory of that night, I had never felt so safe and at peace. I was connected to him, to the stars, to the moon and even to the frog that croaked in the distance.

In that instant, I *did* believe.

But the menacing thunder reminded me something had changed. Things weren't as they should have been. And the ache in my head made me grimace in pain. What was happening to me? Now even White Bird felt it. He stared at me in sudden panic.

Something wasn't right and he felt it, too.

Lightning tore across the night sky over our heads and the distant thunder I had heard before, now rumbled beneath us like the earth was splitting apart. Everything shook like an earthquake. Only this time, it wasn't just in my imagination. White Bird felt it. Our connection to the universe and to each other ended in a terrifying rush. He yelled something at me that I couldn't hear. His lips were moving but nothing came out until seconds later.

"Brenna, help me. I need you. Now!" White Bird grabbed my arm and shook me. "Wake up."

I gasped and stared into his desperate eyes, but the instant I did, his face split in two.

"What's happening?" he cried out. "No! Don't let this happen. Not now."

An intense light emerged from inside him, blinding me. It shot through his eyes, his mouth and through his gaping skull, but he didn't scream. His body went slack and he dissolved into tiny windblown fragments that swirled and dropped into the shadows as if he'd been only a fleeting thought that I couldn't quite grasp. The moon had vanished and the sounds of the creek and the forest fizzled away as if none of it had happened.

White Bird's voice had reached out to me through a cherished memory and made me doubt whether I was awake or asleep—or something far worse.

"Don't go. Stay with me," I pleaded to no one. And I reached out and felt nothing.

This time, my eyes opened wide as if it had been for the first time and I felt my heart slamming against my ribs. I sat and glared into total darkness. It took time to see shapes, enough for me to know where I was.

The Shawano jail.

White Bird begging for my help? That wasn't how I recalled that night by the creek. In a strange twilight—caught between my awareness and a dreamworld—he had called out to me and begged for my help. Had I only dreamed it? Was it one of my nightmares?

Or had the moment been real?

"Oh, my God. What's happening to me?"

Reality was slipping through my fingers like shifting sand and I didn't know how to stop it. I ran a hand through my shredded hair and saw the bars of the jail around me. That part of my reality hadn't been a dream, but the bizarre mix of my actual memories of White Bird and my waking nightmare had been so real that I still felt his touch on my arm.

My skin prickled as if a roach had crawled across my skin. And the hair on my neck shifted like someone had touched me in the dark.

"Where are you? Please…talk to me again. I'm here." I called out to him and peered through the darkness, half expecting him to step out of the shadows like the dead did when they showed themselves to me, but when that didn't happen, I was more depressed than I'd ever been.

"I'm losing it. I'm *really* losing it."

My guilt could have instigated the whole thing, but why did it feel so real? I couldn't shake the feeling that I was missing something. And why had I chosen that particular moment in time? At first I thought that memory had been random, but what if it hadn't been?

What if White Bird was sending me a message…from wherever he was?

And if the past and the present had collided, could I trust those memories? Were they real or cries for help from him? I wanted to believe that I could help him and that he had reached out to me, but maybe that was my guilt talking. And when I thought about my own sanity, schizophrenia could make all of this seem real.

And I wouldn't know the difference.

Before I got my mind wrapped around that little hellish ambiguity, a loud buzzer blared down the hall and made me jump. The harsh sound of a door opening jolted me into the here and now. And with the steady rhythm of footsteps echoing outside lockup, I knew round two was about to begin. I felt as if I had gotten shoved into the deep end of an icy pool when I wasn't ready. I hated what my life had become. And there was no end to the torment.

Maybe I didn't deserve to be happy.

A shadow appeared outside my bars. A man in uniform. And with a jangle of keys, the jailer opened my cell. As much as I'd wished for him to release me, I knew Sheriff Logan wouldn't make it that easy.

"Sheriff wants to see you."

Of course he did. *Why not?*

I gritted my teeth and wished I were anywhere but here. With other prisoners sleeping, the hallway to the holding cells was dark. The only light came from the small wire-meshed window on the door I would walk through. I wanted to stay on this side of the darkness, but that wouldn't be an option.

I had crossed back into Sheriff Logan's world. And that man knew how to twist the knife.

Twenty Minutes Later

At the end of his shift, Deputy Will Tate had stayed to finish his report on the 911 call involving sixteen-year-old Brenna

Nash. Will was writing his report at his desk while he kept an eye fixed on the locked glass door that led to a small reception area outside booking. That lobby was the public entrance to the sheriff's office. The girl's mother would show any minute. And since he'd spoken to the woman on the phone, he wanted to be the one to escort her through the drill of visiting her daughter.

Kate Nash had sounded frantic on the phone. It couldn't be easy being a single parent, especially after what happened two years ago. He'd only glanced at the Heather Madsen murder book, but he'd spent more time reading the interrogation notes of Brenna and her involvement with the case. After reading the file, Will wasn't sure what to make of the kid. He had liked the girl he'd met at the cemetery the other night. She'd been respectful with an acceptable dose of sass that made her interesting.

But the sheriff had painted a very different picture of the girl. And the notes in the murder case that had pertained to Brenna had backed up the sheriff's side of the story. Yet contrary to what Will had seen tonight—the drinking, the fighting and the silent treatment—his gut instinct told him Brenna wasn't some demon hell-bent on the single-handed ruination of Shawano.

The kid didn't strike him as a bad seed, but he didn't know enough about her to argue with the sheriff.

Hearing a commotion from the lobby, Will looked up to see a woman peering through the glass door and calling out to the jailer in booking, "Where's my daughter? I want to see Brenna Nash. Deputy Tate called me."

Will was up on his feet and heading toward the glass door before the woman could sink her teeth into the young officer behind the counter. Outside it had started to rain and the woman hadn't bothered to bring an umbrella or wear a raincoat. Her hair was wet and her clothes were spotted with rain, but she didn't seem to notice. From the look in her eyes, her only concern was for her daughter.

"Mrs. Nash?" he asked. After she nodded, he introduced himself. "My name is Deputy Will Tate. I was the one who called."

He ushered her through the locked door and to his desk.

"Can I get you some coffee?" he asked as he pulled out a chair for her to sit. "And I can get you paper towels to dry off, too."

"No, I just want to see my daughter." The woman sat and leaned an elbow on his desk, not taking her eyes off him.

"Yes, ma'am. We'll get to that."

Wearing jeans and a crimson Oklahoma Sooners T-shirt, Kate Nash was tall and slender with shoulder-length sandy blond hair. Will knew he hadn't caught her at her best, not so early in the morning after a night of worry over her daughter, and after being doused with rain, as well. But her dark eyes had a way of staring a hole through a man. And he'd bet that the lines around her eyes and mouth tipped the scale toward good humor rather than a nasty disposition. She looked like a strong woman with big problems on her shoulders.

"What happened?" she asked. "Can you tell me anything?"

"We got a 911 call about a girl wandering down Highway 12, near the old Thompson ranch at Booker Road. I was first responder." He cleared his throat, trying to figure out how to tell her what he'd found. A mother had a right to know.

"When I found her, your daughter didn't have any clothes on, ma'am. She says she wasn't raped but she refused to let one of our female officers take a rape kit on her. And her blood alcohol level was above the legal limit. She'd been drinking and she had a pretty good shiner and a cut lip. Someone had beaten her up."

Will was thankful he'd gotten to the girl before the rain had hit. Being caught in an Oklahoma downpour would have made things much worse for the poor kid.

"Oh, my God." The woman gasped with a hand over her mouth. Her eyes were already watery and red, like she'd been up half the night crying. "She was supposed to be at a party. I dropped her off at Chloe Seaver's house. I didn't know Chloe's parents weren't there. I swear I never would have let her go if I had known." She bit her lower lip. "This can't be happening."

"Sheriff Logan is taking her statement now."

"No, he can't do that. Not without me being there." She clenched her jaw and glared at him. "You tell the sheriff that we're not having a repeat performance of two years ago. If my daughter needs a lawyer, she's getting one. You tell him that. He'll know what I'm talking about."

"You act as if your daughter's behavior is someone else's fault," a voice bellowed from a hallway that led to the jail.

When Will looked up, he saw Sheriff Logan standing across the room and the man didn't look happy to see Kate Nash.

"You and me are gonna have a talk, Kate. My office. Now."

The sheriff would have intimidated a lesser woman. And Will had seen plenty of men cower at his overbearing nature. Sheriff Logan acted like a father figure to everyone he met. Being sheriff had put the man in the awkward position of feeling like the moral compass to the community.

But Kate Nash didn't back down. And she didn't hesitate to get out of her chair and march down to the sheriff's office. If

Will had the power to reinvent himself as the proverbial "fly on the wall," now would have been the time to do it. After Brenna's mother disappeared around the corner, Will got back to his paperwork, but kept one eye on the Sheriff's office.

Even though it was too early for July 4th, Will had a pretty good notion he'd have a front row seat for the fireworks.

chapter seven

"How dare you interrogate my daughter without me? She's got rights."

Kate Nash tore into him before she'd even crossed the threshold of his office. Sheriff Logan slammed the door to give them privacy and was too furious to sit, especially after she tossed her purse onto his visitor's chair and glared at him with her hands on her hips. Seeing her indignation set him off. She had lit his fuse.

"And this community has rights, too. Where do you get off lecturing me? Your little angel broke the law. She was drunk and parading around naked. That kid has serious problems and you're in complete denial. You have some gall, lady."

It looked like the stark reality of what happened to her daughter had finally hit Kate Nash. She had a hard time looking him in the eye, but that didn't mean she'd keep her mouth shut and listen. *No, sir.* That woman was determined to shed the blame in another direction—anywhere but on her own doorstep.

"I dropped her off at a party. Chloe Seaver's house. How did she get the alcohol?" she questioned. At first, she was more hesitant, but when he didn't answer right away, she became angry and got in his face. "My daughter might have been raped. She could be a victim."

"If she was a damned victim, why didn't she speak up? I tried to get her statement and she didn't open her mouth except to ask if she was being arrested. She demanded to see you and she wanted an attorney."

"Can you blame her...after what happened the last time?"

"And if it was your daughter who'd been murdered two years ago, you'd be all over me to get results. I did what I thought was right. And I won't apologize for that."

When she got quiet again, he heaved a sigh and slumped into the chair behind his desk. He was getting too old for this.

"That kid of yours is a magnet for trouble. And now she even thinks like a criminal. She knows her rights, but she has no respect for anyone else's."

"I don't need a sermon, preacher."

"Sinners never think they do." He swiveled in his chair, not taking his eyes off her. "Did you know she visited that boy at Red Cliffs?" When he saw the shocked look on her face, he smirked. "Guess that's a 'No.' Yeah, someone saw her there... inside the detention center. She had to get through security to do that. So now, you got anything else to say?"

"Are you arresting her?"

"That's it? She went to see the kid who brutally murdered an innocent girl. And all you want to know is how to get her out of jail? You still don't get it, do you?" He shook his head. "You're some piece of work, Kate. You have no idea what you're doing to that girl. You're an unfit mother who's in over her head. I think you know it, but you're just too stubborn to admit when you're wrong."

Kate opened her mouth to argue, but she changed her mind. And the sheriff let the silence build a wall between them. Although she was still a fine-looking woman, Kate had aged since he last saw her two years ago. Raising a wild child will do that to a mother. The woman picked her purse up off the chair and sat down. She clutched her handbag to her chest and waited for his answer.

"I'm releasing her into your custody. You'll have to pay a fine with the booking clerk out front, but she's all yours. And good riddance." He threw up his hands. "You're making things worse by coddling her, Kate. You're screwing this kid up. She's got to take responsibility for her actions."

Kate clenched her jaw and got up from her chair, heading for the door.

"Thanks for the pep talk, Matt. Someday that righteous attitude of yours is gonna bite you in the ass."

After getting another cup of coffee, Deputy Will Tate heard a door slam down the hall and watched Kate Nash leave the sheriff's office. She hadn't seen him come out of the break room. The woman took a few steps before she stopped and leaned against the wall. Her fingers were trembling as she covered her mouth and tears rolled down her cheeks.

"Are you okay, Mrs. Nash?" he asked.

Talking to her only made her cry harder. And she couldn't look him in the eye.

"It's like my little girl's drowning in quicksand," she choked on a sob. "I can almost touch her, but I don't have what it takes. I feel so helpless."

He didn't know what to say. Not having any kids of his

own, he had no idea what she was really going through. So he kept his mouth shut and listened.

"Maybe he's right. I'm making things worse." She shook her head and wiped tears from her face. "I'm losing her. And maybe it's already too late."

"For what it's worth, I don't believe that."

She looked up at him in surprise with fresh tears welling in her eyes.

"I hope you're right."

Without another word, she headed for booking to get her daughter released. And for her and Brenna's sake, Will hoped he was right, too.

After Dawn

Even Mother Nature took it out on me. I'd heard it raining from inside the jail and knew what to expect, but once I got outside, the humidity was suffocating, even this early. And the endless rain made me more miserable, if that was even possible. The thick dark clouds mirrored what I felt in my bones. Heading out of the police station into the rain, I walked with Mom to where she'd parked the car.

She hurried. I didn't.

I didn't give a shit if I got wet. Resembling a drowned rat in my oversize jail threads could only help the way I looked. After I got into the car, I slammed the door shut and slouched deep into the passenger seat with my arms crossed. I braced myself for what she'd say now that we were alone, but Mom surprised me.

She did the worst thing she could have done.

Mom didn't say one word. She started the car and pulled from the parking lot. And we drove to Grams's house in total silence, except for the unending rain pelting our car and the wiper blades fighting a losing battle. I wasn't exactly the one with diarrhea of the mouth anyway. So the odds weren't good that I would be the one to break the ice. But when I caught a glimpse of Mom at a stoplight, I saw she was crying.

And I felt lower than dog poop.

I wanted to say that I was sorry, but not for the obvious. I was sorry that I had turned out to be such a big disappointment. Sorry that I couldn't make things better. Sorry that everything I touched turned to crap. Seeing Mom cry had torn me up.

Until finally she said something.

"What happened to your hair? Did you do that?"

At that moment, I hated Britney Spears. The media had elevated a slow news day into "breaking news" to cover Britney's whacked-out hair shaving fit when she broke out of rehab. But what happened to me was way different. Mowing down every strand off my head would have been one thing, but shredding it like Jade had done to me was off the scale. No way I'd do that to myself.

I gritted my teeth and refused to say anything.

"I need to know what happened, Bren. The sheriff, the kids at the party, they made it sound like you..." She didn't finish. "They all said you got drunk and went off with a couple of guys on motorcycles. So I have to know. Did you do that? Did something happen that you're too embarrassed to tell me? Did they...hurt you?"

Her tears came heavier now. I had the feeling she thought she knew the answer. And she didn't trust me to tell her the truth. And that hurt. But before I could defend myself, she surprised me again. Mom swallowed hard and wiped her eyes.

"I let you down, Brenna. I shouldn't have pushed you to go to that party. And I was so eager for you to go that I didn't even ask whether Chloe's parents would be there. If something happened to you because of me…" She didn't finish.

I waited for her to turn the tables and follow her big admission with some lame justification that completely absolved her of any wrongdoing. But when that didn't happen—when she admitted making a mistake and didn't try to weasel out of it—well, that shocked me. I didn't know what to say. I stared out the window, half watching the rain bleed down the windshield and half watching her from the corner of my eye.

But Mom wasn't done. She gripped the steering wheel and pulled the car over. When we were parked on the shoulder of the road, she turned to me. And her eyes met mine.

"I'm supposed to be your parent, but I have no idea how to fix what's happening to you. I wish I did. I wish—"

"That's just it, Mom. You can't fix this."

My refusal must have sounded like denial to Mom. She didn't stop.

"Did they…rape you? Do you need a doctor? Because I can get you to a hospital, right now."

"God, no. Just quit, will you? I wasn't raped, but I don't wanna talk about it."

Mom had let bad things happen to me, but that didn't mean she did it on purpose. And I didn't see any reason to make her feel worse than she already did. She was asking for me to let her in, but I couldn't do that. Not like this and not because I needed someone to stand up for me.

So keeping my mouth shut, after she'd opened up to me, would hurt her. But it would hurt her more to know that I didn't see the point. I wasn't ready to let her into my life. And I may never be.

But Mom didn't let my silent treatment stop her.

"I want you to tell me what happened because you trust

me…and you want to. You can't bottle stuff like this inside. And if you can't talk to me, I'll help you find someone who you *can* talk to." She reached for my hand. It shocked me, but I didn't pull away. "What I'm saying is that I don't know what the hell I'm doing. I'm in uncharted waters here. And I can't do it alone. I need your help."

I couldn't give it to her. She wanted to be a parent in control again. And I didn't see the point in living *that* lie.

"I'm tired, Mom. Can we just go home?"

I knew when I said it, that I'd done the wrong thing, but I couldn't stop myself. I was being a shit. The only person I wanted to talk to was locked in a mental hospital. But that didn't mean anyone else could take his place.

Maybe what I'd told her was for real, that I was exhausted. I'd been beaten and I ached all over. And my head hurt from the liquor. My first hangover that I hoped would be my last. I wanted to sleep for days. And crawling into bed, buried under my own covers in Grams's house, was the only thing that would make me feel safe.

It was all I could think about.

"That's it?" she asked. "That's all you've got to say?"

I heard it in her voice. The wall had gone up between us again and we were back at square one. And it made me wonder how we had gotten so fragile.

"The other day when you ran errands for me, did you go anywhere else besides the stores?" Mom asked.

I stared at her, feeling the rush of blood to my cheeks as I thought about what I'd told her.

"No. I didn't go anywhere else. I did exactly what you told me." I glared out the windshield and watched the rain, wishing I were anywhere else.

"No, you said you were hungry and had a craving for something. Where did you go? Refresh my memory."

My memory was the one that needed refreshing. Sometimes I lied to keep in practice. And I didn't always remember what I said.

"Oh, yeah, forgot about that."

Stalling gave me time to think. I knew Mom was testing me. If I lost my temper, she'd know something was up. All I had to do was come up with the right answer and act like the whole conversation bored me. Everything would blow over. Mom never really listened to me anyway. She probably didn't remember, either.

"I grabbed a cheeseburger at Sonic with a cherry limeade that had two cherries, my usual."

I didn't hesitate. I blurted it out as if I'd told the truth. When she didn't say anything and merged into traffic, I took a deep breath.

I had either passed her test or confirmed her disappointment in me. And since I didn't feel lucky, guess I knew how I did.

After Midnight

I opened my eyes to pitch black and listened to the sounds of Grams's house as I lay in the dark of my room. I must have slept the whole day and I was still exhausted. I pulled the covers off my face and stared at the ceiling. I don't remember dreaming at all, not about White Bird or anything else. And when I listened to the old creaks and groans of Grams's house, I didn't feel my grandmother and that made me sad.

I didn't want to forget her.

I turned my head toward my window and bunched my pillow under me. The shadows of the old oak tree undulated outside. Its branches cast dark fingers across my drapes. And like an old friend, the tree beckoned me outside. Moving real slow, I got out of bed and changed into jeans, a T-shirt and some old sneaks. I pulled a baseball cap down low on my head to hide what was left of my hair. And I stuffed a flashlight, a small notepad and pen, my cell phone and two things of gum into a fanny pack that I strapped around my waist.

The last thing I tossed into my pack was a box cutter that I'd kept with me since North Carolina. The blade was sharp and Mom had never known what I really used it for. She thought it was something I had to open boxes for our last move. Before I zipped the pack shut, I stared down at the silver cutter and thought about leaving it behind.

But I didn't. I knew I'd need it.

After slipping through my bedroom window, I scaled down the oak tree. I grabbed my old bike from the garage and headed for the stone angels—and Grams. And even though it was after midnight, I took my time getting to the cemetery. I stuck to the shadows on the street to avoid anyone seeing me. And I kept an eye out for patrol cars. No way I wanted more face time with the cops, not even Will Tate.

When I got to the cemetery, I hid my bike and climbed over the stone wall. I located the newer section and read the names on the headstones. It didn't take me long to find Grams. I almost cried when I saw that her grave had the prettiest stone angel I'd ever seen. The angel was a child. A little girl. And I swear she was looking at me. Just me. Her eyes followed me as I walked around my grandmother's grave.

I dropped to one knee and knelt on the ground. And as I stared up at the baby angel, I spoke to my grandmother.

"Oh, Grams. I miss you so much."

I ran my fingers through every line chiseled onto the base

of Grams's stone angel—over and over—as I told my grandmother everything. I huddled against the stone and talked until I was done. Sometimes I cried. Sometimes I even laughed. And I pictured Grams's face and smelled the baby powder she dusted with after her bath. I even caught a whiff of the tapioca she made that I hated but never told her. Memories of Grams flooded my mind like she was reaching out to me.

But finally it was time to do what I'd come to do.

I reached into my fanny pack and pulled out my box cutter. I held it in my hand and stared at it for a long time. The weight of it was familiar and it brought back a rush of dark memories. I had used the blade to cut myself. And each new scar marked a pain I still carried with me in my heart, but what happened today made me see that I was coming to a crossroad.

I had to want to change for myself. And no one else—not even White Bird—could make me happy. I had to do that on my own. And I had to stop letting others dictate how I felt about me. I didn't care what someone like Jade DeLuca thought. She was a total waste of perfectly good skin. And three pounds of brain matter was about two pounds too much for what she did with it. I didn't respect her, so why would I care what she thought of me?

And that went double for Derek Bast. Sure he could pound me into chicken-fried-steak, but he'd always be a charter member of the asshole club. I was tired of feeling awful. And I was fed up with giving jerks like Jade and Derek control over my life. I wasn't sure how I would do it, but I knew what my first step had to be.

I had to stop hurting myself.

I dug a hole near Grams's headstone—under the watchful eyes of her baby angel—and I buried my box cutter. Under the stars, my truth meter, I swore to my grandmother that I'd never cut myself again. And although I had no way of really knowing it, I believed Grams heard me.

Nearly 3:00 a.m.

With a big wad of gum in my mouth, I took my time riding my bike to Grams's house. A couple of lines or a lyric needled me all the way there. I had the urge to stop and write them down in the notepad I had brought with me, but I was still flipping words in different order and working it out.

Forever is never-ending music…

Nighttime is my blanket…

The lines were there, inside my head, for the first time in two years and it felt good. I wanted to write down how I felt whenever I stepped foot in a graveyard. The word *home* came to me, but I wasn't sure what else I wanted to say, so I let it stew in my brain until I was back at Grams's again, ready to crawl under the covers.

But before I climbed up the tree and back through my bedroom window, I saw a strange glimmer of light flickering on the drapes of the living room on the first floor. At first I thought my eyes were playing tricks on me, but when I looked once more, I saw the pale flicker again. I crept toward the window and when I got there, I kept my back to the wall and inched closer to peek inside the bay window. It took me a moment to realize what I'd seen.

Mom was sitting in the dark and watching old family movies. She had a collection that she'd converted to DVD a few years ago. Some were old stuff from Grams, from when Mom was a kid. Light from the TV cast shadows into the living room. I only saw the back of Mom's head as she sat on the couch. But hearing laughter coming from the TV in Grams's living room grabbed my attention.

On the screen, Grams was grinning as she watched me blow out candles on a birthday cake. In these movies, she'd always be young. And Mom looked beautiful. And happy. I'd forgotten how pretty she was when she smiled. Me? I looked and acted dorky, as usual. Some things never change. I still had a weird cowlick in my bangs and was stick skinny.

I also had a tooth missing, right up front. Thanks to the tooth fairy, it grew back and I never needed braces. I used to grin more back then, even with a missing tooth. But somewhere in time I stopped smiling. And I don't remember exactly when that happened—or why it did. It just did.

With a grimace, I crept back off the front porch and headed up the tree for my bedroom. In an odd way, I thought I was intruding on Mom, something private that was only hers. But seeing that old DVD got me thinking.

Even when I was a child, I felt different. I didn't like playing games the way other kids did. And I was quiet. I didn't talk unless I had something real to say and I didn't dress like anyone else. And while other girls played with dolls, I never saw the point. I was off having an adventure down by the creek, up to my neck in mud with lizards and frogs in my pockets. But I guess the real kicker was me hanging out at the local cemetery. Hanging with dead people didn't play well in a small town. Once word got out, I was toast.

Eventually, the other kids stopped inviting me places. I dropped off their radar and they talked about me behind my back. Doing things on my own became a necessity, mostly because I was too stubborn to change. I didn't care if I fit in. And I didn't want to dumb it down to get along. I preferred being in my own head. And as the years went by, it got comfortable for me to stay there—to hide there.

Most days hiding didn't bother me, but some days it did.

After I met White Bird, though, I saw how it could be between two people who were really connected. He made me feel normal. And for the first time, I wasn't just a kid. We really talked about stuff. Real stuff. And he actually wanted to hear my opinions. And that meant I had to have some. He forced me to think. And he really, really listened. When I was with him, I found out something great.

I was actually happy.

But after everything I had with him got flushed two years ago, I was lower than I'd ever been. Had I never met him, I would never have known real joy. But when White Bird got taken away, I sometimes wished I'd never met him. And that killed me.

Now neither of us had moved on from that one gut-wrenching morning. I felt emotionally drained all the time. My life was flat, boring and a lot of nothing. There were no more peaks for me, only valleys of guilt and regret. I wanted to feel better, but I couldn't—not after what I did to him.

Coming back to Shawano had brought the pain fresh to the surface. And I was good at finding different ways to punish myself. I carried my self-inflicted wound with me because I gave myself no choice. And it wasn't because I craved drama. I didn't. I probably would have been content to live my life in boring anonymity, but White Bird changed that. After I'd met him and saw how things could be, I didn't want to settle for anything less.

Did that make me a bad person? Did that make me too weird and unlovable? I really wish I knew.

After I crawled through the window into my room, I thought about going back to bed and forgetting about Mom downstairs, but I couldn't do that. I couldn't shake the sight of her sitting alone in the living room, watching old videos of

Grams and me. I took off my fanny pack, kicked off my sneaks and spit out my gum. And after I got into my PJ bottoms and tank top, I crept downstairs. I still didn't know what I would do once I got there, but something drew me.

Maybe, like Mom, I was looking for answers in the past.

Minutes Later

If I had wanted to peek down from the stairs and watch our homegrown DVD without Mom knowing I was there, that option went away with one step. I had forgotten about a bad creak on the last flight down. I cringed and froze where I was.

"Is that you, honey?" Mom called out from the living room.

"Yeah."

"You slept all day. I thought you were down for the count. What's the matter…you couldn't sleep anymore?"

"Yeah, something like that, I guess."

When I joined her, she patted a spot next to her on the sofa. And she cleared her throat and wiped her eyes, putting on a happier face for my benefit.

"I found these old movies. It's been years since I've seen them." Mom's voice was shaky and her eyes were watery. She'd been crying. "You hungry? I can make popcorn."

"No, thanks. I'm good." Eating popcorn wasn't worth the effort of brushing my teeth again so I sprawled on the couch and curled my feet under me. "I don't remember this one. It looks really old."

The video was real shaky like *The Blair Witch Project,* only no one had snot hanging out their nose…at least that I could see. And the background was of an old mansion with strange gargoyles on the roof that I didn't recognize.

"What's that place?" I pointed. "Kind of weird."

Mom hesitated before she said, "Your father's old family house. He doesn't live there anymore."

Mom pointed to the video, mostly to change the subject away from Dad, like she usually did.

"Oh, my gosh." Mom put a hand to her mouth and gasped. "That's when I was pregnant with you."

I shifted my gaze to Mom's face. The tears were gone and she was actually smiling. Her reaction surprised me. She looked happy.

The video had cut to the sliding doors of a hospital. Whoever was behind the camera was jumping from person to person and zoomed too close and out of focus. And the clips were spliced together, making it hard to follow. But when I saw Mom's young face—and saw her swollen belly—I knew I'd seen the movie before. Hell, I'd lived it.

"Oh, honey, I remember every minute of the day you were born. Well, maybe not every minute, but the best parts, for sure." She chuckled. "And your grandmother was behind the camera. I made her do it. She was driving me crazy."

She didn't have to tell me Grams was there. I heard her screaming over the audio at the nurses when Mom got to the E.R. I couldn't help but grin. Grams barked orders, Mom panted like she was hyperventilating and even before I took my first official breath, I was being a pain. That figured.

"Where was Dad?"

I don't know why I asked that. I blurted it out and should have known better.

"He was traveling…on business. You know that."

That was her stock answer. And like she usually did, Mom tensed up. I could tell she didn't like talking about him. And for her sake, I let it go. She always said the sperm donor wasn't there the day I was born because he traveled a lot on business. But I think she said that to make me feel better. I'd only seen one photo of him and my mother wasn't in it. For all I really knew she'd made him up or they'd never gotten married.

Or maybe his picture came with the frame.

None of that mattered to me. Not anymore. I'd learned how to do without him. If my father didn't want to stick around, I sure didn't need a guy like that in my life. Mom didn't, either. At least, that's what I told myself as I watched the movie.

From day one, it had been Mom and me. And Grams.

"You were a kicker, honey." She laughed and rubbed a hand over her stomach, like she was remembering. "Guess you always have been." A shadow came over her face. And I figured it was a dark memory that wiped away her smile.

We both had plenty of those.

Mom told me more about my first day on the planet. And she was right. She'd only remembered the good parts. And she'd left out how having a baby was like taking a dump the size of a bowling ball. The Cliff's Notes version worked for me. I didn't want to hear about how much it hurt her to bring me into the world.

The real pain would come later and we both knew it.

She reached a hand out for me and I didn't think twice. I laid my head on her shoulder and let her hold me. I'm not sure who needed it more. Guess that didn't matter.

"Tomorrow morning, first thing, we're gonna fix your hair. I'll do it myself. Will that be okay, honey?"

I nodded and didn't say anything. Sometimes I hated when she called me honey, but not tonight. I nuzzled into her shoulder and hugged her back. And I loved how she held me, like she needed it, too. We watched the rest of Grams Scorsese, both of us wrapped in our thoughts. The light from the TV flickered into the dark room and onto both of us. But we just sat there, feeling comfortable with the silence.

It was like we both recognized our truce and neither one of us wanted to screw it up by talking. But I hadn't forgotten what she'd said about me always being a kicker. I pictured a stubborn little kid with a scrunched baby face, thrashing around and demanding to get out. And it made me wonder.

When had I quit being a fighter?

chapter eight

Next Morning

I slept in after my late night and Mom did the same. After a pancake breakfast with an ice-cream chaser, my mother focused on my hair. I knew there wouldn't be much she could do, so I kept my expectations low. She sat me at the kitchen table with a towel draped on my shoulders. After she wet down what was left of my hair, she snipped at the longer strands. I saw blond hairs drop to the floor and I held my breath until I realized she couldn't exactly screw it up. Anything would be an improvement.

When Mom was done, she took a step back and grinned. If she had a more perverse sense of humor, her smile might have been a bad sign.

"Pretty good, if I do say so myself. I always knew you had beautiful cheekbones. You got 'em from your grandmother." She tweaked my hair with her fingers and handed me a mirror.

"If this whole real estate thing doesn't work out, maybe I can open a hair salon."

"I can't look." Visions of Britney still haunted me.

"Trust me, Bren." She grabbed the mirror from my lap and shoved it in my face.

My jaw dropped when I stared at my reflection. I'd never seen me with short hair before. My eyes looked huge and my neck was long. I had the haircut of a boy, but I looked more like a girl than I ever thought was possible, if you didn't count the bruises and cut lip. And with the length gone, Mom had added body and thickness to my normally thin hair. It was scrunched like I'd run my fingers through it. And even though Jade hadn't left me any bangs, Mom had spiked what I had and made the most of it. I looked like a rebellious elf with a serious attitude.

I couldn't help it. I smiled.

"If I had known you would look this cute with short hair, I would have crept into your bedroom at night with the shears." Mom grinned as she swept hair off the kitchen floor.

"Okay, now you're just plain scaring me," I said. I flashed to shades of *Psycho*.

"I'm not done. Stay right there."

After Mom tossed hair into the trash, she raced upstairs. I heard her rummaging through her bedroom and I gave serious thought to finding a suitable hiding place. But in minutes, she was back. And she had a zippered bag filled with cosmetics.

"Makeover time."

I rolled my eyes and raised a hand in objection.

"Oh, no. No, no, no." I shook my head and stood to leave, but Mom shoved me back down.

"Humor me. You can always wash it off. And covering up

those bruises might keep people from asking what happened. I'm sure you'd appreciate that."

I'd given Mom an inch and she'd stretched it into a country mile. My mother was determined to play dress up. And I was her Barbie.

Two Days Later

After Mom made me look more presentable, so I wouldn't scare off little kids or stray cats, I kept a low profile and helped her with Grams's house over the next couple of days. I needed time to heal—both inside and out. The neighbors still spied on us through their miniblinds. And although I'd spotted Derek and his jerk-off buddies parked down the street, they never got any closer.

Except for Mom buying me a new cell phone to replace the one I'd lost at Chloe's party, nothing really happened. And yet I couldn't shake the feeling that would change. Those two days felt like the quiet before the storm.

I was edgy, waiting for the next crisis. Despite the fact that things looked quiet on the surface, there was an undeniable twist in my gut. I believed those feelings had a lot to do with White Bird. I quit daydreaming about him and our past together, mostly because I was afraid of triggering something I couldn't stop.

But at night, he came to me in my dreams.

My nightmares got worse. It would only be a matter of time before I had to do something. The day I had touched White Bird at Red Cliffs had triggered something dark that I didn't understand. I had no idea if it was inside me or if it came from him. And with each passing day that I ignored what was happening, things got worse.

I really had no choice.

"The yard looks beautiful, Bren. You've done a great job, honey." Wearing a bandanna and apron, Mom took a break from her cleaning and brought me a cold Pepsi. She smiled as she looked over the backyard. "The place was really overgrown, but you've made a big difference."

I was sweaty and had a layer of dirt up my arms, but it felt good to work in Grams's garden.

"Yeah, but it could use color. Flowers would be nice."

"Good idea. You feel like making a nursery run with me? We both could use a break."

It surprised me that Mom wanted to come along to pick out flowers. I thought she'd give me the car keys and let me run the errand alone, but when that didn't happen, I had to scramble for plan B.

"I don't know much about flowers. The whole annual/perennial thing confuses me, but I'll plant whatever you buy. How's that?"

"Okay. I'll just change." She turned to head back into the house.

"Hey, Mom? Would you mind if I went to the library instead? I'd like to check my email. I'm sure Dana has sent me stuff. And maybe I can find some books to read." I wiped sweat off my forehead. "I've got my bike. And the library isn't far."

Mom cocked her head with a questioning look on her face as she squinted into the late-afternoon sun, but what parent would turn down a kid for wanting to read? She shrugged her okay and I put away my garden tools and cleaned up, too.

I hadn't lied about wanting to get to the library, but it had nothing to do with checking my email. *Sorry, Dana.*

Shawano Public Library

With my bike, it had been easy to ditch Derek in the street. He never saw me leave. I went around the block and checked.

The only gratifying thing about me having to ditch him was that I knew he'd be in his car baking in the Oklahoma heat while I was at the library.

When I got to the library, I noticed it hadn't changed much, except for a new coat of paint in the entry. The computers were in the same location and the help desk was just as I'd remembered it. Mom used to bring me when I was a kid. I loved the smell of books. And finding my own quiet corner to read was one of my favorite things to do.

Today, it wouldn't be like that. I hadn't come for fun.

Two years ago, the murder of Heather Madsen had been covered in the local papers for months. It had happened during the summer after our freshman year in high school. The violence had shocked the whole community. It was all anyone talked about. And since I had been part of the sheriff's investigation, I'd missed the coverage and had been completely in the dark. At the time, that suited me fine. All I wanted to do was curl up and forget it ever happened.

And even though I had no desire to remember that terrible day now, I had to do it for White Bird's sake. I was the only one who cared what happened to him. It had to start with me. And jogging my memory with newspaper articles at the library was the only way I could do that in secret.

When I first dug through the digital archives of the newspaper, I glanced over my shoulder. I felt someone watching me and I had a hard time shaking the creepy feeling. After a while, I got totally into my search and read every word on Heather's death and forgot about my hinky vibe.

I found it ironic that, according to the newspaper, I was the only witness to her murder, yet I knew the least about it. I'd blocked the trauma from my memory even though flashes of the horror seeped into my brain when I least expected it. I'd see the color red and always remembered the blood. Or I'd hear a fly and I'd flash to White Bird sitting under the bridge at Cry Baby Creek, mumbling and chanting in a daze. That's how my mind worked.

The tiniest thing set off a chain reaction of horrible images. Yet I couldn't replay the mental video of what happened that day from start to finish, no matter how hard I tried. The pieces didn't fit and I had unaccountable gaps. I only remembered what I'd told Sheriff Logan. I went to that scary old bridge looking for the ghost woman and her dead baby. The urban legend had drawn plenty of kids over the decades. It was a rite of passage in Shawano and everybody had done it at least once. That part of my story hadn't surprised Sheriff Logan.

The haunted bridge was on my way home after I'd spent the night in the cemetery. I hadn't told the sheriff how often I made that trek back then. And maybe he sensed I wasn't telling the truth or hiding something. I wanted it to sound gutsy and cool that I'd gone to that bridge on my own—instead of creepy and serial killerish that I was a regular. That morning, I'd heard White Bird's voice carrying on the wind in the gray of morning, just before dawn. And I'd raced to find him. The shock of seeing him over Heather's body stole my breath away. And my heart has never been the same since. *Never.*

That's why I had to read everything I could on what happened that day. I had to fill in the gaps so I could understand. I wasn't sure if any of my research would help White Bird—or me—but I had to do it, even if it made my nightmares worse.

According to the paper, Heather Madsen had been stabbed over a dozen times. And people had speculated that her death had been a crime of passion. That was hard to read. I felt the sting of tears coming and fought it. My head told me White Bird loved me. He wouldn't have hurt me like that, but there was an insecure voice inside me that was hard to ignore. Heather was pretty. I wasn't. People envied her, but shunned me like I was diseased. Even with all my self-doubts, I still found it hard to accept White Bird would betray me, especially with someone that shallow.

And to compound my misery, I saw countless photos of Heather, the beautiful. The newspaper used a school photo for her obituary. She looked gorgeously perfect and she smiled real sweet, but the brunette with long dark hair and green eyes was anything but kindhearted. And nasty Jade had stepped into Heather's shoes for one good reason—*they fit.*

From the corner of my eye, I glimpsed someone moving between the books and that creepy feeling raised the hair on my neck. When I looked up from the monitor, a familiar pair of green eyes stared at me through a bookshelf. Heather glared back, wicked and smirking. She eased down the aisle with her body masked by books, but her movement wasn't normal. She looked like she was…*floating.*

"Oh, God," I whispered.

I stifled my gasp with a hand. And when an older woman looked up from her book, I shot her a shaky smile until she lost interest. I narrowed my eyes at Heather and wanted her to go away, but her lips curved into an eerie grin. In broad daylight, her cruel expression sent chills scurrying across my skin and I had no idea why she'd come.

One second, she was in the book stacks. And the next, she was standing across from my table, staring down at me, messing with my head. Even though she creeped me out, I did my best to ignore her. Seeing the dead came with a price. I had to get used to their humor.

I had always felt sorry for Heather. And with her being dead, that went double. But I didn't put her on a pedestal. She wasn't a nice girl. And being dead hadn't improved her disposition. Alive, the brunette cheerleader took great pleasure in badgering losers like me. She needed to feel superior. But I knew she had to be really desperate to follow me here.

Heather wouldn't be caught dead in a library.

I did my best to ignore the dead girl roaming the aisles in silence, but one good thing came of it. No matter how disturbing it was for Heather to stare at me while I read about her brutal killing, I was glad she made the effort to show up.

Seeing her had triggered my faulty memory.

Two Years Ago

A week before Heather died, White Bird had been secretive. I'd show up at his shelter by the creek and he wouldn't be there. And when he finally showed, he never told me where he'd been. It wasn't like him to keep things from me. And his reluctance to talk about it hurt me even more. I thought he didn't want to see me anymore and maybe he was letting me down easy by avoiding me. Anytime something bad happened to me, I always assumed it was my fault. That's how my brain was wired—then and now—but White Bird didn't know that.

And I didn't exactly come right out and tell him, either.

I took the easy way out. I asked him why he wasn't coming to the creek anymore. I was hoping his answer would be simple, but I knew when he gazed at me with a sad look in his eyes that wouldn't be the case.

"I won't lie to you, so please...don't ask me again," he had said. "Just give me space, okay?"

I wouldn't let it go. I couldn't. He meant too much to me.

We argued and I said terrible things. After that, I spent more time in the cemetery at night and avoided the creek. All the good memories we had together were spoiled. I felt lost and I spent hours thinking over what I had done to ruin it.

After I had confronted him, he stopped showing up at his shelter. I had made him a peace offering—a special friendship bracelet that I had woven for him out of embroidery thread and beads—but when I went to the creek to find him, he wasn't there. I hung it on a branch near his fort and left.

And I never saw him again—not until that day.

That's why I ran to him when I heard his voice. I couldn't believe my ears. I thought I was dreaming. I ran along the dry creek bed, tearing through the brush to see him…and talk to him…and touch him.

But that never happened.

I was the only one who had seen him there. A part of me still wanted to run to him, but something held me back. Something terrifying. White Bird was ranting like a madman. He wasn't the gentle boy I knew who had healed a bird with a broken wing. He wasn't the boy who wanted a family badly enough that he had asked me to be part of his tribe. I saw a man that day, covered in blood and holding a knife in his hand.

And the smell of blood and the never-ending buzz of those damned flies hit me like a sledgehammer, but that wasn't nearly as bad as seeing Heather staring at me with her dead eyes. Her mouth was gaped open and fear had frozen on her face like a death mask. Seeing her like that, I had to do something.

I reached for my phone and made the call that would change my life. Heather wouldn't be the only victim that day.

Shawano Public Library

It took me a long while to recover from that dark flash of memory, triggered by Heather and all the news articles I had read. Cold sweats had given me a chill. And I hadn't realized that I'd been crying. I wiped the tears off my cheeks and looked for Heather. I really wanted to see her, like even seeing her dead would make that horror go away.

But she was gone. And that left me feeling hollow inside.

I had never considered her a friend, but no one deserved to die like that. I took a deep breath to clear my head. And to get out of the dumps, I kept reading and found a strange article published almost a month after Heather's death. It grabbed my attention even though it was on the back page—because it showed White Bird's booking photo.

I stared at that photo for a long time, looking for any hint of the boy I knew. His eyes were half-shut. And with his messed-up long hair, he looked like a drugged-out homeless guy. If I didn't know better, I would've sworn the photo wasn't of my friend.

And yet it was.

In the article, a reporter had written a short piece on a local theft that had been linked to White Bird. Joe "Spirit Walker" Sunne was a Shaman and Euchee tribal elder. He claimed that he'd been robbed a week before the murder. His burglary report would barely hit the papers on a slow news day, but after the police ran fingerprints taken from the scene, a hit came back on White Bird. According to the paper, the police had solid proof that he had stolen tools from Sunne.

I got angry when I read this. White Bird stealing? That made no sense. But the weirdest part was that I could reject the idea that he could steal, yet when it came to killing Heather,

I had serious doubts about his innocence. I couldn't get past seeing him over her body and holding that knife. The gory image had horrified me. It still did. It had branded my psyche. And I couldn't shake that sight, not enough to keep an open mind.

What kind of a friend was I?

I scribbled Sunne's name in my spiral notebook. And I looked him up in the online White Pages and printed off directions on how to find him. It couldn't have been a coincidence that Joe Sunne was a revered member of the Euchee tribe. White Bird wouldn't have stolen from the man unless it had been for a very good reason—or a very big misunderstanding.

And I had to know which.

I had a hunch that talking to the man face-to-face was the next step I'd come to the library to find. I had to piece together a puzzle that had been a long time in the making and resurfaced on the day I touched White Bird at the hospital. Those days that White Bird had kept secret from me—the week before Heather was killed—were a good place to start.

Next Afternoon

I hadn't seen Derek all day. Even though I had no idea what it meant for him to be missing in action, I hoped that he'd gotten bored with watching me over the past several days with nothing happening. He could have learned not to be so obvious or gotten smarter about keeping an eye on me, but that idea made me laugh. Using the words *learned* and *smarter* to describe Derek sounded like a ridiculous waste of my valuable worry time.

Still, I had to admit that not knowing where he was made me tense. I thought about telling Mom about him stalking me, but that would only stir things up with the sheriff. And I liked the peace and quiet. I needed it.

With Mom keeping me real busy, that helped get my mind off my stalker. She had painters coming the next day and had me clearing space for them to work. We moved furniture away from the walls and covered things with sheets to protect the important stuff from paint splatter.

But the hardest thing we had to do didn't require muscle.

By late afternoon, Mom was clearing the last boxes of my grandmother's clothes. By the end of the week, not much of Grams would remain. And with everything I had on my mind, I made room for more sorrow in my heart. The pain of losing my grandmother gripped me hard.

When Mom told me what she had planned, I helped her get everything done even though I hated it. I got real quiet. I knew the day would come when closets had to be cleaned and clutter had to be tossed, but boxing up a lifetime of memories was hard to do.

And until today, I'd been so wrapped up in myself that I'd forgotten how hard this would be on Mom, finally saying goodbye to her mother. I found her alone in my grandmother's bedroom sitting on the bed. And from the reflection in the mirror, I saw she was crying as she looked into a box. I turned to leave and creaked down the hall. Being really sad wasn't exactly a team sport, but Mom heard me.

"Brenna, you got a minute?"

"Yeah, I was just…" I came back to the bedroom and sat next to her. "What's up?"

"I saved some things for you. If you don't want them, let me know."

Mom had set aside the best stuff for me. I had my own box and everything. My grandmother's costume jewelry was in a shiny onyx jewelry case that opened into tiered velvet drawers. And every piece I picked up reminded me of playing dress up with Grams on rainy Sunday afternoons or stolen hours when she had spent time with only me.

"And I picked out her funkiest clothes. You can sew them into something new, with your special touch. I think Grams would love that." Mom ran a hand through my short hair. "I'm sure of it."

Grams had been into real drama when she was younger. And her taste in clothes showed it. She had great hats, stylish vintage evening jackets, and belts and scarves that looked glittery and magical. Of all the things Mom could have given me to lift my spirits, I wouldn't have asked for anything better. She'd boxed up the best of Grams—and she'd given it all to me.

"I don't know what to say." I felt my eyes water as I stared into the box. "Thanks, Mom."

She kissed me on the forehead and smiled.

"I'll help you load the boxes for Goodwill. You mind dropping them off? I'll get you the address." Mom got her purse and handed me the car keys. "And if you feel like it, you want to pick up a pizza?"

"Yeah, sure." I nodded.

I'd have my freedom and Mom's car again. Although that should have made me happy, it didn't. Sneaking behind her back to see the Euchee Shaman felt wrong, especially after what she'd done for me today, but I really had to do it.

I was scared to face a man who could shed light on White Bird's secrets. My friend had been up to something that he couldn't tell me and he'd needed tools to do it. And by week's end, he would be charged with a vicious murder. I had to know what he had been up to.

Yet even though Joe Sunne might have answers for me, I wasn't sure they'd be something I'd want to hear.

Outskirts of Shawano

After I dropped off the boxes of Grams's life at Goodwill, I checked out the internet directions to the home of Joe Sunne. I figured pizza could wait. Even though I liked it best cold, Mom didn't. I could pick it up on my way home. When I got to the address I had listed for Joe Sunne, I couldn't drive up to the place. I don't know what I expected to find—maybe more suburbia like Grams's hood—but the man didn't live in an old Victorian with neighbors close by.

He lived on the fringes of town where the houses were more like ranches with barbed wire instead of cyclone fences and dirt roads replaced asphalt. I saw a house hidden by trees in the distance, but I wanted to be sure. House numbers weren't exactly posted on imaginary curbs.

Here I stood out, me and my little Subaru. I'd have no place to hide once I drove onto the man's land. I clutched the steering wheel tight as I sat parked on the road outside his property.

"Oh, White Bird. How did you find this guy?" I muttered. "And what kind of stuff were you into with him?"

The dusty gravel road I was on led to a few turnoffs behind fences. I put the car into Reverse and checked out a stand of mailboxes behind me. When I saw "Sunne" written on one, I figured I'd come to the right place, but what I hadn't counted on was driving smack into the middle of *Deliverance* country. Hell, I even heard banjo music in my head—that's how edgy I was. I stared out the windshield at the turnoff for Joe Sunne and ran my tongue over my cut lip.

"What are you gonna do, Bren?" I whispered and gripped the steering wheel with sweaty palms.

It didn't take long to decide that I'd driven too far and taken too much risk to chicken out now. I turned onto the drive marked Private—No Trespassing and drove in. Ruts in the road jostled the Subaru and tossed me around, forcing me to grip the wheel hard to keep the car from getting stuck.

I drove by a crop of plants near a creek. The earth was mounded in rows, bordered by tall cedars. Dusk had brought shadows, making it hard to see, but I felt more than a bad case of nerves. I sensed the draw from a world not my own, like when I stepped foot into a graveyard. Spirits of the dead who cross my path leave their mark. Sometimes I hear or feel the dark breeze from the other side, a sign they've crossed a portal between their world and mine. And when I feel their presence, my skin tingles and my senses go on hyperalert like I had just downed mass quantities of Red Bull.

That's what I felt now. I didn't have to see the dead to know they hung out with Joe Sunne.

When I rounded the last turn, I came to a small wood-framed house with a tin roof. It looked dark and ominous with the dying sun behind it. Spears of bright orange filtered through the dense trees and made it hard to see details in the deepening shadows.

An open garage to the right sheltered an old blue truck with the hood up. When I spotted greasy rags and tools nearby, I figured someone had been working on the engine. Clay pots, plastic jugs and rusted metal buckets littered the front of the house. They hung off the walls and were piled near a wooden rain barrel like they were worth something. And tons of glass jars were stacked under the overhang, but they weren't empty. Someone had a thing for collecting roots, tree bark, leaves and other weird stuff I didn't want to know about. Real Voodoo Hoodoo.

Stray cats darted into the scrub brush as I drove closer. I was already on edge, but when I almost hit one of them, I skidded to a stop. I sat gripping the wheel, reconsidering what I would do next when I saw something familiar. Joe Sunne had a medicine wheel. An elaborate pattern of stones, shaped into a large wheel, was positioned on the ground near the front of his house. White Bird had a smaller, less-complicated version near his shelter in the woods and he'd told me about it.

Feeling a connection to White Bird, I got out of the car to get a better look at the medicine wheel. That's why I missed him. When I looked toward the house, I gasped. A man sat stone still—staring at me.

Dressed in jeans and a black T-shirt with a worn cowboy hat on his head, he sat on a cluttered front porch. He was tilted back on a wooden chair with his dusty boots on a railing. And he glared at me without flinching. He reminded me of a cougar eyeing prey on the National Geographic channel.

He watched me with keen eyes that looked black as coal. His long hair was worn loose and had gray streaks in it. And I was close enough to see age lines cut deep into the dark skin of his face, but something more bothered me about the man.

I swear to God, Joe "Spirit Walker" Sunne—Shaman to the Euchee tribe—looked like he'd been expecting me.

Chapter Nine

"Are you Joe Sunne?"

The man didn't answer. He didn't even move. Or blink.

"My name's Brenna Nash."

"I know who you are."

The sudden sound of his deep gravelly voice grabbed me. It reminded me that I was alone with this strange man in the middle of nowhere—and that I had intruded on him. And the awkward silence that followed made our meeting even harder. All I wanted to do was get in my car and drive away…real fast.

If the guy meant to mess with my head, then mission accomplished.

"You do?" I shrugged and stuffed my hands in my jeans. "How do you know who I am?"

"Why are you here?" His lips barely moved.

And with Joe Sunne ignoring my question, he was sending me a clear message that he was in control. And as long as he tolerated me, he wouldn't kick me off his place—for now. His question had been direct. And I had to admit that my brain scrambled for a lie.

Lies came automatically, especially when talking to strangers. But something in the man's eyes made me rethink my normal reaction. It was like he was testing me. And one of his superpowers was a hypertweaked bullshit detector.

"I'm a friend of White Bird. And I came for your help."

For the first time, the man showed signs of being human. He blinked. Once. And for an instant, his stern expression softened. I had him right where I wanted him.

"I can't help you."

I had been very deliberate in my wording. Since the man hadn't asked who White Bird was, that told me he knew him. Score one for me.

"With all due respect, sir, I think you're underestimating your potential."

I surprised even me. I kept a straight face and fixed my eyes on his. That's how I saw it. He actually flinched with a weird smile. Score two for the visiting team.

"Is that so?" Straightening his chair, he sat up and planted his boots on the porch with his hands on his knees. "Then you better tell me how I can help, 'cause I ain't seein' it."

When I leaned against the Subaru, a cool breeze blew by me. It made me shiver. As I crossed my arms, I saw a drape move in the house, like the wind had blown it.

Only it wasn't the wind.

A woman's face peered at me from behind the glass. Her blanched white skin glowed from the shadows. And her haunted eyes were nothing more than dark circles. She stared at me before she faded into the darkness. The moment happened so quickly that I thought I had imagined it.

But I hadn't.

"You live here with family?" I turned toward him.

"No one lives here but me. Unless you work for the census, that's none of your business. I think you should go."

I cleared my throat and caught a glimpse of the window again. No one was there. Not now, but tell that to the goose bumps on my skin. Joe was sharing his digs with some dead woman and I wondered if he knew that, but not bad enough to ask.

"I need to know what White Bird was up to the week before he was arrested," I said, getting back to the reason I had come. "He was behaving strange. He had something secret going on and I have to know what that was."

"I still don't see how I can help you. Why come to me?"

He stood and hitched a leg up on the wooden railing of his porch. The man was muscular and lean with broad shoulders. And he was taller than I expected. The word *intimidating* came to mind. He had a real poker face, but since he wasn't asking me questions, I figured he knew a lot more than he was letting on. Although I had no doubt that I was on the right track, Joe Sunne could still derail me.

"I read in an old newspaper that White Bird stole tools from you, that the police found his fingerprints here."

"So?"

"Well, you're not exactly Home Depot. And your place isn't on the main drag of town. How did he know to come here?"

"You should ask him."

"I can't. In case you haven't heard, he's locked away in a mental hospital. And he hasn't spoken a word since that crappy day." I heard the anger in my voice. The man didn't give a shit and it showed. "I need to know why he came here. What's your connection?"

The sun had slid below the horizon and steep shadows swallowed what was left of the light. I felt like my time was running out—in more ways than one—and a bad case of the jitters hit me hard. I didn't want to be caught out here in the dark with this man.

"Like I said, I can't help you."

"Or won't?" I argued. I felt the heat rise to my face, like how my arguments started with Mom. "You know, I have no idea why White Bird wanted to be part of your stupid tribe. He's better than all of you."

I felt it happening. My mouth had taken over and I couldn't stop.

"All he wanted was to belong somewhere…anywhere. But no one from your tribe accepted him. What would it hurt to let him feel a part of something? His parents were dead. He had no one who cared about him. I don't understand any of this."

"He had you."

"Well, he deserved better."

I wanted to cry. I dragged fingers through my short hair and swatted the bugs flying around my face, fighting back the lump in my throat. I paced the ground around my car, taking deep breaths. I had flared out of control in front of this stranger.

In a weird way, it felt liberating. And I wasn't done.

"I don't know why he chose your tribe, mister. Maybe if you'd given him some of your precious time, none of this would've happened. He's not a throwaway kid, you know. He deserves better than you…and me."

I didn't wait to hear anything the man had to say. I didn't care anymore. I jumped into the Subaru and hit the gas. And I kicked up dust and gravel on my way out, not caring if I dinged Mom's car. All my frustration welled up inside me and it felt like I was suffocating, but none of this was about me anymore.

I'd been so focused on how everything that had happened affected me, that until I got back to Shawano, I'd almost forgotten about White Bird. Even though I didn't always show my appreciation, I had my mother along for my never-ending roller-coaster ride. But White Bird was the one suffering alone, stuck in a mental hospital.

I guess I had high hopes that Joe Sunne would care. He was a tribal elder and a healer, too. Even if White Bird killed Heather, didn't anyone else want to know why? What motive did he have to do such a thing? And what had he kept secret on the days before Heather's death? I had to have answers, but after my one-sided conversation with Joe Sunne, I was more in the dark than ever—literally.

Once again, I'd let White Bird down. And I had no idea where I'd go from here...except to pick up a pizza that I wouldn't feel like eating.

The Next Morning

I had tossed and turned all night. And when I finally did get to sleep, White Bird filled my dreams. In the two years since I'd left Oklahoma, I had thought of him, but not like this. Ever since I'd first seen him at the hospital and touched him, my dreams now were much more intense, as if he was really with me and we were linked somehow. When I imagined him kissing me, I felt his lips on mine. And when he playfully tapped my nose to tease me, I felt the nudge even in the dark of my room.

But my dreams of him always turned darker.

In the early-morning hours, he would beg for my help

with such urgency that I would wake up gasping and crying. I swear to God, I even had red marks on my arm from where he reached for me. Those nightmares were so vivid and powerful that I had no idea if I was losing my mind or if he was really with me.

And not knowing the difference was the worst part.

Time felt like it was running out. If I were going crazy, I was scared Mom would notice. And once my secret was out, there'd be no turning back. She'd line up more therapists, like she did before, and she'd expect me to actually talk to them. I didn't want to go through that again.

I had set my alarm to go off early. Mom had painters coming today. I rolled out of bed exhausted and trudged to my bathroom. When I looked in the mirror, I had a terminal case of bed head and I noticed dark circles under my eyes. I didn't recognize my own face. I looked like a stranger. Staring at my reflection, I searched for the parts in me that had changed. Did schizophrenia make you look different? I made weird faces in the mirror, practicing my crazed psycho look.

After I scared myself, I hit the shower.

Afternoon

Mom had an army of painters working the inside and outside of Grams's house. The outside guys were prepping the wood and scraping stuff. They'd do the painting tomorrow, but the inside guys were hard at work. I stayed outdoors to avoid the fumes in the house and planted the rest of the flowers Mom had bought. When I was done, she found me in the backyard.

"You've been working really hard, Bren. You wanna go to the movies?"

"You mean, with you?" I said it like she'd insulted me, but Mom didn't notice.

"No. These guys are almost done. I've got to stick around until they leave, but you can go. The matinees start soon."

"Can I have the car?"

"Wish you could, but no. I've got to pick up groceries. I called the movie theater near the interstate. It's the closest one. You should be able to ride your bike there, right?"

She handed me a list of the movies and times that she'd written down. I looked at the list like I was interested. With Mom thinking I was at the movies, I could be gone for hours without her expecting me home. And the theater was on the way out to Red Cliffs. As long as I was home by dinner, I'd be golden. Even if I was late, I could blame it on the bike and guilt her into giving me the car next time. *Perfect!*

I shrugged. "Yeah, okay. I'll clean up."

I pretended to look bored as I shed my garden gloves and headed for the house, but inside I was twisted into a nervous knot. I wasn't scared about sneaking into the hospital again. I knew what to expect now.

The part that had me jumpy was seeing White Bird again.

I knew I had to do something. And although I wasn't necessarily convinced he was sending me a message from wherever he was, I did feel sure of one thing. I couldn't move on with my life unless I confronted my past by helping him.

White Bird might be the key to opening the door that could save both of us.

Red Cliffs Hospital

If I had gone to the movies, I would be sitting in the air-conditioned dark eating popcorn mixed with peanut M&M's

and drinking a big thing of Pepsi. Of course I would have been miserable, kicking myself for being a self-centered jerk who had picked a stupid movie over helping a friend. With White Bird quietly dying behind locked doors, nothing was more important than helping him. And I had an urgent feeling this would be my one big chance to turn things around for both of us.

I pushed up the last steep hill on my bike then coasted down to the driveway into Red Cliffs Hospital. After I secured my wheels, I hit a restroom inside to wash up. My T-shirt was soaked with sweat and I looked like shit, but that didn't matter. Not today. I washed my face and put my dark glasses back on to cover my black eye. I didn't have any big strategy for getting in. I figured I'd rinse and repeat.

Like I did last time, I watched the routine until I could make my move, only this time I couldn't wait forever. Visiting hours would be over soon. I scribbled my name in the visitor's log so no one could read it. And for the patient's name that I was there to see, I again picked the name of someone who had visitors earlier in the day.

Once I got behind the locked door, I didn't waste my time looking in the visitor's area. White Bird had no one who would visit him. I went straight to the fenced-in gardens where the patients enjoyed the outdoors. And my pace picked up as I searched all the faces. For some reason, I felt this urgent need to find him…now. I went to where I saw him before, along the far fence, but he wasn't there. And when I saw a nurse staring at me, I pretended not to notice and kept moving.

White Bird wasn't anywhere. And a feeling of dread gripped me hard.

If he were locked in his room, I'd have to find another way in, but what if I couldn't? I went back inside anyway and came face-to-face with the locked part of the ward. I faked like I was coming in and out of the visitor area, where other outsiders were, and I eyeballed the setup of the secured rooms.

And my frustration to find him was making me think of really stupid stuff to settle my nerves.

I could pretend to be a crazy person and get myself locked up, just like in the movies. That wouldn't be a stretch. And White Bird would be so grateful I'd come to rescue him that he'd kiss me. And we'd make our big escape using my genius plan. Avril Lavigne would play me. Zac Efron could be White Bird. And the sound track would be from Kimya Dawson, whose songs always made me laugh and cry.

It would have been perfect, except life wasn't a friggin' movie. I headed back into the visitor's area. I had no idea what I would do and needed time to think, but I'd never get that chance.

"You're Isaac Henry's friend, aren't you?"

A man's voice echoed down the hall and I heard his quickening footsteps behind me. I should have ducked outside and pretended not to hear him…or faked like I didn't know the name Isaac Henry. But now that I'd flinched and stopped cold, I had to turn around. A tall slender man in a white doctor's coat with grayish-blond hair had his eyes on me.

"Who?" I shook my head. "I think you've got the wrong person."

"No, I don't. I remember seeing you the last time you were here. Your hair is shorter, but it's definitely you. My name's Dr. Sam Ridgeway. Isaac Henry is my patient."

He was White Bird's doctor. And once again, I couldn't hide my surprise. I had so many questions for this man that I ditched the idea of playing it safe. I might not get another chance to talk to him.

"You're his doctor?"

"Yes, I am. And I have to tell you. When I saw the reaction he had with you on your last visit, it blew me away. I've tried everything and gotten nothing from him. But you? You got him to actually look at you. You have no idea how big that was, do you?"

I should have taken off my sunglasses, but I couldn't. I wasn't ready for this man to see me.

"Why is he like that? It's like he's…brain-dead." I chewed the corner of my lip and winced. I'd forgotten about the cut.

"He's catatonic. I believe he experienced something highly traumatic that made him that way. It's like his mind can't accept what happened. He's not ready to face it. And if you're a friend of his, you might have an idea what I'm talking about."

Yeah, guess I had firsthand knowledge of what he was talking about.

"It's not fair he's locked up here. It's like he's doing the time for something he's never been convicted of. Will he ever get better?"

"Before you came along, I might have told you something different. But you got a reaction from him and that's why I was hoping you'd come back, so we could talk." He took a deep breath and fixed his eyes on me. "I could use your help."

"Me? What are you talking about?"

I felt my heart racing and the hospital corridor closed in. This man had kind eyes and he wanted to help White Bird, but something didn't feel right about him. I couldn't put my finger on why I was so anxious.

"I'd like to schedule time for you to visit with your friend, under my supervision, of course. You'd have to follow my instructions to the letter, but I think you'd make a difference in his treatment."

"I don't know." I shook my head and my throat was suddenly dry.

"But you're his friend. Don't you want him to get better?"

"Yes, but..."

I knew what he was doing. I'd used his move before. The guy was using my guilt against me like a weapon. I was White Bird's friend. Why wouldn't I want to help? But I didn't trust this man.

"If you want him to get better, I'm only asking for a little bit of your time. Is that too much to ask...for a friend?"

The jerk in the lab coat was trying too hard.

"No, it's not. But I want time to think about it."

"What's there to think about? You're his friend."

"Yeah, mister. I get it. You don't need to whack me over the head with your guilt hammer. You could let me see him. Why do you have to be there?"

"Because I'm his doctor."

The way he said it—like him being a doctor trumped my friend status or aced any other job on the planet—turned me off. It was like arguing with Mom and her big comeback would be "because I'm your mother." *Big deal!*

And he glared at me now. The kindness in his eyes that I had seen before was gone.

"Not good enough." I raised my chin. "How about a show of good faith? Will you let me see him now...just for a little while?"

The man clenched his jaw and didn't say anything. I knew he was mad, but I kept my mouth shut until he came back with an answer.

"No. I control who visits him. And if you won't cooperate, then I'll make sure you don't see him again. I'll alert security." He had the nerve to hand me his business card. "Call me, but only if you'll play by my rules."

This guy made sure I knew he was White Bird's gatekeeper and in control. And he was used to getting his way. I looked at his business card and gritted my teeth when I saw his big shot title. He was in charge of stuff and wasn't just a doctor handling White Bird's case.

And yeah, he had the authority to let me see White Bird if I changed my mind and played his game of intimidation, but I didn't like him and I was too stubborn to give in. I didn't say another word. I walked by him and headed back to the reception area.

And that made Dr. Ridgeway mad.

"Do you want to see him spend the rest of his life in an institution?" he called down the hall after me. "Because that's what could happen if you don't help him."

Why was the guy trying so hard? If he really wanted to help his patient, he would have given in on letting me see him. He was the adult and the man in charge, but he'd resorted to playing hardball. And that made me wonder what he was up to.

I needed time to think. I left the hospital feeling more down than before. Not seeing White Bird—not even a glimpse of him—tore at me. But knowing that damned doctor would keep me from seeing him pissed me off. I didn't think I could feel any worse until I looked up.

Mom was standing where I'd locked my bike. And she didn't look happy.

"Oh, shit," I mumbled and took a deep breath.

"I thought you were at the movies." She crossed her arms, daring me to lie to her.

"Didn't feel like it." I crossed my arms, too. "Were you spying on me?"

Mom was seething. She glared at me, as mad as I've ever seen her. Accusing her of spying wasn't my smartest move, especially considering that I'd proven she couldn't trust me.

"You came to visit that boy, didn't you?" She didn't wait for me to answer. "Is this your first time here?"

I could have lied, but I didn't.

"No. I had to see him, Mom. You don't understand."

"Put your bike in my car. We're leaving. And when we get home, you're going to explain why it's so important for you to see him."

She turned and didn't wait for my usual drama. And without an audience, I had no choice but to get my bike and follow her. I didn't know what I would say. Maybe it was time for the truth—whatever that was.

Mom didn't say a word to me all the way home. It was the quiet before the storm and we both knew it.

My mind raced with all the things I could tell her, but nothing sounded right. A part of me wished we could just talk. I needed someone to listen and not judge me, but that definitely wasn't my mother. Mothers always had an answer for everything. And it was never something a kid wanted to hear.

When we turned onto our street, I saw the painters were gone, but an old blue pickup truck was parked in front of Grams's house. In the lengthening shadows of early evening, it took me a minute to recognize the man behind the wheel.

"Oh, hell." I cursed under my breath and Mom heard me.

"Who's that?" she asked. "You know that man? He's parked in front of our house, Bren."

I heaved a sigh and stared at the long-haired, dark-skinned man in the truck. Wearing a cowboy hat, he watched us with interest as we drove toward him. His dark eyes never wavered. And he intimidated me as much as he'd done the other night.

Joe Sunne had come to see me. And now I'd have to explain his visit to Mom, too. *Joy!*

"Yeah, I know him." I turned toward her when she pulled into our driveway. "And I can explain everything, but I need to talk to him first. Give us a minute."

"Oh, no, you're not talking to that man without me. You have anything to say to him, you'll do it in front of me." Mom was done talking. She threw open her car door and got out.

"Oh, brother." I rolled my eyes, but Mom was long gone.

She was heading for the old beat-up truck as Joe Sunne was getting out. Not knowing what brought the man to my door was bad enough, but what he'd say to me in front of my Mom made me sick with worry. As I walked toward the truck, heat rose to my face when I saw both of them staring at me.

I had a bad feeling that I was heading for another crap shower.

chapter ten

"Mom, this is Joe Sunne. He's a tribal elder and a Shaman for the Euchee tribe." I spit out the man's full pedigree, hoping Mom would be impressed and not so mad at me. A long shot. "This is my mother, Kate Nash. We're from Charlotte, North Carolina. Just came back to fix up my grandmother's old place. She died not too long ago."

When I played the grandmother card again, I hoped he'd take pity on me. I had a hard time looking the man in the eye. He had a way of staring that made me feel like he could read my thoughts. You'd think that keeping my mind a blank slate wouldn't be hard, but it was.

"Sorry to hear about your grandmother," he said.

When he directed his comment to me, I looked up and met his gaze. The stern expression I had seen the other night—after I'd intruded on him—was gone.

"Your daughter came to see me yesterday evening. I'm saying this because, if she's like most kids, she didn't tell you."

He shifted his focus to Mom. "She came to ask me about White Bird. You might know him as Isaac Henry."

"Is that so." Mom crossed her arms and glared at me. She'd done the math and knew I'd taken the car to run my little side trip. I knew that choice tidbit would add another log onto the fire of our argument, once our visitor left. "And what brings you here, Mr. Sunne?"

"Please…call me Joe." He took off his hat and tossed it through the open window of his truck. "I came to talk to Brenna and ask her a question, Mrs. Nash."

"Kate. Call me Kate. You want to come inside, Joe?"

"No, thanks. This may not take long."

I didn't like the sounds of that. One question and he'd be gone. My dread at seeing him had shifted to worry that he'd come for a good reason and I'd have to prove myself for him to stay and help.

"What did you come to ask?" I'd gotten tired of them talking around me.

"Why do you care so much about White Bird?"

"Yeah, Bren. Tell us both."

Two sets of eyes stared at me like I'd farted in church.

"It's complicated." I stalled.

"Then simplify it for us." Mom wasn't cutting me any slack, but the edge had gone out of her voice. She really wanted to know.

I could have told them that I loved him and that the guilt of me turning him in had gotten too much for me to handle, but my feelings for White Bird were deeper than that and what we shared was private. So I told them what I could and spoke from my heart.

"I'm part of his tribe. He asked me to be his family and I said yes."

Mom cocked her head and I had a hard time reading her face. Did she feel betrayed that I had chosen White Bird as my family? I wanted to tell her that saying "yes" to him didn't mean I had disowned her, but I wasn't sure she'd believe me.

Joe Sunne's expression was easier to read.

"A tribe has to do with blood." He shook his head. "You can't say 'yes' and make that happen. It doesn't work that way."

"Why not?" I asked.

Even Mom turned to him for an answer, but when he only shrugged, I had something to say.

"You act like you don't even know him. Why is that? He's Euchee, like you. Even if he's not full-blooded, why would you treat him like shit?"

"Brenna." Mom grimaced. "Watch your language."

The man stood silent for a long time. He fixed his eyes on me and I did the same back to him. After what seemed like an eternity, he blinked and looked human.

"Your daughter's right, Kate. And she deserves an answer." He cleared his throat and glanced away. I knew whatever he'd say would be hard for him. "I've been a coward when it comes to this boy. And your daughter came to me the other night to speak up for him. That took guts. And I respect that."

Mom looked at me and narrowed her eyes as if she was seeing me for the first time.

"It looks like we've got things to talk about," my mother said. "Why don't you come inside, Joe. Please."

He nodded and followed Mom to the house and I walked two steps behind them. I had a strong feeling that White Bird was with me. And I pictured him smiling.

* * *

Deputy Will Tate had started his shift with more of a purpose than his usual patrol duties. The incident with Brenna Nash had been bugging him ever since it happened. That kid was hard to forget. And when she kept her mouth shut about what had happened, that worried him. His gut told him that he had to watch out for the quiet ones—the kids who took a beating without complaining. That meant someone else posed more of a threat than cop trouble.

And it didn't take him long to find out who that might be.

Being a liaison officer to the local high school, Will knew plenty of the local kids. The sheriff had assigned him the job as part of his rookie duties. And with him being a young deputy, the assignment fit. He had a small office on school property with regular hours for him to interact with kids. And with his visibility, he not only kept incidental crimes to a minimum at the school, but he also had become more visible to the community. The program was innovative and he liked being a part of it.

Putting his connections to good use, Will spent his past few shifts calling on the kids who owed him a good turn, ones who might be honest with him. But when even those kids played it cagey—and kicked out the same story verbatim—he was even more worried for Brenna.

"You're hiding something about that Seaver party. What's got you spooked?" he pushed Tyler Dixon for an answer. "Since when do you keep your mouth shut, Tyler? It's not in your nature, man."

Tyler was heading into his junior year and was the editor for the school paper. He was a bit of a big mouth with an ego to match and prided himself on reporting the truth. Maybe his rebellious nature only went as far as the cafeteria menu and parking lot issues.

"I told you. I wasn't there until later, but I heard stuff." The kid sprawled on a bench along a hiking path by Walnut Hill pond. He'd been playing Frisbee with his dog, Taco, a border collie–terrier mix. Will had seen the kid from the street and drove into the park to talk to him, one-on-one.

"Like?" Will leaned against a tree with his thumbs hooked into his duty belt. "Come on. You know you're dying to tell me 'cause you like stirring things up. You've got the instincts of a big city reporter, so talk to me."

Tyler sat quiet for a long moment and stared down at the black-and-white-spotted dog stretched out at his feet. The dog's long tongue dangled from its panting mouth.

"I heard Jade DeLuca and Derek Bast made things happen. I don't know how far they went, but those two don't have limits, if you know what I mean. And they fed their concocted story to the other kids to stack the deck against that Nash girl. But I have to tell ya, I wouldn't want to get on the wrong side of either one of those idiots. Derek is a mean son of a bitch, but Jade is worse. She's a backstabbing snake and not even her bodacious boobies make up for that."

The kid smirked and gave him a visual, holding out both his hands. Taco wasn't impressed. The dog groaned and went to sleep.

"Why would they want to hurt Brenna Nash?" He knew enough about the Heather Madsen case to suspect this was all connected, but he wanted to hear what Tyler had to say.

"You weren't in town when Heather got whacked, but it's all linked to her, dude. In my opinion, that girl had serious issues. And she'd pissed off plenty of folks to make a hefty list of enemies, including Jade DeLuca, *numero uno* on Heather's hit parade."

"Jade? I thought she was Heather's best friend."

"Well, you know what they say. Keep your friends close and your enemies closer. That pretty much described those two. Heather was one mean bitch and anyone in her inner circle knew that firsthand."

"Then why would anyone want a part of that?"

"Good question, dude. I heard she dealt out the good with the bad. Personally, that wouldn't be my thing, but some folks don't know how to stand on their own two feet. They get desperate to belong, you know?"

"So if Heather had plenty of enemies, are you saying someone else might have killed her?" Will cocked his head and grimaced. "Because from what I've seen of that investigation, Isaac Henry was a clear front-runner."

"I'm not saying anything. We're just two guys talking here. *Capisce?*" Tyler raised his voice, clearly uncomfortable with his line of questioning. "I'm just into conspiracy theories, okay? And that Indian kid seemed like a convenient suspect. The investigation was over before it began. Considering your boss had a connection to a kid who should have been questioned, I just think that's funny, is all. And that's all I'm gonna say."

Will knew what Tyler was suggesting. And he had to admit that he'd thought the same thing about Sheriff Logan's conflict of interest since Derek Bast was his nephew and had been part of Heather's circle.

"But why pick on the Nash girl? If what happened at the Seaver party was about retaliation for what happened to Heather, why go after Brenna Nash? She was the one who turned in Isaac Henry."

"Who knows how psychos think? But if I had to take a

guess, I'd say someone wanted to point a finger at Brenna because of her Tonto fetish. White on brown doesn't always play around here with some folks. That's no big deal for me, but each to his own." He twirled the Frisbee on his finger and kept talking. "This town got real riled up when they heard about those two hooking up. If I was writing this movie, I'd say that playing the race card made a good smoke screen for the real killer to hide what might have happened."

"And what was that?" Will asked. Tyler definitely had his interest.

"Don't know. That's why it's a mystery."

When the kid laughed, Will slumped onto the bench next to him. With Derek Bast being related to the sheriff and Jade DeLuca's family being well connected in town, he would have an uphill battle to dig into this thing with Brenna Nash. He had a bad feeling he'd be unearthing something dark and ugly. And if he did run his own investigation, he'd be alone in pursuing it. The sheriff would be all over him. Second-guessing his boss's case—a case everyone in town thought was a done deal—would really muck up the works.

He should have let things go, but keeping his mouth shut when things weren't right wasn't in his nature, either.

"So if you were plotting this movie—" he grinned at Tyler "—who would you put on the suspect list for Heather's murder and why? Hypothetically speaking, of course."

Tyler smiled back and kept talking. Guess the kid had guts after all.

Bricktown Ballroom—Oklahoma City

Known for its live music, the Bricktown Ballroom was a converted warehouse of red brick with massive exposed wood beams jutting through its tall ceilings. Colored lights were dim, barely bright enough to see faces. And even though the place smelled like smoke and alcohol, Jade DeLuca loved the casual vibe that focused on the music.

And tonight would be no exception.

The ballroom was packed and Jade felt the electric mood that ran through the crowd. Everyone was talking and drinking and stealing glances at the stage as they waited for any signs of the band, Brain Crush. Lucas Quinn played lead guitar and was the front man for the hot new group. His band was on the fast track and Jade thought they were way better than the Flaming Lips, a very popular alternative music band that originated out of Oklahoma City and had made it big. And that was saying something about Lucas.

Brain Crush had played in Bricktown many times, a sweet gig and a hot spot for entertainment that was located near the downtown canal in OKC. And when Chloe had told her about Lucas playing there, Jade really wanted to go. She had used her fake ID in Bricktown before and she knew she could get into most places. And it took only two hours to drive there from Shawano.

But messing with Chloe was the main reason she was here. Jade took advantage of the fact that the girl didn't want to drive to OKC alone. Chloe had already offered to pay for her gas and all her expenses if she drove, including the cover charge, drinks and food after. So Jade took advantage of her pathetic excuse to buy friendship and invited Nicole and Brandy—telling them all their expenses would be paid for, too.

Chloe never objected. That's what a total loser she was.

Jade had bought drinks for a crowd of strangers, using Chloe's tab, and was passing the drinks around when an announcer came on the stage and introduced Brain Crush. And as she expected, Lucas was amazing and the first set was incredible. Elbow to elbow, the crowd jammed to the music and screamed after each song. With cool videos playing on a big screen behind him, Lucas was in his element and he was crazy good.

"He looks yummy," Jade screamed to Chloe over the music.

The girl nodded and hadn't said a word since the music started. She only stared up at the stage with buggy blue eyes, drooling over her crush. She had it bad. Real bad.

"You gonna talk to him at the break?" she asked. When Chloe only grimaced back with a crazed look that was a mix between deer in the headlights and pure panic, Jade came up with an idea. "You should let him know you brought a group down from Shawano. He'd like that."

Even in the dim lights off the stage, Jade saw Chloe smile. She had dangled the bait and Lucas Quinn made an enticing lure. When Chloe went back into ogling Lucas onstage, Jade got to work. She moved through the crowd until she spotted the person she was looking for. After everything had been arranged, she sat back and waited for the band to take a break.

Jade didn't have to wait long.

At the break, Lucas made his way through the crowd. He was stoked and grinning, looking cuter than ever. Hands reached out to touch him and people called out his name and waved. Chloe was rooted where she stood. Her eyes were glued onto Lucas, but she was too scared to approach him until Jade waved her hands and gestured for her to go. Even though it was too loud for Chloe to hear, Jade mouthed the words, "Go! Talk to him!" And good little Chloe did as she was told.

To get a better look at the train wreck that was about to happen, Jade crawled onto a bar stool and craned her neck over the sea of heads. Chloe worked her way through the masses, but so did some chick named Misty that Jade had met near the bathrooms. She'd paid the stacked blonde—who had the best rack money could buy—to plant a deep wet kiss on Lucas and pretend to know him intimately.

And everything played out like Jade had planned.

Misty wrapped her arms around Lucas, yelling, "Baby! You played our song." And she even grabbed his ass as she drove her tongue down his throat. With Lucas still working off his stage adrenaline, he took full advantage and kissed her back.

The crowd went wild, but Chloe didn't.

She had broken through the hordes just in time for a front row seat. She stood next to Lucas, so close she could touch him. Even from a distance, Jade saw the shock on her face… and the tears that followed. Chloe melted into the mass of people and got swallowed up. And Jade lost sight of her. She plopped down on the bar stool and smiled.

Seeing the hurt on Chloe's face should have made her feel bad, but it didn't.

It only brought back terrible memories of the same crap Heather used to pull on her. Lashing out at Chloe—to make up for Heather's sins—was never enough, but she'd become addicted to the power of controlling other people's lives. Hanging with Heather had been the stepping stone she'd needed. And now it was her turn to be on top.

Outdoing Heather's cruel pranks really got her off and the other kids hadn't seen anything yet. She was only getting started. Jade loved how everyone talked about *her* now and not that dead bitch anymore. Erasing Heather's memory in everyone else's minds was like a drug she couldn't get enough of.

And Chloe had made it way too easy.

Shawano

Mom had fixed hot tea, something Joe Sunne had asked for. We sat at the small table in the kitchen, one of the few areas of Grams's house that the painters had left intact. And the Shaman's deep voice captivated me, especially when he talked about White Bird.

"The first time White Bird came to me, he wanted to know about vision quests. And with me being Shaman for my people, it was natural he would come to me. I explained to him that a vision quest is a rite of passage for boys before they reach puberty and that he was too old for the ritual. But when he insisted on knowing more about it, I told him that I couldn't help him. I turned him away because he wasn't a tribal member and I didn't want responsibility for an outsider."

"An outsider?" I let my anger show. "He took pride in being Euchee. You don't know what it meant to him."

"I know that now, but at the time, I didn't realize how strongly that boy felt about being without a tribe." He looked into his mug of tea as if he was staring into the past. "Weeks later, I found tools stolen. A shovel, an ax, a knife that my grandfather had made, and some other things were missing from my shed, like tarps and tanned hides and some old blankets. I swear that I didn't know it was him. If I had, I would've kept my mouth shut. But I thought it was some white kids down the road from me and I wanted that knife back."

When he realized that he said "white kids," he looked at Mom and me and said, "No offense."

"None taken," Mom said. "Go on, Joe."

"After the police told me the fingerprints they found were White Bird's, I felt real bad. I knew he'd taken those things to do his own vision quest. And he took them to make a point with me. He was building a sweat lodge somewhere. He knew enough about vision quests to know he'd need one."

"Once you found out those fingerprints belonged to him, why didn't you explain to the police that he'd come to your place looking for help?" I asked. "You let them believe he'd stolen your stuff. That's not right. Maybe he was only borrowing them."

"Brenna." Mom jumped to Joe's defense.

"No, she's right, Kate. That kid could have borrowed my stuff. And I should have said something to the police, but by that time, he'd been arrested and charged with murder. My tribe wouldn't have wanted trouble with the whites. I was afraid they'd blame my people and our customs for what happened."

Joe took a long gulp of tea before he continued.

"You see, White Bird may have taken peyote or mescaline to enhance the visions on his quest. That was an old custom practiced by the ancestors of many tribes. It was considered a sacred medicine. I would not have recommended that for the boy. Fasting and sleep deprivation would have been sufficient, but without my guidance, he didn't know." He hung his head low. "I had no idea what would happen by turning him away. If I had it to do over again, that never would've happened."

"But you let them file theft charges against him. I don't understand." I shook my head, not letting it go.

"I figured if the theft case ever went to court, I'd recant my story. Those charges never would've stuck. But they had him for murder. And as volatile as Shawano got over one half-breed boy murdering a white girl, imagine what it would have been like if my tribe had been drawn into the investigation. Guilt by association can get real ugly, especially in a small town."

"Believe me, we know about that," I said. I could totally

see his point. And I also knew what it was like to live with guilt and regret.

"But what's eating me alive is that he might have killed that girl while under the influence of a hallucinogen. And all because I said no." He clenched his jaw and stared at his hands. "That's why I came to see you, Brenna. I can't sit back and watch that kid take all the blame. And I think you might have what it takes."

"What it takes for what?" I leaned forward in my chair and put my elbows on the table.

"The other night when you came to my house, I saw something in you. I know this will sound strange…"

I was BFFs with strange. And all ears.

"Go on," Mom said. Even she was getting into this.

"I sense you have a gift that you keep secret. Am I right?"

Holy shit! Didn't see that coming.

Mom did a double take and stared at me like I was a friggin' alien. I'd seen the look before. And Joe Sunne waited for me to confirm something he might already know. *A gift?* My life was more like a damned curse. I was a borderline schizophrenic who saw dead people and was channeling a great guy who had only two flaws—he'd been arrested for murder and had a room at the local asylum.

What part of me was a gift to anyone?

I had no idea what the man was talking about, but with him being mystical and all, maybe I didn't stand a chance of fooling him, a guy who could probably bend a spoon using only his brain. He'd see right through me. And with him and my mom both staring at me—waiting for an answer—I didn't know what the hell I'd say.

chapter eleven

"I don't have a gift for anything except getting into trouble." I shrugged at Joe Sunne, who sat across from me at our kitchen table. "I don't know what you're talking about."

Mom grimaced, but I noticed she didn't contradict me. And when Joe glanced at Mom and back at me, I could tell he felt the awkwardness of talking in front of her, too.

"I sense you are a very perceptive girl. You see things that others don't. I was the same way when I was your age," he began.

"My sympathies," I said. "Go on."

"Your ability to see things might help White Bird." Joe set his mug of tea aside and leaned across the table. "I can't be sure of this, but I believe he is trapped in a vision. If he ingested a drug to enhance his quest—and his vision was interrupted by something traumatic while he was under the influence—he may be trapped in his own mind and unable to find his way back."

"What?" Mom asked the same time I did, but she wasn't nearly as shocked.

"This'll sound strange to both of you. You aren't familiar with the spiritual beliefs of my people." He hesitated. "But if you promise to keep an open mind, I'll explain."

"Please. I'm very intrigued. And I'll keep an open mind, Joe," Mom promised and I nodded.

He took a deep breath and went on.

"I've seen this only once before. And it was decades ago. A rattlesnake bit a boy while he was alone on his quest. He nearly died. These things can happen, but the strange part was that he stayed in a coma for weeks. And the doctors had no explanation for his condition. Later when the boy regained consciousness, he remembered that he'd gotten separated from his spirit guide and lost his way. That was bad, but good eventually came of it. When he had grown into a man, this same boy had greater insights into the spirit realm because of what he had survived. White Bird's condition reminds me of that boy."

"Spirit guide? Why would a boy need a guide to wake up from a vision quest? Couldn't he just open his eyes?" I asked.

"Something like what happened to that boy is rare. Maybe what happened to White Bird was part of his test. That's why I believe we must help him find his way back. And I think you can reach him…as his friend," Joe explained. "When a boy goes on a vision quest, he is in search of his spirit guide. My people believe that a person needs a guardian for the journey they will take in life. Such a supernatural being is similar to your Christian guardian angel. They give us special prayers and songs and symbols that protect us against evil and help us transition to the next life."

I decided that White Bird must not have connected with his spirit guide. No guardian angel would have let him cross paths with Heather Madsen.

"White Bird would have fasted and prayed until his guide was revealed," Joe said. "To whites, this would sound like superstition, but my people believe we must open our minds and hearts to know when the spirits are speaking to us. Like all living things, we're a part of the earth and the universe. And we are connected to our ancestors, too."

"You sound like him." I smiled. "White Bird told me something like that. And he said that he'd chosen his clan. The *Dala*. He told me that was the bear clan. He'd picked it because the bear was strong and symbolized Mother Earth. And it's a totem sign for a healer," I told Joe. "Would the bear have been White Bird's spirit guide?"

"The clan name is spelled with a *D* but it's pronounced *Tala,*" Joe corrected me. "Our language is nearly forgotten and difficult to learn."

I'd heard the pronunciation from White Bird. He'd gotten the clan name wrong, too, but without a Native speaker to help him, he probably got lots of stuff wrong, but that didn't stop him from trying.

White Bird talked a lot about the Euchee. He said that the tribe kept their language pure and did not teach it to outsiders or take on the influences from other cultures. But in the mid 1900s, when Native children were forced into boarding schools to teach them how to be white, the language was all but lost. The Euchee were forced to use English as their main language. But just like White Bird clung to his beliefs without giving in, so did the Euchee tribe. The language exists today, even though it's spoken by only a few.

"And the *Dala* is a good clan for him." Joe smiled. "That

boy has the spirit of a healer. I felt it in him. But the spirit guide in his quest could have been different. The quest is very personal and private. And only White Bird would know his guide. It would be up to him to share that."

"Is that why you didn't tell me you knew him the other night?" I asked. "You were keeping his vision quest a secret, huh?"

Mom looked confused, but she went with the flow.

"Yes. I didn't think it was right to tell," he said. "It wasn't my place. And Euchee ceremonies are sacred. They are not spoken of outside the tribe. I hope you understand."

"Yeah, I do. And I respect that." I nodded and smiled. "He would have, too."

The pieces to the puzzle were falling into place. Now I knew that White Bird had been preparing for his vision quest during the week before Heather died. I was sure of it. And even as close as I thought we were, he might have felt that the secrecy was part of the ritual and an ancient tradition. I breathed a sigh of relief, but another question hit me.

"Tell me about how he'd prepare for his quest. I have to know. Please."

"I can only guess what he did, but how is that important to you?" Joe asked.

"What are you thinking, Bren?" Mom chimed in.

"Because I know White Bird. He would've done his research preparing for his quest. He'd even told me that he needed some space and I wouldn't see him for a while. I thought he was breaking up with me, but now I don't think that was it."

I narrowed my eyes and dug into my memory.

"He had no patience for someone as shallow as Heather Madsen. And she would've been a complete distraction from something he wanted more than anything, to become a man with the Euchee tribe." I turned to Joe. "Even with the Euchee not claiming him, he would've gone through the ritual on his own. He wanted it that bad. So tell me what he would've done to prepare. Please, I have to know."

Joe shared as much of the ritual as he could. And as he did, I pictured White Bird in my mind.

He would've picked a very secluded and special spot near water to build the sweat lodge for his vision quest. And he'd taken Joe's knife to cut, strip and sharpen the sapling branches he'd need to frame the lodge. And once he had constructed and shaped the outer shell, he would have used the tarps, blankets and hides he'd "borrowed" from Joe to keep the inside dark and watertight. And the floor on the inside would have been covered with grasses, leaves or wildflowers to make it soft, like the little hut he'd built near the creek.

Once he'd built his sweat lodge, he'd dig a pit outside for the fire he'd need to heat the large stones for steam. The sweating part of the ritual, to cleanse his mind and body. I thought about all he had to do to prepare for one of the biggest events in his life. It would've taken him time to build his sweat lodge, fast for days and gather wood and water for the steam, enough to last for his quest.

No wonder he needed space from me.

"That sounds like a lot of work. Amazing," I said.

"It is. It takes a strong boy to do this, especially by himself and without guidance from an elder." Joe's expression grew dark. "And under the influence of peyote or mescaline, his quest would have been very risky."

Joe told us how White Bird would have stripped off his clothes and remained in the sweat lodge, praying and sitting cross-legged near the steam, fending off hunger and the never-ending heat and his growing hallucinations to pray for his spirit guide to come. It was a grueling ritual that required real commitment and courage…and faith.

White Bird really believed his soul was connected to all living things, past and present. And he believed in the power of his mind and had faith in his senses. His quest was spiritual. Something bigger than he was. I had nothing like that in my life. I didn't have his passion. I wanted to belong somewhere and got good at complaining about what I didn't have. But White Bird saw what he wanted and went for it.

"I had no idea he did that," I whispered.

Although anything Joe told us about what White Bird might have done was pure speculation, it helped me to imagine what was in his head as he prepared to endure the physical test to become a man in his tribe. It made me even more proud of him.

But it also reminded me of our first and only argument. It was the last time that I saw him before I made the call to the sheriff that got him arrested.

Two Years Ago

When White Bird had told me he wanted his space and didn't tell me why, I was sure he was letting me down easy and that he'd grown tired of hanging with a girl like me. And it hurt worse because he'd told me at his shelter by the creek. I always looked at that spot as our place.

But instead of asking him why he didn't want to see me anymore, I got mad. Losing my temper had put him on the defensive. It was the only way I could handle the hurt.

"This has something to do with your tribe, doesn't it? They don't want you with a white girl."

"Brenna, that's not it."

"I thought I was your tribe. Why do you want to be an Indian when they don't want you? They never have." I felt the heat on my face as tears drained down my cheeks, but my misery didn't come close to matching the pain I saw in his eyes.

"I need to belong, Brenna. It's important to me. And I want you to respect that. I hope you can." He turned his back to stuff something in his knapsack. He was packing to leave. I took a deep breath, but I couldn't let it go.

"I don't know why you care about a tribe who has been so cruel to you. I wouldn't want people like that in my life… people who can hurt me. I don't need that." I reasoned with him while he grabbed his stuff.

We were very different when it came to needing other people. We both felt the urge to belong somewhere and fit in, but when others made that impossible, that's where our differences showed. I'd get pissed and ditch them before they rejected me. Lashing out made it my choice, not theirs, even though it still hurt.

But White Bird had a quieter way. He knew what he wanted and patiently focused on getting it, one way or another. He didn't blame others for what made him miserable. Any changes he made were inside him.

After he'd stashed his things, White Bird slung his rucksack over his shoulder and turned to me one last time.

"I know there's a bigger picture, Brenna. We belong to the tribe of man first," he said, without anger. "Our humanity is what we share and it shouldn't matter what our skin color is or what language we speak. But it makes me feel special to belong to the Euchee. It makes me happy. I thought you had accepted that."

I thought I had accepted it, too, until I realized that his

becoming Euchee might mean I'd be out in the cold. I didn't belong anywhere. He'd asked me to be his tribe, but that was when he thought he had no one else. Maybe he got a better offer and had changed his mind.

"I don't see the world the way you do, White Bird. I just see my little corner of it. And I don't understand why you can't be satisfied with…that."

I wanted to ask why he wasn't satisfied with *me*—why I wasn't good enough—but I wasn't sure I could handle what he might tell me. So I didn't wait for him to say anything at all. Before I left, I looked into his eyes and saw that I'd hurt him.

I also knew I'd never forget what that felt like.

Even now, I felt a lump welling in my throat when I remembered the hurt I saw in his eyes that day. Of all people I should have understood him. Why didn't I? He could make me bleed with just a look. He still could. Everything that he felt was in his eyes.

And that made him beautiful.

Without making a big deal about it, White Bird had the courage to stick with what he wanted—what was right for him. He didn't whine about not belonging anywhere or feel sorry for himself like I did. He took charge of his destiny and made things happen. And he would have done it too if the tragedy of Heather's death hadn't happened. Whether Joe and his tribe accepted White Bird for the man he'd become, that didn't matter. Not to him and not to me.

And I loved him for that. Even gone from my life, he was teaching me.

"I wanted to understand what he'd been doing during the

week before Heather died, because he'd been secretive with me. After what you've told me, I know his vision quest would have been his whole focus. Nothing else would have mattered." I fixed my gaze on Joe. "So with all he had going on, why would he kill Heather?"

"What are you saying, Bren?" Mom asked. Joe kept quiet and waited for me to finish.

"How did their paths cross, Mom? Heather wasn't a nature girl. She wouldn't have been caught dead in the woods."

When I heard what I said, I gasped and nearly choked. Mom snorted a tension laugh and Joe raised an eyebrow.

"Sorry, I didn't mean to...say it like that." I heaved a deep sigh and rolled my eyes before I went on. "Anyway, White Bird was totally into his quest. He would've been at his secret location in the woods for days before. How would they get together...him and Heather?"

"But he was found over the body," Joe said.

"Yeah, by me. And I didn't see a sweat lodge near the bridge at Cry Baby Creek. That would have stood out. It would've reminded me of White Bird."

"Maybe his lodge is near that bridge," Joe said, smiling. He finally got my point.

"Maybe it still is." I grinned.

"What just happened?" Mom was confused. "Will one of you fill me in?"

"Tomorrow, Joe's gonna take me to look for White Bird's sweat lodge," I said. "If it's still there, like I think it is, we may find proof that could help him."

"But if you find any real evidence, it won't be admissible in court unless the police find it as part of their investigation. Some chain of custody thing," Mom said. When we both stared at her, she shrugged. "What? I watch a lot of cop shows. You pick up this stuff."

"Your mom is right, but I'm not sure about getting Sheriff Logan involved." Joe was the first to say the sheriff's name. It creeped me out.

"Not the sheriff, but maybe there's someone else. Someone who wasn't in Shawano when all this went down." I grinned. "That deputy, Will Tate. I think we can trust him."

"I'll call the sheriff's office on my way home. A call from me wouldn't alert the sheriff, not like one from you or your mother. I'll ask the deputy to meet us at the bridge tomorrow morning. I can be very persuasive."

"I'll bet." I smiled. "That'd be great, Joe. Thanks."

I knew we had a solid first step to help White Bird, but our plan didn't go far enough. He was trapped in his mind. And even if we could get the police to reopen the investigation into Heather's murder, that wouldn't free him from his misery.

"Earlier you said that I could help him. What did you mean by that?" I asked Joe. "Even if we get the cops to reopen the case, he's still trapped in his head."

From the look on his face, Joe knew what I was talking about, but Mom was in the dark.

"Brenna, it's gonna be hard enough to get the sheriff to move on this," she said. "If the people in this town find out how much you're involved, things could get uglier. Are you sure you want to chance that?" Mom reached for my hand. By the expression on her face, I knew she wasn't telling me not to help. She was only concerned for me. "This sounds… risky, especially for someone your age. You've already been hurt so much. I'm worried for you, honey."

"Someone's got to stand up for him, Mom. He can't do it the way he is." I gripped her hand. "Joe came here because he thought it was important. And I do, too. Ever since I turned White Bird in to the sheriff, I haven't been able to get past it. I'm stuck at fourteen and I can't move on without dealing with this."

"It's just that I'm scared for you, Bren. I want to help, but I don't know how."

"I know you do, Mom. But I need you to trust me. For real. Can you do that?"

Mom didn't answer right away. If she'd nodded too fast or made promises she couldn't keep, then I would have seen it in her eyes. But when she kept silent and thought about the gravity of what I'd asked, that meant a lot to me.

"I'll try," she said. It was the only answer Mom had. And it touched me more than if she'd said yes.

I knew I couldn't say what I really wanted to tell Joe with Mom around, so I waited for him to leave and walked him to his truck. Mom gave us privacy this time, even though I knew she was peeking out the window. In the moonlight and under the stars, Joe didn't look as scary as I had remembered him from the other night. I felt comfortable walking with him in silence, just like I used to do with White Bird.

"I want to thank you for coming, Joe."

"I should be the one thanking you. What happened to that boy has been eating me alive. Guilt can consume you."

I knew exactly what he meant.

"You walked me out here for a reason. Tell me what you think I should know." The man didn't beat around the bush.

"I visited White Bird in that hospital when I first got here. And something...happened." I chewed on the corner of my lower lip, thinking of how I would explain something I didn't understand myself.

But Joe made it easy.

"You saw his vision, didn't you?"

"How did you know?" I almost choked. "Yeah, I touched his arm and I got sucked into something really nasty. And I felt how scared he was."

"You see? I knew you could do this." Joe grinned and shook his fist in the air. "When I met you the other night, I saw the strength of your gift and I knew."

"Yeah, well, don't get too excited. There's more," I said. "I don't know if it's because of me that we connected, or because he's trying to reach out from some weird dimension."

I told him about the images I saw in White Bird's vision, and I shared my continuing nightmares. I even told him about Dr. Ridgeway and what he'd asked me to do.

"The link you share is probably coming from both of you. It's hard to say. Do you trust the doctor from Red Cliffs?" he asked.

"No, but he's barred me from seeing him until I cooperate. If I want to see White Bird, I've got to go through Ridgeway."

Joe nodded as he leaned against his truck and stared up at the moon, then said, "I will think about what you've told me. And we can talk more tomorrow. If White Bird is reaching out to you, it takes great strength to do that. I'm not sure how long he can keep that up." He heaved a sigh. "We have to help him…now. And like I said, I sense that you are the only one who can do this thing."

When Joe first asked me about seeing White Bird's vision, I was shocked. I didn't know how he'd make such a leap. And I remembered what he'd said about the gift I had. It took me a moment to make a leap of my own.

"That boy you were telling me about, the one who got

separated from his spirit guide. If quests are so private, how did you know about what happened to him decades ago?" I didn't wait for him to answer. "That boy was you."

Joe only smiled and said, "White Bird picked you as a friend for a reason. And he chose wisely. I'll call that deputy tomorrow morning. And if he's agreeable, I'll pick you up, eight o'clock sharp. We'll start at the bridge and work our way out, before the heat comes." Joe climbed into his truck and started the engine.

"I'll be ready." I waved as he drove away. And when I turned to head back into the house, I saw the drapes move.

What happened with Joe had taken the sting out of the talk I owed Mom after I'd lied about going to the movies, but I was sure she'd have plenty more to say. I wouldn't get off that easy. When I got back into the house, she was the first one to speak up.

"I had no idea what you've been going through, Brenna. You've been trying to help that boy on your own. Guess you thought it was the right thing to do, huh?" After I nodded, she said, "Why didn't you tell me?"

Mom only knew a fragment of what was happening and that was good enough. The truth would have only hurt her, so I told her what I thought she could handle.

"It was something I had to work out on my own. I still do."

I couldn't make up for the past between Mom and me. It was what it was. And I didn't know what our future would be like, either. All I knew was that I felt different about her this very second. Huddled on the couch where we'd watched home movies the other night, we talked until I got too sleepy to keep my eyes open. I kissed her good-night and went to bed. And although we'd talked about a lot of things, I hadn't told her about seeing into White Bird's visions or about my conversation with Dr. Ridgeway.

All of that was mine. It was private and I had to make the decision on what would happen next. I knew that if I told Mom, she'd only want to fix it.

And I couldn't let her do that.

Hours Later

After Joe's visit, I welcomed White Bird into my dreams. I wanted to feel close to him and remember the good things that had happened between us. But as they usually did lately, my dreams of him turned into nightmares.

I thrashed under my blankets and woke up screaming, drenched in sweat. I didn't know where I was at first. The blackness of my room was no different from the empty void I had left behind. It wasn't until I heard Mom's voice and saw her come into my room that I realized I was at home.

"Brenna, it's only a bad dream, sweetheart." She wiped my forehead with her cool hand and whispered to me. And with my heart pounding real hard and my panting so loud that I couldn't hear anything else, I strained to listen for her voice. "You're safe, honey. I've got you."

Mom crawled into bed with me and held me as she whispered, "Shhh. You're okay, sweetheart. I'm here. I love you so much."

I don't know why, but I cried and hugged her as hard as she hugged me. After I calmed down and got my body under control, I heard her say, "You know, Bren. I don't have to believe in the same things you do, but I do believe in you."

That was the first time she had said that. It touched me so much that I couldn't say anything and the tears came stronger. I think Mom cried, too. We held each other and it felt good.

I wanted to tell her how much I loved her, but I think she already knew. I didn't leave the house to go to the cemetery that night. I fell asleep with Mom holding me, exhausted.

The nightmare never came back. And I think I had Mom to thank for that.

chapter twelve

Next Morning—8:00 a.m.

Abandoning my usual fashion circus, I kept things simple and dressed in jeans and a white T-shirt with sturdy boots. Today would be about searching hard and I didn't want to hold anyone back because of blisters or the heat. When I saw Joe's blue truck rolling down our street from my upstairs window, an army of butterflies pinged off the inside of my belly. I was anxious to get started. I finally felt like I was helping White Bird by doing something real. And I had my fingers crossed that Joe could help me turn my luck around.

I blasted down the stairs to find Mom.

"Joe called while you were in the shower. He said Deputy Tate is on board. He'll be at the bridge by eight-thirty," Mom said as she ran a hand through my wet hair, touching up her handiwork. "Please...be careful."

"I will. And I'll call you if we find anything, okay?"

She nodded, but she didn't look happy. I knew she wanted

to go with us, but she couldn't. The painters were already working and they wouldn't be done for days.

"And don't forget the things I packed for you and the guys. It's gonna be hot today. You'll need 'em."

Mom had made breakfast to go for all of us—scrambled eggs and bacon wrapped in flour tortillas. And she'd packed bottled water, snack bars and a thing of sunscreen in the knapsack where I carried my spiral notebook and my collection of sunglasses. After our late night, I didn't know when she had time to pack the goodies.

"Thanks, Mom." I kissed her goodbye and she walked me out.

When I got in Joe's truck, he waved at Mom, who stood on the front porch.

"I packed us water and other stuff." He pointed his thumb to the bed of his truck where he had three knapsacks. And I laughed.

"Mom did, too. Guess we'll have plenty H_2O, but I bet you don't have these." I unwrapped his breakfast and handed it to him so he could eat and drive. He looked happy after his first bite.

"Mmm. Good. Be sure to thank your mother." He nodded. "Since my wife died, I don't cook much."

"You were married?"

I should have said, "Sorry about your wife," but I was more shocked that he'd gotten someone to marry him. He was such a…*guy.*

"Is that so unbelievable?" He smiled and took another bite of his breakfast. "We were married for twenty-one years. She was a good woman."

"How did she die?" I asked.

Joe got real quiet. And I wasn't sure he'd answer me. Eventually, he said, "It was sudden. A brain aneurysm."

"How awful."

I flashed on the memory of the dead woman I had seen at Joe's place, the first time I'd met him. I had only caught a glimpse of her at his front window, but the image of her sad eyes had stayed with me. I suddenly knew who she was. And I also got a strong flash that she had died at home, alone. I don't know where these thoughts come from, but I'd learned to trust them.

A part of me wanted to ask Joe if he knew his wife was still with him, but that felt like a major intrusion—a line I shouldn't cross. The way I saw it, the dead had rights, too. No matter how curious I was about her, it wasn't any of my business. And besides, when he didn't say anything more, I knew it was time to change the subject.

We talked about my nightmares and what they might mean. And although I saw that Joe was concerned for me, he held back his real thoughts on how White Bird had reached out to me. I had to accept that his tribal and spiritual beliefs were deeply personal and not easy to share with an outsider. Eventually we got around to talking about Dr. Ridgeway and the Red Cliffs Hospital.

"I know this is your decision, but if you visit White Bird at that hospital, you should tell your mother. She's got a right to know. What you'd be doing is risky. And she's still your momma."

"But what if she stops me?"

"I don't think she will," he argued, without taking his eyes off the road.

"You got a better crystal ball than I do?"

Joe didn't answer, but I saw the corner of his lip twitch.

"Will you go with me?" I asked. "I don't trust that doctor."

"Oh, but you trust *me?*" He smiled for real. "Yes, I'll go with you."

"With you as the Grand Pooh-Bah of the Euchee tribe, maybe we can mess with the doc's head," I said. "I'm sure the guy usually gets his way, but I'd like to see how he handles being off balance. It might be our best shot at doing what's right for White Bird…our way."

I stared straight ahead with a grin on my face, but from the corner of my eye, I saw that I had Joe's attention.

"Sounds interesting. What do you have in mind?"

I turned to catch a glint in Joe's eye and I knew he'd go along. Dr. Ridgeway would get a taste of Shaman magic, whether he wanted it or not.

Outskirts of Shawano—8:35 a.m.

Like he'd promised, Deputy Will Tate was parked near the mouth of the trail that led to the haunted bridge over Cry Baby Creek. He'd ditched his uniform and was dressed in a blue T-shirt, an OSU ball cap and faded jeans with hiking boots. And his patrol car was nowhere in sight. With arms crossed, he was leaning against a red SUV. I was glad he'd downplayed the cop thing. Police cruisers drew attention and I didn't want anyone else to know what was going on until we got good news.

Word traveled too fast in this town as it was.

"Deputy Tate, glad you could make it." Joe held out his hand and they shook. "We appreciate you coming before your shift."

"Call me Will." And when he turned to me, he said, "Hey, Brenna. Joe says you have a theory about a sweat lodge?"

Even though my theory wouldn't free White Bird, I hoped it would cast enough doubt to reopen the case. And that was good enough for now. I told him what I suspected.

"Interesting." Will nodded. "I've seen the case file and there wasn't anything mentioned about a sweat lodge or the boy's vision quest. If we locate this lodge, we might find more evidence, but you have to be prepared. Whatever we find might make things worse for your friend."

"Can things get worse?" I asked.

The deputy smiled. I didn't mean my question to be funny. I really wanted to know.

"And whatever we find," Will added, "if it pertains to the case, don't touch it. Let me handle any evidence. And I'll have to tell the sheriff. It's my job."

"Okay."

"Then let's go." The deputy led the way.

We grabbed our gear and headed out. And even though I sounded sure about White Bird, I had my doubts. My luck was for shit. If there were anything in these woods that could make things worse for him, I'd find it.

We started at the bridge where I'd found him kneeling over Heather's body. It had been hard for me to be there again. I never thought I would've returned in a million years. But there I was, acting tough like I could handle it.

Inside, I knew better.

That old rusted bridge had stood in silent witness to what had happened underneath it. I stared at it as I walked under. Rust stains bled down gray, bleached wood like blood. And the reason the bridge had been built no longer mattered. It spanned the dry creek without a purpose, going nowhere for decades. *Why had White Bird come here?*

"This is where you saw him?" Will asked and pointed to a spot under the bridge. I told him what I remembered.

"Yeah. I was over there, behind those trees. He didn't see me." Flashes of terror rose hot in my stomach when I told them what I knew. It wouldn't have taken much to make me throw up. And the heat wasn't helping. "He was staring off, like he didn't even know where he was."

I caught Joe watching me. His concern told me all I had to know about what he was thinking. He was looking out for me like Mom would've been. And right now, I was worrying him. After taking a deep breath, I told them what I knew and my voice sounded like someone else was talking.

"After I called 911, he didn't run. I don't think he heard me. He was chanting something I didn't understand. And he was rocking back and forth. It scared me." Even though it was already hot, a chill raced up my spine. "He was acting… crazy."

"Was White Bird tested for drugs after his arrest?" Joe asked the deputy.

"Yeah." Will nodded. "He was definitely under the influence. Notes in the murder book said the kid was really messed up. But something else was going on, 'cause drugs would've worn off. That's when he went to Red Cliffs for evaluation."

The deputy took a good look around and pointed down the creek. "Let's spread out, but keep each other in sight." After he explained a grid pattern to organize the search, he finished by saying, "Call out if you see anything. And keep hydrated. It's gonna be a scorcher."

We didn't say much after that. We kept our heads down and worked it hard, feeling the gravity of what we were doing. I looked for Heather, but she never showed. Although I never saw her, that didn't mean she wasn't there. She'd found another way to haunt me. I felt her under my prickling skin and flashes of her battered my mind with images I'd never forget.

Heather was just as cruel dead as she'd been alive.

Hours Later

When the sun beat down on us directly overhead, I knew it was close to noon as I sucked down more water. In the sweltering heat, my boots felt heavy and sweat clung to my skin like a fine layer of grit. Sunscreen had helped for a while, but it had melted off.

Cicadas buzzed in waves from the scrub oaks and mesquite trees, nothing more than a mind-numbing white noise. We worked our way along a rocky ridge, peering down into a red clay gorge near a tributary of the old creek. Even though I drank water, I didn't have to pee. Mainly because I didn't want to deal with the inconvenience, but I was battling dehydration. We all had slowed our pace and were taking more breaks.

It was on one of my rest stops that I saw a glint of something that had reflected in the sun. It caught my eye.

"What's that…over there?" I called out to Joe and pointed. "Something metal."

I didn't wait for Joe or Will to see it. I stayed on the ridge and headed straight for where I had seen the reflection. As I rounded a bend, I heard the sound of creek water and followed my ears. The ridge overlooked the rolling hills below. And the water made the view an oasis in the heat. Without seeing a sweat lodge, I knew White Bird would have picked this beautiful spot for his vision quest.

"It's here. I know it." I called out to Joe and the deputy. And I heard the smile in my voice. "He'd camouflage it, so look real good."

Within minutes, we'd found what we came looking for.

"Oh, my God. This is it," I called out to the others when I found the entrance. I pulled back the layers of blankets over the opening and looked into the dark lodge.

"You did it," I whispered to him and pictured his smiling face.

White Bird had his sweat lodge in a dense stand of trees and it had been hidden in thick brush. We almost missed it. The structure he'd built looked undisturbed, but the fire pit was in a shambles with the stones shoved away and the ash pile filled with debris. It was yards away from the hut and closer to the creek.

"He did a fine job." Joe nodded as he looked over what White Bird had done. "As good as I've ever seen."

Joe was as interested in White Bird's accomplishment as I was, but Deputy Tate looked on the scene with a cop's eyes as he knelt at the fire pit, putting on latex gloves he had stuffed in his pants pocket.

"Looks like someone kicked these stones out. And I see a charred watch in the ashes. It's caked with clay, but it looks like a man's watch. Do either of you recognize it?" the deputy asked.

After we both shook our heads, Joe said, "Usually a boy on a vision quest has no need for a watch. Time means nothing. Did White Bird have one on him when he was arrested?"

"I don't know. I'll have to check." The deputy gazed into the stone pit. "We'll take this one as evidence and clean it up. Hikers might have left it."

Joe shifted his focus back to the sweat lodge.

"These are my blankets and hides. And that's my shovel." He grabbed the blankets at the entrance to the sweat lodge then pointed inside the hut. "And that's my grandfather's knife…over there."

"You found your knife?" I asked him, then turned to the deputy. "I thought I read in old newspaper clippings that investigators found the murder weapon and had taken it as evidence."

"They did, yeah," Will agreed.

"Then why would he have two knives here?" I shrugged. "I can see him taking Joe's knife because it was made by a Euchee elder. He would have used it for everything. It would've been special to him. So why bring another knife?"

"Good question," Will said.

"What kind of knife was used on the girl?" Joe asked.

"A hunting knife. Pretty common," the deputy told him as he went inside the sweat lodge to retrieve the knife that had belonged to Joe. When he came back out, he looked closely at the blade, holding it in his gloved hands. "We'll have to test this, but it doesn't look like there's blood on it." He shook his head. "It doesn't make any sense that he'd have two knives here. You're right."

"I'd always assumed my grandfather's knife had been the murder weapon, especially after they found White Bird's fingerprints at my place after the robbery." Joe grimaced. "I wasn't certain, but I was too afraid to ask. I figured if I drew attention to the weapon being my knife, that would only strengthen the case the police had on him."

"And it would have," Will agreed.

"But finding it now isn't enough, is it?" I asked. From the look on the deputy's face, I knew what he'd say.

"No, it's not. But I'll get a team out here to collect evidence. With your positive ID on the knife, Joe, we can link this site to White Bird. If nothing else, we can cast doubt on what happened. But I don't think it'll be enough for Sheriff Logan to reopen the case. People would string Matt from the highest tree once details of this case came out."

"It's not fair," I argued. "If he was white, I bet the sheriff would look into it."

Will narrowed his eyes and I wasn't sure if he was mad at me or not.

"The sheriff is a hard man, but a fair one. I know you don't agree, but if we brought him a solid reason to reopen this case—something the D.A. could sink his teeth into—I think the sheriff would listen."

"You're right, Will. I don't agree." I'd had enough.

I was tired and frustrated and the heat made everything worse. I couldn't let things go. I argued with the deputy, even when I knew he was only doing his job and had done us a favor by being out here before his shift started. Joe kept quiet, but he nodded his support and let me talk without interfering.

"Look, I hear what you're saying, Brenna," the deputy said. "But there's one thing you don't know that could really blow up in our faces if we don't come up with something more solid."

"What's that, Will?" Joe asked.

"There's a reason that the sheriff and anyone who investigated this murder wanted to hang Isaac Henry on the spot. And this didn't get into the papers. The sheriff held it back, so I'd appreciate it if you wouldn't talk about this to anyone." After we both nodded, Will heaved a sigh and rubbed a hand over his face before he went on. "It was bad enough that Heather Madsen had been stabbed so many times, but—"

The deputy stopped and looked at both of us.

"That girl had been scalped, too."

Shawano—An Hour Later

Derek Bast had sent several text messages to Jade DeLuca, but after her late night with Chloe, Nicole and Brandy in Oklahoma City, she'd slept in and missed his first few attempts to reach her. By the time she got up and cleared the fog from her brain, she was coherent enough to get really pissed at him for not picking up the damned phone and calling her. All his text messages had been the same.

we got trouble—call me

After she got dressed, she would call Derek. With her mom out of town on business, she was staying at her father's place. But after he had left her a note taped to her bedroom door that he had to work early and didn't know when he'd be back, she was relieved that she was on her own as usual. Sitting on her bed, she dialed Derek's number and when he picked up, she didn't bother to say hello.

"If this is important, why didn't you just call me?"

"Well, good morning to you, too." He didn't sound in a good mood. "You got a lot of nerve bitching me out. You asked me to follow Brenna Nash. And I don't get one thank-you?"

Jade ignored the drama of Derek's faked hurt feelings. The jerk always demanded attention and constantly needed his ego stroked.

"Look, you've got just as much at stake here. So quit your whining." Jade looked into the mirror on her dresser and wiped a corner of her mouth, tweaking her lipstick. "What's the texting all about?"

"I got up early and parked down the street from the Nash

place. If I hadn't done that, I would've missed what happened," Derek said. She heard the smile in his voice.

"So tell me already."

"She had a visitor. Some old Indian guy in a blue truck. He picked her up and I followed them."

"Where'd they go?"

"You're not gonna like this."

She heard Derek sigh on the phone and she rolled her eyes.

"Spit it out, Derek!"

"They drove to the bridge at Cry Baby. And they met up with one of my uncle's deputies. He wasn't wearing a uniform, but I recognized him."

"What? Why would they be out there with the cops?" She jumped off her bed and walked to her window. "They're gonna find out what we did."

"Not if we keep our mouths shut," Derek said. "How could they?"

Jade used the word *we* so she wouldn't be alone in this, but she really only cared about covering her own ass. Even though others had played a part in what happened that night, no one knew how far she'd gone. What she'd done to Heather—no one could know. *No one!*

"What did they do?" she asked. "Did you see?"

"No, I didn't hike in there. I was afraid they'd spot me."

"I knew that little bitch came back here to stir things up. She's gonna get them to reopen Heather's case, I just know it. And we'll get dragged into this. That can't happen, Derek." Jade paced her bedroom floor. "*Shit!* This can't be happening."

"Nothing's happened yet. We don't know what they're looking for. What could be up there after all these years?"

"Why didn't you find out? You should have followed them."

"I told you…they would've spotted me. We gotta play this smart, Jade. That Indian will fry for killing Heather. My uncle and this whole town are ready for that to happen."

"Too bad Isaac Henry doesn't know that. This thing is never gonna be over as long as his trial is hanging over our heads. He could stay in that loony bin forever."

"So what?" he argued. "With him locked away and not saying anything to the cops, that's as good as a life sentence. Nothing's gonna happen to us. This whole thing will blow over. You'll see."

"Not if that little bitch doesn't let this go. She's messing this up for all of us." Jade fell back onto her mattress and stared up at her ceiling. "We gotta teach her a lesson. And this time, we're rampin' it up."

It didn't take Jade long to come up with an idea. And Derek was psyched when she told him what she had in mind. He had a mean streak that she could always count on.

"Are you calling Chloe?" he asked.

"No. She's out of it." Jade didn't bother to explain that Chloe was too weak to handle something like this. "Call some of your buddies. Tell them to meet us at our usual spot, the old culvert at midnight. Operation Warpath starts tonight."

chapter thirteen

Outskirts of Shawano—Late Afternoon

"I'm okay, Mom. We'll be home soon."

I ended the call to my mother, knowing I hadn't told her the truth. I wasn't okay. None of this was okay. I told her about finding White Bird's sweat lodge and she was real happy until I gave her the bad news—that none of it mattered. We were back at square one with little to show.

Now I had to watch as strangers tore through the only thing I had left of him. Crime scene cops took what they wanted of his sweat lodge and bagged stuff. But when I saw one guy with a beaded leather pouch in plastic, with a strand of a colorful woven bracelet sticking out, I grabbed the sealed bag from his hands.

"Don't take that. It's…mine."

"Brenna?" Joe Sunne rushed to me when he heard my angry voice. "What is it?"

He looked down at the plastic bag I had in my hand.

"That's his medicine pouch. And the bracelet that's sticking out? I made it for him." My eyes welled with tears. "I left it… somewhere else, but he brought it with him. I can't believe he did that."

I knew without looking that the medicine bag held the twig he had taken from my hair the day we first kissed. With the twig would be a small feather, a remembrance of the day we had set the little wounded bird free. And now my friendship bracelet had been worthy of his special pouch. I held back how personal all this was. My time with White Bird had been private until now. No one would understand how sad I was, watching these men tear apart everything he had worked so hard to do. The sweat lodge was a big deal to him and no one treated his things with respect. No one.

"That's evidence. I've got to take it," the crime scene investigator argued.

When I didn't give the medicine pouch back, Will Tate stepped between us. "Sorry, Brenna. You knew this would happen."

With trembling fingers, I handed the plastic Baggie back to the CSI guy. Will gave me a sympathetic look and got back to work. This whole thing was unfair and wrong. I needed today to turn out good, but all I saw was that daring to hope had been a mistake. And after I'd found the friendship bracelet that I'd made for him out of embroidery thread and beads, I realized he'd brought it here. He had a piece of me with him when he did his quest to become a man.

And knowing that made me sick, especially after how things had turned out.

"A boy doesn't usually bring personal things with him on a quest," Joe said. "You must mean a great deal to him."

The first time we'd met, the man had scared me. Now his deep gravelly voice felt like a hug.

"This has been hard, Joe." Tears spilled onto my cheeks as I watched the police work. "I have to see him. If there's a shot at him getting better, I have to find a way to reach him."

"I know, Brenna." He squeezed my shoulder as he stood behind me. "Since there's nothing more we can do here, you want to pay a call on that doctor? We can do it together. And maybe your mother will be done with those painters. We can pick her up on the way. What do you say?"

Joe had a real subtle way of being a friend. And at that moment, when I needed to feel better, he found a way to lift my spirits.

"Yeah, let's do it." I wiped my face and smiled. "Thanks, Joe."

Red Cliffs Hospital—Early Evening

This time I didn't have to sneak in to see White Bird. I walked up to the receptionist outside the detention unit and signed in, saying, "I'm here to see Isaac Henry."

I didn't look up to see her expression. I pretended like I'd visited a hundred times before. And with Mom and Joe standing behind me, it looked like I meant business, but the woman at the desk wasn't impressed. She looked up something on her computer and narrowed her eyes before she said, "I've got a flag that he's not receiving any visitors. I'll get his therapist, Dr. Ridgeway."

She didn't wait for me to argue. The woman in the white uniform made a call and in minutes Dr. Ridgeway came through the locked door with a loud buzz.

"It's you." He looked relieved that I'd come. "And I see you've brought people with you."

I wasn't used to anyone being happy to see me. I made the introductions. And when it came to Joe Sunne, I stretched the truth a little.

"And this is Joe Sunne. He's a Shaman and tribal elder of the Euchee. He's here as an...official. He's checking into White Bird's treatment...for his tribe."

"White Bird?"

"That's Isaac Henry's Indian name. He prefers it."

"I didn't realize that. Are you here to help your friend, like we discussed?" The doc was playing it cagey in front of witnesses. With a kid, he hadn't thought twice about throwing his weight around. But with Mom and Joe here, he was acting all professional.

"Yes, that's why I brought Mr. Sunne. He's a tribal...representative. He's here...like a priest."

Sometimes I don't know how I come up with my brand of bullshit. It was a gift and a curse. And today, it was a little bit of both. I kept my face real serious and I avoided looking at my mother, but Joe was hard to ignore. He stood with his chest out and chin up with both hands clasped behind his back. His eyes were fixed on the doc in the same scary way he'd glared at me the other night. And he didn't flinch or say a word.

He almost cracked me up.

"Oh? I've never seen anyone from his tribe here before. Your friend has never had a visitor, except for you." The doc avoided the use of White Bird's Indian name. "But no matter. As long as you follow my instructions, I'm sure we can..."

"Our tribal customs are very important, too, Doctor. Nurturing the boy's spirit might heal his body." Joe spoke for the first time. And he sounded impressive. "Ms. Nash and her mother were kind enough to notify the tribe that this young man was Euchee. We hadn't known that before now. That's why he's had no visitors."

"Really?" Ridgeway cocked his head and looked confused. "And you're aware of the boy's history and why he's here?"

"Yes, we are." Joe nodded. "Can we see him now?"

"I'm sorry, but he's under sedation." The doctor grimaced. "He hasn't been sleeping the last few nights, so today we gave him something to help. I wished you had called ahead."

Nothing had gone right today. And if what the doc said was true, about White Bird being sedated, he wouldn't have been strong enough to reach me in his condition. I hated this and it showed on my face. Seeing my frustration, Mom put her arm around me.

"What about tomorrow?" Joe pressed and laid it on thick. "The tribal council is waiting for my report on his condition."

"Tomorrow is fine. I'll change his meds, but I'm his attending therapist. I'll supervise your visit. Is that understood?"

I opened my mouth to object, but Joe nodded and said, "That'll be fine. We only ask that you respect our customs, as well."

"That shouldn't be a problem." The doctor told us to come back at one o'clock tomorrow afternoon and left.

I stood there staring at the locked door and it killed me to know White Bird was on the other side. I wanted to be with him. Touch him. And I wanted him to really see me, but I'd have to wait until tomorrow—an eternity in my world.

Shawano—7:20 p.m.

On our way home, we stopped at Denny's off the interstate. So much had happened that day, I think we all needed time to talk and let things sink in. We sat in the back and picked a megabooth so I could stretch out. The next RV that pulled up with a herd of human clones would have to sit somewhere else.

Joe and my mother ate for real and I faked it.

At first, I caught Mom up on what had happened at the bridge and the crime scene, but eventually our conversation drifted to the hospital and what would come tomorrow. Mom sensed I was holding back and Joe knew I was. He glared at me until I finally got the message. He expected me to be honest and spill my secrets.

And the only way I could do that was over lemon meringue pie.

"Mom? I've got something to say and I want Joe to hear this, too. After tomorrow, I've got a feeling we won't have any more secrets between us, so here's a sneak preview."

I told her everything; that my reading the obits had a purpose and I confessed that my occasional night trips to the graveyard were visits to my home away from home. Her jaw dropped on that one. I had to think up something to make her feel better.

"Hey, it's not like I constantly hang out with dead people." I grimaced and shrugged. "It's just that most of my friends aren't exactly breathing, is all."

That didn't make her feel any better, but at least she'd stopped asking questions. It didn't do any good spelling out every detail. I could tell by the look on Mom's face that she'd reached the saturation point. And Joe had given me the sideways glance that told me my mom had had enough.

Even though having Joe there had helped, it felt strange to talk about dead people and visions at Denny's. He understood what it was like to be different. And the "gift" he'd been given as a small boy, surviving his vision quest, gave us common ground. I had no idea if I was actually losing my mind, but I knew that I was a far cry from being "normal."

"Oh, my gosh, honey. I can't believe you went through all that…alone. You thought you were schizophrenic?"

When her eyes filled with tears, I knew what she was thinking.

"Mom, I'm sorry I didn't say anything. But I thought I'd put you through too much already. I was really scared I'd be a burden—more of one—and I couldn't do that to you." I reached for her hand. "But if what Joe says is right, maybe I can help White Bird. I have to try."

"But isn't that risky?" she asked me, but turned to Joe for an answer. "I don't understand any of this."

"Yes, there's risk. And most people would think this is pure mumbo jumbo. But I've experienced it. And I know what I know," he told her. When I glared at him for being too honest, Joe narrowed his eyes back at me. "We talked about this, Brenna. Your mom has a right to know. And a casual conversation over pie won't cut it. The two of you should talk more."

"Okay already. I get it." I took a bite of pie. "All this talking is wearing me out."

Although I'd resisted telling Mom the truth until now, it had felt good to finally have everything in the open. I was still worried sick for White Bird, but I allowed myself a moment of feeling good. Lying and hiding stuff took a lot of energy. No wonder I was so friggin' skinny.

Hours Later

Lemon meringue pie and Mom's smile—a real smile that let me see the girl she used to be—had given me a false sense of security. After I got home, I took a long hot shower to wash off the grime and what was left of my hope. In denial, I got dressed in my T-shirt and boxers and went straight to bed, pretending I could sleep. Acting like I was normal.

I was exhausted. And the walls of my room had closed in and my mind wouldn't let me relax. But this time I didn't run away to be with my stone angels. I had stayed to face my fears, which felt like a mistake.

I wasn't ready. Maybe I'd never be.

As I lay on my bed in the dark, I stared at my ceiling and all my insecurities hit at once. I'd wanted something more today. I'd counted on it. And when nothing much happened, I felt the hollow ache of failure. For White Bird's sake, that couldn't happen tomorrow. But what if it did?

What if I couldn't reach him like before? With all the hype over me having a gift, what if I had nothing except plain vanilla schizophrenia? The strain of being back in Shawano had hit me. I was faced with the stark reality that I might not be able to fix any of this. Not even having Mom and Joe on my side would matter if I couldn't help White Bird. Our paths had been linked from the first time we'd met. I felt responsible.

And I was scared as hell that our fate had already been decided.

This time when I closed my eyes, I didn't feel White Bird at all and that terrified me. In the dark, we were both invisible. We didn't exist. And all that I wasn't, and would never be, stared back at me through the blackness. What if he'd given up or had lost the strength to reach me? Maybe he'd blown through and wasted the only freedom he'd ever have and the emptiness inside me was all there was. I didn't want to think about the tie between us being severed for good, but in the dark of my room, that's all I saw.

After Midnight

I jerked awake to the sound of my mother screaming.

"Brenna! Get down and stay down!" The sound of loud pops forced me off my bed. And I fell onto shattered glass. Cracks in my window glinted in the moonlight. And the lamp on my nightstand had tumbled to the wood floor and busted. Had someone shot through my window?

"What's happening?" I yelled, but Mom didn't hear me.

Her footsteps thudded down the hall outside my room and the door swung open. She found me cowering in the dark. I was on the floor by my bed with hands over my head.

"Was that a gun?" I wasn't making sense, but everything I said had come from gut instinct. It felt like we were under attack. "Is someone shooting at us?"

"I don't know. I can't tell," she whispered and shielded me with her body. That scared me more than I already was.

In the distance I heard the screech of tires and the house got real quiet, except for dogs barking across the street. Mom stayed still and stopped me from moving.

"Turn on some lights," I said.

"*No!* Not until we know they're gone."

Mom had used the word *they,* and Jade, Derek and his terrible friends flashed into my head. Waking up from a dead sleep, I must have heard something that had scared me awake. I had sat up in bed with my heart hammering, like my nightmares.

Only this time it had been real.

"I think they're gone, Mom." I got to my feet, even with her grabbing me.

"Don't go. They might still be in the house." Panic had gripped her hard, but she got up with me. "Get some shoes on. There's glass on the floor. And no lights. They could be down the street waiting to shoot whatever moves."

I slipped into the unlaced boots I had tossed onto the floor by my bed. And I grabbed the only weapon I had in my room—a pen I had in my purse, the kind with a pointy fine line. I gripped the pen in my hand like a dagger. When I crept from my room, I was clinging to my mom's back and we moved together down the stairs. Her breaths came in pants, like mine. And I was shaking out of my skin. I peered through the dark and found monsters in every shadow. When we got to the front room, I saw broken glass everywhere. Windows had been shattered and rocks littered the floor. Maybe we'd only heard the pops of glass breaking, but I still didn't flip the lights on. If they were watching down the street, I didn't want to give them the satisfaction of knowing that they'd scared us.

Stupid, I know.

With a trembling hand, I peeked through the drapes of the bay window and stared onto the front lawn.

"Oh. My. God," I gasped.

Grams's house had been trashed. Garbage was strewn on the lawn. And someone had spray painted our windows and torn apart all the planting I had done. They had tossed dirt and plants down the street and smashed flowerpots. And toilet paper hung from the trees. I could only imagine what Grams's old house would look like in daylight and it made me sick.

After a long silence, Mom finally said, "We've got to call the police."

"Do we have to? You know what's gonna happen."

I knew reporting what had happened would be a waste of time—especially if Derek Bast had played a part in the vandalism. He'd spent his entire life flying under the radar of his cop uncle. And only Sheriff Logan knew how many times he'd looked the other way to cover for his nephew.

"I don't care." Mom crossed her arms. "Matt Logan might have this whole town fooled, but it's time someone stood up to him. The next time I see him, he's gettin' a double shot of me."

chapter fourteen

2:40 a.m.

Obscenity spray painted in black marred the outside of Grams's old Victorian. And the crude words were meant for me. I was ashamed and embarrassed. I'd never had sex, but if anyone looked at the huge letters sprawled on my grandmother's house, they'd think I was lying. It was bad enough that bad news traveled fast in Shawano, but soon everything would be on the internet. I wanted to run, but there'd be no real place to hide and I wouldn't leave Mom alone. Besides, with all four tires on the Subaru slashed, neither one of us could escape.

The police cruiser parked at the curb drew attention like flashing neon. The spiraling red-and-blue lights shone in neighbors' windows and cast eerie shadows on the front of our house, reflecting off the shattered glass. And the deputy's radio blurted codes in copspeak. None of this was low profile.

Even at this insane hour, neighbors got in line to watch the circus. They stood on their porches and sidewalks and stared at us like we were freaks. I was used to gawkers, but Mom wasn't. I saw their dark faceless shadows, but none of them came over. We were outsiders. If anyone had witnessed what happened, I knew they wouldn't get involved.

We were totally screwed.

I stared up at the house and whispered, "I can't believe this."

All we had done had been ripped to shreds or destroyed in minutes. The new paint, the flowers and plants, and the clean windows—all of it ruined. And at my feet was a little white petunia that had lumps of soil clinging to its tiny roots. I bent down and picked it up, cradling it in my hand.

"Ah, poor baby."

It would cost time and money to fix things, but the pain of seeing Grams's house destroyed took a higher toll. Even if we fixed it, there were no guarantees that Jade and Derek wouldn't target us again.

Since I'd come back to Shawano, everything had come at me fast—like I was stalled on the tracks of an oncoming train and locked in my seat belt with no choice but to wait for the wreck. And I was sick and tired of just watching shit happen.

"You said you heard a car. Did you get a look at the vehicle? Or see a tag?" Deputy Sanford's voice carried on the muggy night air.

He went down his standard list of questions and did his best to finish his incident report, but we had little to say. Since the destruction looked like kids had done it, the deputy had tried to pull me aside earlier, but Mom had gotten real protective and took control. After that, he directed all his questions to her.

My mother knew what would rain down on us from all

directions if she accused the sheriff's nephew without any real proof. Our suspicions wouldn't be enough, especially in this town. We were in a no-win situation and we both knew it, so we stuck to the facts, even though it was killing us not to say more.

"No, like I said, we were asleep. We didn't see anything," Mom repeated. "We only heard it."

"We'll get statements from your neighbors and let you know if they saw or heard anything," the deputy said as he looked at our house. "In the meantime, you should take photos for your insurance. That's always a good idea."

His attempt at being thorough and helpful fell on stunned, numb ears. Not much was getting through. I couldn't stand seeing my grandmother's home trashed, a place filled with memories. I knew Mom probably didn't blame me, but everything I had done since I got back to Shawano had brought this down on her. Was she sorry that she'd brought me…or sorry that she got stuck with me as her kid?

Maybe I'm an alien.

"I know what you're thinking," Mom said.

"I doubt it."

"This wasn't your fault. Whoever did this will pay, in this life or the next."

Mom didn't go to church much, but she always got religion when she couldn't explain really bad stuff. And when the situation called for it, she made God out to be a really angry guy who got revenge in the afterlife—like he was a badass hall monitor with a whack sense of timing. I wanted to tell her that God would get a whole lot more satisfaction if he took care of business now and bitch slapped anyone who got out of line.

Me being an alien made more sense.

Shawano Sheriff's Office

Sheriff Matt Logan wasn't surprised to see his deputy, Will Tate, in the office this early before his shift. Most guys his age valued downtime, but Tate was real dedicated. This wasn't the first time he'd come in early.

Matt was working on his fifth cup of coffee when he saw Tate sitting at his desk in the bull pen, looking at a silver watch in a plastic bag. It had a striking blue watch face on it. Even from a distance, something clicked with him. And a slow gnaw in his belly started working.

"What's that?" Matt asked. "Mind if I take a look?"

"No, go ahead. We found it in a fire pit, covered in mud and ash. The wristband's broken, but the lab got it cleaned up. No usable fingerprints, but I'm still working it. We could get lucky." He hesitated a minute before he added, "It's new evidence in the Heather Madsen case."

Hearing Heather's name caused Matt to tense. That case was a black mark on his career, the one investigation that still plagued him. Heather had been a close friend to his nephew, Derek. A girlfriend, in fact. The investigation would have turned uglier if he had to put Derek on a suspect list. Boyfriends always hit that list, but the Nash girl and that Indian kid made things real simple.

Until now.

As Matt stared down at the silver watch in plastic, the walls closed in on him. He recognized the timepiece, especially the unique colored face. He'd ordered it special, online.

For Derek. It had been a special gift, for his nephew's thirteenth birthday, a rite of passage for a boy turning into a man.

"You said you found this. Where?" Matt tried to sound

casual. After Tate told him about the location of the crime scene, he asked, "And it's part of the Madsen case, you say?"

When Tate confirmed his worst nightmare, Matt pursed his lips and nodded.

"You got a minute, Will?"

He waved his deputy into his office. When Tate came in, he closed his door and offered his deputy a seat.

"I hear you've been asking questions about what happened to Brenna Nash at the Seaver party." His question was a smoke screen to get his mind off the watch, but he also wanted his deputy to know that nothing got by him. He had ways of keeping tabs.

"Yeah, I have been. You got a problem with that?"

"No. Just keep me in the loop. That's all." He rocked in his chair and steepled his fingers as he stared at his deputy. "Tell me about that sweat lodge you found, the one that the Henry kid might have built."

"No maybe about it. Joe Sunne ID'd the knife that kid stole from his place. And some of his other stuff was there, too." Tate nodded. "That was the boy's sweat lodge all right."

His deputy filled him in on what he'd found. And he told him about the second knife at the lodge. The question of why the kid would've needed two knives was a valid one. And it had always been a mystery why Heather had been in the woods that night, but none of this was enough for him to reopen a case that would have the whole town up in arms. No, sir.

Will Tate was a good young cop. He had an easy way about him that Matt liked. And despite the fact Will had not heeded his advice on Brenna Nash—that the kid was trouble—he respected his deputy's instincts to pursue his own investigation. At his age, he might have done the same.

"I saw that Kate Nash filed a complaint last night. Vandals

hit her mother's old place," he said. He hoped his deputy would see the connection. The Nashes were magnets for trouble, both of them.

"Yeah, someone did a lot of damage, Sanford said. From what he told me, it sounded like kids. Maybe it's linked to the incident with the Nash girl, after the Seaver party." Will shook his head. "That woman and her daughter have had more than their share of crap to deal with."

Matt's natural instinct was to lecture his deputy on believing a mother with parenting issues. Kate's little darling was never responsible. But after seeing Derek's watch in that evidence bag, he didn't feel up to it. His sister was a single mom who had survived a really rocky divorce. He'd wondered about his nephew after seeing uncomfortable signs that the kid gave his mother regular snow jobs about what he was up to. But kids were kids.

Kate Nash's girl was another story. She'd been involved with a half-breed kid who had killed a real promising young woman. Heather Madsen had been an upstanding girl from Shawano who had a bright future taken away from her and her family.

The Nash woman was no comparison to his sister.

"Is that all, sir?" Tate's voice yanked him from his doubts. "I've got paperwork to do."

"Yeah, that's all." He nodded. "And good work on uncovering the new evidence in the Madsen case. The D.A. will need it when the time comes."

For his sake and for the town's, he hoped that time would come sooner rather than later. With the Nashes in town, things had come to a boil real fast. All he wanted now was a quick trial to put that Henry kid behind bars where he belonged.

The Madsen family needed closure. And he'd breathe easier when the case was officially closed.

Red Cliffs Hospital

After we got a tow truck to pick up Mom's car to fix the tires, we hitched a ride with Joe, and we got to the hospital half an hour early, but that didn't do us any good. Dr. Ridgeway kept us waiting outside the detention unit. *Forever!* He was making a point that he was in charge. But after what had happened last night—and with all the things on my mother's mind—she looked antsy and a little pissed. Her show of attitude covered up her jangling nerves.

Mom sat next to me, but Joe kept moving. With hands clasped behind his back, he paced the hall like he was a shark in open water. His eyes took everything in the way a predator looked at the world. His face was always calm. Only his eyes hinted at the coiled spring of tension inside him. The man knew how to keep his emotions in check.

Until today, I wouldn't have bet a dime that Joe owned a tie much less a sport coat. His jeans and boots offset his adult gear, enough to avoid the whole "Look at me! I'm a good Christian heading to church" thing. Mom wore a blue sundress and sandals. And I had on jeans, my best vintage sneaks, a T-shirt and vest, with a short brimmed straw hat pulled down around my ears. And I wore my biggest aviator shades that made me look like a fly.

I'd changed ten times.

"No matter how this goes, you're a tough, gutsy kid, Bren," Mom said. "And I'm proud of you."

"I'm an idiot."

"You get that from your father's side of the family."

I couldn't help it. I snorted a laugh. Sometimes Mom cracked me up.

"Okay, this waiting is driving me insane." Mom sighed.

"I wouldn't say that too loud. Not in this place."

She didn't hear me. Mom jumped off the couch like it was on fire and said, "I'm gonna find out what's going on." She zeroed in on the nurse behind the desk.

After she left, Joe came over and stood in front of me with his hands stuffed into his jeans.

"Are you nervous?" he asked.

"A little." I wrung my hands and my knee got fidgety all by itself.

I didn't bother to hide my twisty nerves from a guy who knew exactly what it took to survive a hellish vision that probably had felt like being gutted like a fish.

"Tell me what will happen, Joe. I need to know." I thudded the back of my head against a column and kept my eyes fixed on him from behind my dark glasses. "Mainly, I just need to hear your voice."

He smiled. A real smile and not just a lip twitch. When it lit up his dark eyes, I could totally see him being married.

"Every journey is different." The rich tone of his voice rumbled like distant thunder. I leaned my head back and shut my eyes to listen, until he said, "I hope he's strong enough to reach out to you one more time."

My eyes popped open and I jerked my head straight. The thought of White Bird being too weak had me picturing him hanging off a cliff. And the only thing holding him there was me.

"I wish you hadn't said that." I grimaced. "Positive thoughts, okay?"

The man nodded and sat next to me.

In a low voice, only loud enough for me to hear, he said, "You've already seen the inside of a vision. It's like a string of illusions, symbols meant as a message. Everything is important."

"Wait a minute. What about him? I don't care about road signs in hell. I just want to find him and break him out of wherever he's at."

When Joe hesitated, I got worried.

"You're hiding something. What is it?" I pressed.

"Remember when you first came to me and I said that I knew who you were?"

"Yeah." I figured he'd heard the town rumors or seen something in the papers from two years ago.

"I knew you were coming," he said, fixing his dark eyes on me, "because I'd seen you in a vision."

"You're scaring me, Joe." I glanced over to Mom. She was still talking to the nurse at the desk. "What did you see?"

"White Bird is locked in his mind, but even if you reach him and show him the way out of his torment, he still won't be free." Joe reached for my hand. "Inside the memories you share with him is the key. That's why you're the only one who can truly free him."

"What does that mean? I don't understand."

"That's why I want you to remember everything you see after you connect with him. Nothing is too small. The dream signs could come from you or from him, but all of them will be important."

"Why? I don't get it."

"Everyone assumed he killed that girl. Maybe even… you did, too." Joe took a deep breath. "But what if he was only a witness, Brenna? What if the real killer still lives in Shawano?"

What Joe said hit me like a jolt of electricity. It charged through my body and tingled shame down my fingers and toes before it shot out from every follicle of my hair. It never felt right that White Bird was capable of killing, but with him kneeling over Heather with that damned bloody knife in his hand, what was a kid to think? I was fourteen then. And I thought I'd done the right thing by calling 911. Now Joe made me doubt everything.

"I hadn't said anything before now because I didn't want you to second-guess yourself and get distracted."

"But I was the one who turned him in, Joe. Did I do the wrong thing?" I stared at the tips of my sneaks and everything blurred. I heard Joe's voice, but not what he said. I couldn't get past what I'd done. "They arrested him…because of me. If he was a witness, why didn't he tell them what he saw?"

"He couldn't. But now, with you, I think he's strong enough. You both are." Joe pulled at the tie hanging around his neck and unbuttoned the top button of his shirt. He looked tired.

"I've learned to stop questioning the tests that are put in my path," he said. "I think folks are given what they can handle and are stronger for it. You and White Bird have an extraordinary journey in front of you. Keep your eyes set on the horizon and quit looking over your shoulder. Guilt and regrets are a waste of time."

I shut my eyes tight and took what he said into my brain, letting his message roll around in the void. When I opened them again, I was still shaky.

"I'm scared, Joe."

"Just trust your feelings and follow your instincts."

"My instincts? You got a plan B?"

Joe ignored me.

"Above all, you must believe that your gift is real. If you falter or doubt yourself, you could lose him. And there are no promises that you'll have a next time. Do you understand what I'm telling you?"

"I've got one shot? That's it?" I heaved a sigh. "So…no pressure."

"One shot is all any of us have. Make it count."

I didn't think he was talking about vision tripping anymore. Joe put a strong hand on the back of my neck and lent me his strength.

"You're very strong, Brenna. That's why he can reach you. You're like a beacon. Use the strength you share and rely on each other."

He pulled my chin toward him to make his point.

"And believe in your bond," he said. "Trust me when I tell you that you have a very special gift. You have no idea how extraordinary you are."

I stared at Joe and filtered what he said through my bullshit detector. The guy wasn't blowing smoke, but he'd given me the equivalent of keys to a priceless Maserati, with only a five-minute pep talk on how to drive a stick shift.

"The doctor is on his way." Mom came back with a grin. "He'll be here any minute."

"Great. Just…great." I swallowed, hard. Even though Joe had delivered a last-minute bombshell, it needed to be said. And if I had dwelled on his message overnight, who knows what a basket case I would have been by now.

I'd never gotten very far trusting my own instincts before. Guess there was a first time for everything.

Shawano Sheriff's Office—Afternoon

With a half-eaten sandwich sitting on his desk, Sheriff Matt Logan had called his sister's work number at the bank and had to leave a message. She was in a meeting that would take her through the lunch hour and then some.

He was looking for Derek.

If the school year were underway, he'd know where to find his nephew, either at school or the football field. But with summer here, he needed help from his little sister. When she finally called him back, he was eager to talk to her.

"Hey, bro. You calling about the barbecue this weekend?" Before he answered, she kept talking. "Just come over whenever. We'll be cooking all day. And bring beer. That way you won't have to hit the store. I know you always have brewski on hand."

"You know me too well. Sounds good." He forced a smile into his voice to sound casual. "Hey, I'm looking for Derek. You know where I can find him? I've got chores at the house. And I could use his strong young back."

"Emphasis on *young*." She laughed. "Normally I couldn't tell you, but it's your lucky day."

Matt didn't feel lucky.

"I just got off the phone with him," she said. "He's working out in the garage with one of his buddies. The only thing that boy has on his mind these days is next football season."

That's not the only thing, he thought.

"Thanks, sis. I'll talk to you later."

After he ended the call, he dumped the sandwich that was still on his desk and headed out. He went to the evidence lockup and waited for the desk clerk to leave before he went behind the secured door without bothering to sign in. It didn't take him long to find the Madsen box. He knew it well. After he pulled out the plastic bag with the watch in it, he put it in his pocket and slipped out to find Derek, not telling anyone where he was going.

The fewer who saw him leave, the better.

It took fifteen minutes to get to his sister's place. And when he pulled into the drive, he saw the garage door open. Derek and his sidekick Justin were lifting weights. For a split second, he caught a surprised expression on his nephew's face. The kid looked worried.

Being a cop, Matt knew what that look meant. He'd seen it plenty. *Damn it!*

"Hey, Uncle Matt." Derek waved as he walked toward his police cruiser. "What's up?"

The kid's face flushed red and his sudden color didn't appear to come from exertion.

Matt got out of his squad car and leaned on it with arms crossed. Justin had stayed in the garage pretending to be busy, but the kid kept eyeballing him. Normally Justin was real friendly. Not today.

Using his skills as a cop, he chatted his nephew up and got him feeling real comfortable. They talked about football and the family grill party on the weekend. And they even talked about girls. That's when he took a detour.

"Hey, what's up with that plastic watch? What happened to the one I bought you for Christmas a few years back?" He forced a smile. "I thought girls were into…bling."

Derek looked down at his wrist and the red splotches on his face came back. The watch Matt had given his nephew had been a nice one. And the kid used to wear it all the time. A watch like that should have lasted him. But plain as day, the kid wore a cheap sports watch now.

"It's in my room. In my dresser." He shrugged and laughed it off. "It's too nice to wear every day. You know, all the sweatin' and stuff."

"Yeah, you're probably right." Matt nodded. "Listen, your

mom has a phone number in her address book that I need to get. I know where it's at. I'll only be a minute."

He headed through the garage door and into the house, without waiting for Derek to say anything. His nephew was probably exchanging nervous glances with Justin and whispering for him to keep his cool. Matt knew the drill.

Once he got inside his sister's house, he searched Derek's room looking for the watch. It wasn't in the dresser like he'd said, but Matt looked everywhere. The kid's room was a mess and smelled like feet. After ten minutes, he gave up his search. The watch he'd given his nephew was missing.

"Damn it," he cursed under his breath and headed back to his cruiser.

On his way out, he decided not to confront his nephew. He had too much to consider. If Derek had been an official suspect, he would have pressed him harder. The kid was being evasive and his body language had given away telltale signs that the boy was hiding something. His gut instincts and experience told him that Derek had lied about the watch. But why?

Matt wasn't sure he wanted to know the answer. And with his being responsible for the Madsen case, how far would he go to protect his own family?

Red Cliffs Hospital

"Sorry to keep you waiting," Dr. Ridgeway said.

Funny. He didn't look sorry.

The doctor led us behind the locked buzzer door to the detention unit and walked with a quick pace. His white coat whisked the air and I had a hard time keeping up. I never moved that fast. *Ever.*

"An orderly is bringing him to an observation room. He

should be with us shortly." The doc smiled over his shoulder as he walked, dangling White Bird as a carrot. "You'll be able to see him through a two-way mirror. He won't know you're there."

"But—" When I opened my mouth, Joe raised a finger and took charge.

"We'll need to talk to him. Pray over him. If that's a problem, I'll take it up with the tribal council...and the media."

"No need for threats, Mr. Sunne. You'll have time with him, but I'll be observing from the next room. And I'll step in if I determine it's necessary. Understood?" He didn't wait for an answer.

When the doctor opened a door and went into a small dark room off the hall, I took off my sunglasses and grabbed Joe's arm, mouthing the words, "What the hell?" And Mom did a silent double take. Although Joe and I hadn't worked out any signal, I was fairly sure he understood my WTF distress call.

The last time I touched White Bird, it had been powerful. Inside his hellish vision, it was pure torture. And I had no idea if my body mirrored what I was doing in that waking nightmare. I was afraid if I screamed or tumbled through the black void again, that I'd be fitted for a straitjacket. I'd look like I was having a fit.

Behind the doctor's back, Joe held up a hand, a signal for me to hold on. I knew he wanted me to trust him. And I did. It was the tall guy in white that I had problems with. I turned my back on the two men behind me and stared into the empty room next door, the one White Bird would be brought to. And with my nose pressed to the glass, I pictured him there.

I trusted Joe. I really did.

"Can you share what you've tried for treatments?" Joe asked the doc.

"That's confidential, I'm afraid."

"Then what's his prognosis, Doctor? Surely you can answer that?" Joe insisted. "I've got to report back to the tribal council that White Bird is receiving the proper care."

Joe had picked his words well. The word *proper* riled Dr. Ridgeway. It showed on his face. And the man definitely didn't like being second-guessed, especially by a Shaman.

"We've tried everything. The normal protocols have had no effect." Dr. Ridgeway took a deep breath and let doubt show in his eyes. It made him look human. "Quite frankly, I'm at a loss. That's why when Ms. Nash got the boy to look at her, that was a real breakthrough."

The doctor turned his attention to me.

"I don't know what your relationship is with this boy, but he really needs your help. If we can get his attention and keep it, we may see results finally. I'm not talking about a complete cure, just a first step toward recovery. What do you say?"

"You may not want to talk about a cure today, but I do." Joe narrowed his eyes at the man. I'd seen that look before. "Tell me, Doctor. Are you a betting man?"

"What?"

"Stacked up against all your science and this fancy hospital, would you bet money that a sixteen-year-old girl and one old Indian could completely cure this boy?"

"You mean, right here and now? Today?"

"Yes." Joe nodded and his lip twitched. "Superstition against science."

Joe had lured the man like catfish to stink bait.

He knew that stacked up against Dr. Ridgeway being in charge with a tight stranglehold on White Bird as a patient, we wouldn't stand a chance at coloring outside the lines. But with his "superstition versus science" bet, the doc might give us more leeway. I held my breath waiting to see what Ridgeway would say.

"You want to place a wager on the boy's health?" Dr. Ridgeway grimaced and acted like he was above being goaded into a silly wager. But after Joe nodded, the doc said, "You're on. What's the bet?"

"Oh, brother." I rolled my eyes at Mom. "No pressure."

That's when I heard a door creak in the next room. I turned in time to see a Hispanic guy dressed in a white uniform rolling in a boy slumped in a wheelchair. The sight of White Bird made my heart lurch with every ounce of joy and every stab of pain I had ever felt for him. I wanted him to be that boy by the creek, the tall one with the gentle hands, the soft voice and the sad knowing eyes.

But he wasn't. *Not like this.*

I pressed my forehead to the two-way mirror and touched my hand to the cold glass. It was impossible to forget he was trapped in the past—a past we shared. And now I had to have faith in something I'd never believed in before. *Me.*

The gravity of what we were attempting hit me hard and I couldn't breathe. I had to save him. *I had to.*

chapter fifteen

Red Cliffs Hospital

Dr. Ridgeway finished giving Joe last-minute instructions on what he expected from us—*his rules*—but all I heard was, *"Wa, wa, wah, waaah."* My eyes were fixed on White Bird sitting alone in the next room until I forced myself to turn away and look for Joe.

When my eyes met his, words weren't necessary. And the nod of his head was subtle. I wasn't even sure I'd seen Joe move at all. His gesture drifted between us like a puff of smoke, there one minute and gone the next. With eyes the color of shiny obsidian, he held my attention like the first time we'd met, when I was afraid of him.

Only this time, I drew from his strength.

Mom was the one who needed words. "Are you ready, honey?" she asked.

Even though Mom had good intentions, her voice doused me with ice water. I loved her, but she wasn't part of this. She'd always be an innocent bystander. And I hadn't realized how true that was until now. For her sake, I nodded and forced a smile, but I kept my eyes on Joe.

He was my gatekeeper.

He was the one I trusted to get me through this.

And he was the one who would save us both, if we weren't already too late.

I heard the white noise of the doctor talking again as he led Joe and me out the observation room door. We were about to join White Bird in the next room. I took a deep breath before the doctor opened that door and without thinking, I grabbed for the pinkie of Joe's hand. I clutched both hands around his finger as if it was the most natural thing to do. Joe didn't look as if he minded being my lifeline.

When the door opened with its annoying creak, the doctor let us in but didn't stay. Even though Mom and the doc would be listening in the next room, we were finally alone with White Bird and I saw him for real this time. His back was to me. And his head was slumped forward as he slouched in his wheelchair. I moved across that room, not knowing how I did it. I was just there, kneeling in front of him, too afraid to touch him—knowing what even the slightest contact would start.

Dressed in a pale blue robe with white pajamas and slippers, he smelled like soap, fresh laundry and the unforgettable aroma of boy. I breathed him in and held my breath to keep him inside. When my lungs burned, I let him out and went for seconds. His dark hair was still damp. It had grown and curled at his neck. Finger worthy. And his half-lidded brown eyes stared at the floor, a sweet gift that was wasted on hospital linoleum.

I fought the persistent lump of guilt wedged in my throat

and White Bird's face blurred with my tears. I wiped them away to see him.

"Hey, it's me."

This time I didn't say my name and introduce myself as if we were strangers, like I'd done before. Too much had happened since then. He'd invaded my dreams too many times.

"Joe Sunne is here…but maybe you know that."

I whispered the last part, so the doctor in the next room wouldn't hear me. From the corner of my eye, I saw Joe take off his jacket and tie and toss them onto the only table in the room. When he rolled up his sleeves, Joe looked ready, but I sure wasn't. I wanted White Bird to lift his head and see me, without needing the intimacy of my touch to know I was there, but that didn't happen. And it scared me that I didn't feel him like I did when I dreamed.

Maybe Joe was right—it was too late.

Doubts were killing me and poisoning my mind. My gut instinct told me to focus and shove the negativity aside. And when I looked at Joe, he nodded at me again, as if he'd read my mind. But this time when the man opened his mouth, he mesmerized me when he spoke.

He chanted the nearly forgotten Euchee language and it sounded like an ancient prayer. With each word, I heard the distant thunder again and I felt a spark of energy surge through me. I knew that strong sensation came from Joe. Spirit Walker was his Indian name. When the Shaman eased around White Bird, he waved his dark hands over him with his eyes closed.

But when I felt this incredible urge to touch White Bird, the room blurred to an intense brilliant white. I gasped and squinted, raising my hand to shield my eyes. Still sitting head down and slumped in his chair, he was the center of the light.

I couldn't tell if he'd caused it to appear or if Joe had summoned it. The boy in the wheelchair was all I saw, until he slowly ebbed away like low tide.

The intense light was feeding on his edges and sucking him into the milky void. I had to make it stop. I had to keep him from disappearing. I reached for his hand and pulled with all my strength, like a treacherous game of tug-of-war.

But when we touched, everything went black. And deathly still. I didn't feel White Bird anymore.

I'd lost him.

Dr. Ridgeway watched the Native Shaman and the girl react to seeing Isaac Henry. He knew in an instant that the girl was in love. Maybe that was all this visit was—a girl who wanted to see her first love before he got sent to jail for the rest of his life.

It was a good thing he hadn't called the sheriff about the kid's visitors today. His old friend Matt Logan would have given him hell if he'd made a trip to the hospital for no good reason. Matt didn't like calling attention to the fact that Isaac Henry was confined to a mental ward with criminal charges still pending.

"Something's happening in there. I can see it, sort of." The girl's mother stepped closer to the observation window and put her fingers on the glass. "Is it hot in there? Joe's got sweat on his forehead. What's happening to them?"

Although Kate Nash had a better view, Ridgeway did a double take into the observation room and looked closer. Sunne had blocked his view with raised arms and his back darkened the two-way mirror. The man's body was rigid and his head shook with strain. And the girl was kneeling in front of the Indian boy. Her hands gripped his so tightly that her knuckles were blanched.

But something much more interesting was happening to the boy.

Once again, Isaac Henry had straightened his head and stared into the eyes of Brenna Nash. With eyes wide, the kid looked fully aware, except for the fact that he hadn't moved. His face was ghostly white and his mouth was gaped open. Whatever he saw in the girl had terrified him.

"I gotta make a call." Ridgeway yanked his cell phone off his belt. "I'll be right outside. Come get me if anything changes."

Kate Nash yelled as he left the room. "What are you doing? You can't leave now."

As the door shut behind him, he hit speed dial for Sheriff Logan. When the man answered, he didn't bother to identify himself. "Matt, you gotta get out here. Now! That Nash girl is in with Isaac Henry. And I think he's coming out of it."

Ridgeway didn't wait to hear what his friend would say. He ended the call to the sheriff and went back inside the room, joining Mrs. Nash by the two-way mirror. His mind catapulted into the future and he envisioned writing a book on what he was witnessing. He had to know more.

And with Sunne making a bet with him, the Euchee Shaman knew this would happen. How could he have been so sure? Ridgeway had way too many questions to break this up now. He had to see it through.

"This is…amazing," he gasped.

The Indian kid had never reacted this way in any of his treatments. His head now lolled from side to side and his breathing had escalated, but Isaac Henry looked as if he was on the verge of waking up. He was coming out of a stupor he'd endured for the past two years.

Whatever this was, it was truly remarkable.

"Shouldn't you do something?" Kate Nash kept her eyes fixed on her daughter.

Ridgeway had no idea what to tell her. The woman had no appreciation for what was happening. They were witnessing a major breakthrough that could mean a boost to his career. What was going on in the next room was beyond the medicine he'd studied. And being a man of science, he had to know more.

He wasn't about to stop it now.

After White Bird vanished before my eyes, I lost track of time. I saw nothing and an aching emptiness filled me up. I wondered if this was what death felt like—a vast barren abyss where time meant nothing—where a soul in limbo waited for something to happen, only vaguely aware of its existence. Wherever I was felt like a one-way trip. I was a lab rat in a maze with only one way out. I had focused so much on helping White Bird that I never imagined that touching him would blow up in my face. What if I never found him and got stuck here?

Suddenly, I missed Mom. And I wanted my crappy life back.

So I got down to the business of survival. I had to focus on something. The sooner I found him, the sooner we could put our heads together and find our way out. Joe had said to rely on the bond we had and I believed him.

And when I heard the steady beat of my heart, I knew I'd been wrong about being dead. I felt better already. But even with me hearing the blood rushing through my veins, everything else was oddly still. And with sounds muffled in the dense vacuum, I resisted the urge to call out White Bird's name. I didn't think he'd hear me. I sensed he was too far away.

But not so far that I couldn't draw him from my memory and imagine him.

An image of him flashed in my mind. I saw his face wavering in front of me like a ripple on water, but he disappeared as fast as he came. I wasn't strong enough to hold him. Was that how White Bird had done it? Had he just imagined me asleep in my room and linked to me that way? Maybe he'd been too weak to hold me long enough to find his way home.

When my head filled with memories of him, a warm feeling welled inside me and I felt his presence—really felt him—all around me and through me. I'd never experienced such peace. And the rich smell of the earth and a faint aroma of pine bark and wildflowers reminded me of the shelter he'd made by the creek, even though I couldn't see anything but a bleak white. I wanted to believe these triggers were meant to calm me, that they were a message from him to let me know he was with me, but maybe that was only wishful thinking.

Where are you?

I concentrated on finding him, trusting my senses to point me in a direction. But when I peered through the brilliant white, I felt a growing tension behind my eyes that sent shards of pain shooting through my head. I'd never experienced snow blindness, but that's how I imagined it would start.

Or maybe my throbbing discomfort was a warning that I was not welcome here.

I hovered like a weightless mass of molecules, connected and yet not. I felt the confines of my body and yet I was connected to everything, as far as I could see. Even the vast expanse of time didn't feel like a barrier. I wasn't a kid in this place. I was a sentient being without age, linked to the past yet driven toward the future.

And I didn't think like the girl that I used to be, not exactly. I was the same, yet different. Like I understood the word *sentient* without having to look it up on Wikipedia, but I also totally knew all the lyrics to Kimya Dawson's "I Like Giants" song. A real crowd-pleaser for someone who hung out with weirdos like me. The way I felt reminded me of what White Bird had described years before when he first told me about keeping an open mind to the messages of the universe and about being connected to the past and present.

Had his obsession with his tribe and mystical dream symbols created the illusion that trapped him here now? Or had he truly found his way here because it existed like an alternate universe?

I picked a direction without a point of reference in the stark white. I moved as straight as I could and hoped I wouldn't be traveling in circles. After what felt like an eternity, I came across something of substance.

It knocked me on my ass.

My face smashed into an invisible barrier that felt like I'd run into closed sliding glass doors. The impact messed me up so bad that when I fell down I stayed down. I lay there in shock, wondering. If I was so hooked into the past *and* the future in this place, why hadn't I seen *that* coming? *Shit!* I rubbed my nose and waited for the Fourth of July sparklers to stop spinning over my head.

When I finally got up, I placed both hands in front of me to feel what I'd hit. Everywhere I turned, my fingers found a solid surface that mirrored the bleak dreamscape. I had run out of places to go and stood on the edge of White Bird's vision, getting mad.

What was the point of imagining a dreamworld with boundaries? I'd had enough of peace and tranquility. I balled my fists and pounded the invisible wall. And when that felt good, I kicked it, too. Mom always said that when I was in her belly, I had mad skills with my feet. So I got after it, kicking and hitting that damned wall until I felt it give way and a burst of color shot through. It streaked in like a laser beam.

"Holy shit!" I squinted and tried to peek through the crack, but that wasn't happening. I'd have to do more.

I pushed my way through the white serenity wall. And when I climbed in, a rush of heat swept over me. It was muggy hot, but I felt White Bird here, more than ever. I had to be in the right place. That was a good thing, because when I looked back the way I'd come, the stark white was gone. One door had opened and another one had slammed shut in my face. There was no going back, even if I wanted to.

But this new dreamscape really got my attention.

"Oh, wow," I gasped as I looked around.

Everything was in vivid 3-D and insanely cool. I stood in the middle of a beautiful yet eerie forest. And the colors were intense, like I'd had a black-and-white TV my whole life and now I saw everything through a color plasma screen. But with the serene world of white gone, I knew there had been a barrier for a reason. On this side of White Bird's vision, there was evil. And it lurked beyond where I could see. I don't know how I knew this, but I did. I tasted danger and it seeped through my pores.

When I sensed it coming, I stopped to listen really hard. I should have run, but I was rooted where I stood, waiting. It didn't take long for the danger to find me. A low menacing growl came from behind and it sounded like the deep throaty growl of a lion about to pounce. I didn't want to turn around, but I had to. My instinct for survival took over.

I forced myself to run and when I gaped over my shoulder to see what had made the noise, I saw the huge grizzly bear from White Bird's nightmare. My feet got tangled and I fell to the ground. And when I turned over, I stared up at the monster that towered over me. The twelve-foot beast reared up on its haunches and swiped its front claws at me. It bellowed a roar and gnashed its teeth. And I knew I wouldn't stand a chance if it got hold of me.

I scrambled to my feet and looked for someplace to hide, watching the predator over my shoulder. I expected the bear to follow, but it didn't. It plopped its butt down and watched me run with its head cocked. Guess I looked goofy.

I stopped where I was and turned to face it. We glared at each other for what felt like forever. Maybe it was, but eventually the beast tossed its head and turned to leave. And when it trudged back the way it had come, I got the distinct impression that it wanted me to follow.

"Hey, something I said?" I yelled. With a fresh shot of adrenaline in my veins, I gave the grizzly bear attitude. And it felt damned good.

All my instincts should have told me to run the opposite way, but since none of this was normal and I wasn't at some whack petting zoo, I did as Joe had said and trusted my gut. I took a risk and trailed the animal from a safe distance. After all, White Bird's adopted Euchee tribe was the *Dala,* the bear clan.

With my new traveling companion, I drifted through a dense monochromatic forest awash in shades of lime-green. It was as if I saw everything through polarized sunglasses. Trees towered over me with light flickering through their trunks. And a thick green fog swirled at my feet and clung to tree bark before it drifted into the branches. The mist brought a muggy stillness to the forest.

And even though I wasn't sure if that was a good thing, I kept walking with the grunting bear, searching for any sign of White Bird. The farther I trekked, the stronger the sense I got that he was very close. And when the bear eventually broke free of the dense vegetation, it took me into a vast field of charred trees rooted in a sea of blood-red flowers. And the fog followed me. It spread its billowing clouds and the intense humidity made it hard for me to breathe. It was an annoyance I couldn't shake.

"Get a life." I swatted at the trailing mist. My swipe didn't do any good, except to make me feel better.

Ahead of me, the burned field stretched over rolling hills. And beyond that, a steep rock face lurked in the shadows with its peak shrouded in a dense haze. And although the blood-red flowers made me flash back to the violence of Heather's death, I trusted my instincts to stay with the slow plodding bear as it lumbered across the open field. But the minute I stepped on the flowers, they gave off a foul odor.

"Oh, God. What the hell is that?" I checked the bottom of my shoes until I realized the stink was coming from the flowers.

What I smelled was the coppery stench of blood. It was so toxic that I had to hold my breath. I pressed my arm over my nose and kept the bear in sight. The animal was headed for a trail into the dark mountains. As we climbed, the fog snaked down to meet us, making it hard to see ahead. And when visibility got tough, the bear slowed even more. Eventually, it strayed off the path that had split in two. One trail led down and the other way climbed higher and was much steeper. The grizzly plopped down and groaned. It bobbed its head and swiped a paw at me.

"So...you're a low road kind of guy. Is that it?" I shrugged and mumbled, "Guess that leaves me the high road. That'd be different."

The bear had taken me as far as it would go. The rest was up to me. I stared into the thickening mist and took a deep breath to steady my nerves. From here on, I'd be on my own.

Dr. Ridgeway had called Matt Logan earlier and delivered the bombshell that Isaac Henry was coming out of his catatonic state. Time would tell whether that news would be good or bad. Sam Ridgeway had explained the medical jargon before, but he'd never placed any credence in a condition that got the kid out of serving the jail time he deserved. Up until now, that boy had gotten off light. Red Cliffs was no posh country club, but from the kid's perspective, the mental hospital was better than being locked in a box with hardened criminals.

After Matt got the call, he dropped everything and headed out. And hospital security rushed word to the doctor that he'd arrived. It didn't take long for him to be ushered into the observation room where he'd get to see it all for himself.

One thing he hadn't counted on was coming face-to-face with Kate Nash. He would have bet money that Brenna had come alone, leaving her mother in the cold again. The kid had no sense, but maybe he shouldn't blame her.

Apparently, that trait was hereditary. Kate had been a headstrong kid, too. She had been no shrinking violet. Even though he was older, he'd remembered that much about her.

"You and your daughter shouldn't be here, Kate."

The sternness in his voice reverberated in the small observation room. And he sounded angrier than he'd intended.

"And you're like a vulture on roadkill, Matt. Why are you here?" Before he answered, she figured it out. Kate glared at Dr. Ridgeway and shook her head. "You're both feasting on this kid like he's raw meat."

Wisely, Sam Ridgeway stayed out of the argument. He backed off and kept his eyes focused on the next room.

"In case you forgot, he killed an innocent girl," Matt reminded her.

"Don't you have to convict him in a court of law first? Or does that silly notion not apply in your town?" The woman crossed her arms and cocked her head. "You've got a lot of nerve getting all preachy with me."

"What's that supposed to mean?"

"Your nephew is a bully and those kids he hangs with think they're above the law. And you can't see it." She raised her chin in defiance. "So don't act all holier-than-thou, Sheriff. Not until you clean your own house."

"You got any proof, Kate? 'Cause that sure would be nice for a change."

Kate Nash always got him riled. She knew how to push his buttons.

"I know Derek and his friends trashed our house but, no, lucky for you, I've got nothing real to back me up, only my gut feeling." She heaved a deep sigh. "But would it hurt you to look into it? I need help here, Matt. I think those kids hurt my daughter. And now they've trashed my family home. This has *got* to stop. You're not doing any of those kids a favor by ignoring their behavior. They'll only grow into mean, manipulative adults."

Matt clenched his jaw and stared at Kate. The silence that

filled the room was only broken by the static from speakers and the occasional voices coming from the next room. After the watch incident with Derek, plus the suspicions about his nephew's character that he'd had for a while, Matt had a strong feeling that Kate was right.

And that meant he was wrong, a notion he didn't like at all.

"Look, I know you've had your share of trouble since you've been back. My deputies will investigate the vandalism at your house and what happened to your daughter. I'd like to get to the bottom of all this myself." He softened his tone. "I'm doing the best I can with what I've got, Kate."

"So am I, Matt." She narrowed her eyes. "So am I."

Kate looked tired and a hundred miles past worried. And when Matt looked at what was happening in the next room, he understood why. What kind of whammy hoodoo did they have going on with that kid?

After the bear and I had parted ways, I climbed the steep trail until I got to a rock ledge that flattened for a stretch. It was wider than the path up and might have been a good spot to catch my breath, until I got a better look. The ledge was mottled with fissures in the rocks. And each crack glowed red with steam rising from the molten lava that seeped out and spilled onto the earth. With the stench of hot gases and sulfur, I couldn't stay here. I carefully stepped through the minefield of spewing hot lava, choking on bad air.

It smelled worse than gym class after Taco Tuesday.

But a sound made me stop and look up. Through the belching steam and thickening fog, I saw red, glowing eyes homing in on me. And a huge dark shape cut a swath through the fog. A fierce black stallion burst through the mist, its hooves pounding like thunder. Its eyes looked like hot embers and it breathed fire from its nostrils. When the demon horse hit the clearing, it reared up and flailed its sharp hooves. That's when I saw the tiny bird. It came out of nowhere and flitted too close to the menacing horse. I thought it would get trampled.

"Shoo. Go away!"

I waved my hands at the little bird, trying to protect it. The bird was helpless, like the one White Bird had healed at the creek. And for a second, I thought he had sent the tiny creature as a messenger, to let me know he was here, even though it wasn't the best time to reach out and touch someone.

But I didn't have time to think about what the bird meant. When I dodged the raging horse, I lost sight of the bird, but came face-to-face with the fire-breathing animal that was bigger than a Clydesdale.

"Easy now." I spoke to it in a calm voice, but that only made the fierce horse more enraged. It charged and forced me down the trail. I wasn't going to get by it.

And I couldn't go back the way I came, either.

From the corner of my eye, I saw a grinning jackal baring its teeth and growling at me. The hair on its neck bristled out from its head and down its back. The mythical guardian of the dead closed in, creeping slowly as it maneuvered around me. It stared at me with strange gray eyes, licking its chops. I knew the sly hunter would strike when my back was turned.

"Back off, mutt face." I glared at the mangy fleabag, but it hadn't come alone.

Next to the four-legged scavenger was a black hairy spider. Way bigger than a tarantula, it was the size of a small dog. Besides its ginormous size, it had two other distinctive features. A splatter of blood red on its back and glittery green gems on its head that looked like eyes. And when the giant bug crept toward me, I heard its legs hit the ground, sounding like the clicking clack of fingers on a computer keyboard. The noise really got to me. And worse, the spider was spewing its web-like barf. It would soon trap me in its slimy lace. Not cool.

I had my back against the wall—literally—and had nowhere to go. The fiery black stallion, the cagey jackal and the barfing spider with the green Day-Glo eyes had joined forces to stop me. And that left me with only one way to go. *Up.*

I didn't consider myself athletic. Forget about me being a rock climber, but there was a first time for everything with the right motivation. When I gazed up at the towering rock face behind me, it was the only option I had left. Without much of a plan, I scaled the rocks fast. The jackal leaped off the ground to catch me and barely missed nipping at my ankle. And the fierce horse charged and snorted a flame that roasted my butt as I climbed.

Once I got beyond the reach of those two, I breathed a little easier, but I still had one more fugitive from bizarro world to worry about.

The spider clacked after me and skittered up the rocks with more agility than I had. It wouldn't be long before the eight-legged freak caught me. My fingers grabbed for anything that would hold me. And the muscles in my legs burned from exertion. I climbed faster and harder, my lungs on fire. And with sweat pouring off me, my hands were real slick.

Below, I heard the stallion shrieking and stomping and the jackal howled its haunting threat, but the spider had gained on me. I had no time to turn around and see where it was, nor did I have to. The clacking had gotten louder.

It was right behind me.

And I couldn't go on much longer. I wasn't strong enough to outpace a monster with six more legs than I had. With sweat stinging my eyes, I looked up to see that the fog had cleared and I saw another ledge above me. Had I reached the peak?

I couldn't check that out. I heard the spider behind me and I had to move. I hoisted my body onto a rock and made my last climb. When I got to the top, I doubled over with a painful cramp, panting out of control. And I saw a shimmer of blue-green behind me, but I'd run out of time.

The spider had closed the gap and was heading straight for me. I had reached the summit and had nowhere else to go. And I was too exhausted to run. There was only one thing left for me to do. I grabbed a rock and hurled it at the green-eyed mutant, but the stone only bounced off.

"Shit, metal head. Why don't you die already?" I grabbed a bigger rock and raised it over my head. "Come on, bitch. Show me what you got!"

Instantly, I regretted saying that. And I also wished that I hadn't stepped on every bug that had crossed my path in my other life. It was way too ironic that I might end up as spider food. I was about to hurl the heavy boulder, when a flash of white streaked down from the sky and attacked the bug.

Without a sound or a screech, a snow-white owl dive-bombed the spider. It tore chunks of flesh off the bug with its sharp claws. And as the spider bled, it gave off a foul stench that reminded me of the field of blood-red flowers. I nearly gagged. After the white owl ramped up its aerial attacks, the gross spider lost interest in me. I could have stayed to see what happened, but I took advantage of the distraction the owl created. I left the spider to its fate and sneaked away to find White Bird.

I felt him strongest here. The mountain had drawn me and I knew he was close. I stood on the precipice with the rumble of thunder in the distance and I stared into an immense crater below. Its valley held a pond of bright aqua water, the color of a glacier.

"You're down there, somewhere. Aren't you?" I whispered, hoping White Bird would hear me and would know I was coming.

Like Joe had told me, I followed my heart and headed down toward the water. And with every step, I thought about what he'd said about my journey, that it wasn't only about finding White Bird. I had to remember every encounter, every incredible sight, every sound and every creature from hell. Joe had said everything would be important to remember and I trusted him.

As I made a mental list of what I'd seen—picturing me doodling in an imaginary notebook so I wouldn't forget things—I hiked down to the water's edge. I trekked the rocky bank and peered into the depths of the gem-colored water. On the pond's calm surface, I saw the reflection of the brewing storm. The dark clouds rolling in were a striking contrast to the cool serene water.

Something on the glistening water brought images of White Bird to my mind. Glimpses of our past bubbled to the surface as I gazed into the shimmering pond. I should have felt at peace here, walking beside the still water, but I didn't. Nothing was normal in this place and a bad feeling gripped me hard. I picked up my pace and my search grew more frantic. Something lurked beneath the water and when I peered into the depths, I wasn't sure what I was looking for.

Until I found it.

"No! Oh, God. Please." I gasped and collapsed to my knees. When I stared into the murky bottom of the pond, I was shocked at what I saw.

White Bird's body floated just beneath the surface of a deep underwater chasm.

He wore only jeans and his dark hair was long, as I'd always remembered it. Tiny bubbles dotted his eyelashes and clung to his lips. His handsome face looked pale, blanched by the water. Suspended beneath the surface, he lay perfectly still.

He looked more dead than alive.

"Oh, no. Please…no."

The blow of seeing him like this took my breath away and my eyes brimmed with tears. I don't know how long I cried, but I was still sobbing when I finally waded into the water. Nearing the edge of the chasm, I wasn't sure the underwater rock ledge would hold me, but I didn't care. I had to see him. And if I could reach him, I wanted to hold him in my arms. He looked at peace in his watery grave like someone lying in a coffin. A rush of grief and shock welled inside me and I couldn't believe it was over.

"Why did you do this? *Why?*" I screamed. And the echo of my voice carried across the mountainous crater.…

I slipped my hand into the water to touch him. Rings of shimmer lit his face before my outstretched fingers cast him in shadow. And I swear to God, I saw something move. I yanked my hand back and gasped.

White Bird's eyes had opened wide.

I'd scared the shit out of him—and he'd returned the vor.

'Oh, my God. It's really you." My voice cracked. "And… e alive."

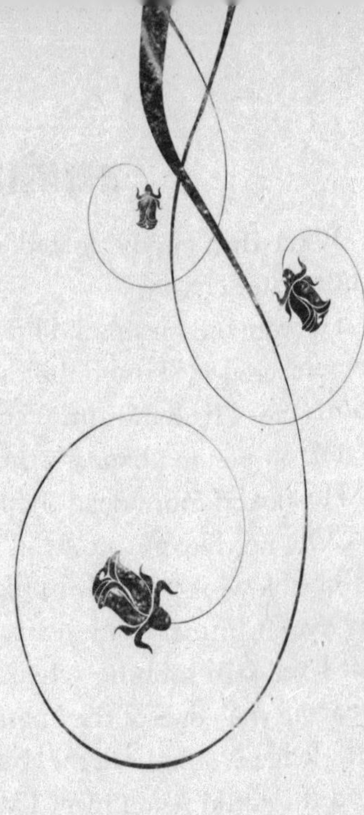

chapter sixteen

When I held out my hand to him, I expected White Bird to swim toward me and grab it, but he just stared at me with a pained expression. Only his eyes moved. His arms and legs floated limp beneath the surface of the water. He showed no relief that I had found him, and looked more worried for me than about what was happening to him. That made no sense.

"Can you move?" I yelled. "Blink once for yes, twice fo no."

With a strained look on his face, he slowly blin

He was beyond my reach. And after I lo didn't see a lifeline that could help me ha about doing the whole lifeguard th shore, but maybe I'd get stuck guarantees of normal in biz

"We don't have a lot of optio of my lip and considered my ne down at him, he looked even mor

"Are you tied down? Once yes, twice no," I asked, but none of my game of twenty questions was getting us anywhere.

There was a very good reason I hated charades—because I was friggin' bad at it. Besides, my thinking was wrong. The guy was submerged and still alive. The water where I'd waded into was cold, but not unbearable. But the deep chasm where White Bird floated, that was as frigid as glacier water. And in this strange place, he didn't have to be anchored to anything. Nothing in this damned nightmare was like anything I'd ever seen. I had to think out of the box. And whatever I decided to do, I'd have to do it really fast.

What the hell! I sucked in a deep breath and jumped in.

Shawano Sheriff's Office

Will Tate took an early shift break and spent it at his desk, checking the messages dispatch had told him about. He'd gotten a return phone call from the customer service department at TimeOnMyHands.com, an online seller of watches. A guy by the name of Jon Fischer had left his direct dial number.

"Hot damn." He grinned.

Will had the urge to rush to his desk and play his end of phone tag, but it might be helpful to have the watch with him when he called the retailer back. Even at this hour, these East Coast businesses had twenty-four-hour customer service departments. Maybe Jon Fischer was a night shift guy like he was. Will headed to the evidence locker to retrieve the watch he'd found near the crime scene.

After placing a few earlier calls to Bulova, the manufacturer of the watch, he'd lucked out in learning that the timepiece was pricey enough to be unique. Its striking blue face was distinctive and it had a stainless steel band with a clasp, but the real identifier was etched inside. The watchmaker had told him how to retrieve a number etched on the back, inside the mechanism. That number could ID the specific watch and by backtracking transactions, they could isolate the retail seller. With any luck, eventually he'd find out who had bought it and where it had been shipped.

And Will had been able to speed up the process by telling the Bulova customer service guy that the watch would have been purchased longer than two years ago. Because his inquiry was part of a murder investigation, the manufacturer had fully cooperated and expedited their response. It hadn't taken long to isolate the online seller as TimeOnMyHands.com.

Will was getting closer to finding out who owned the property that was now evidence in a murder investigation.

"Hey, Walter. How's it going?" Will smiled at the evidence clerk as he signed the log to retrieve the watch. "I need the Madsen box."

"Comin' up." The clerk flipped the sign-in sheet around and glanced at what Will had written. The guy was a stickler for rules. And that was a good thing.

After Walter pulled the box and shoved it over the counter, Will opened the lid and reached inside the case file. The watch would have been on top, where he'd left it. But it was missing.

"Did anyone check this box out today?" Will looked more carefully. Maybe the timepiece had slipped deeper into the box.

"Don't know. I'm night shift, but I'll have a look." Walter read through the log and shook his head. "No. You're the last signature I have for that case. You missing somethin', Will?"

"Yeah. Most likely, my mind." He narrowed his eyes and

backtracked over what he'd done with the evidence, but came up with the same answer.

The watch was missing. And no one had signed out for it. *What the hell was going on?*

"You want me to leave a note for the morning crew?" the clerk asked.

"No. I'll come in early tomorrow and look into it. No problem."

Will had taken photos of the watch, but without the real deal those digitals might not hold up in court and be difficult to place in the context of the investigation or the crime scene. Will grabbed one of the photos and headed back to his desk. When he called Fischer, he got good news and bad news. The good news was that the guy worked night shift, but the bad news was that he was taking a dinner break. And he hadn't left word on the watch with anyone else. Will had to leave a message.

Although he was disappointed that he'd have to wait, Will had hopes that he was onto something. Soon he'd know the name of the person who'd purchased the watch and where it had been shipped.

With any luck, he'd still hit pay dirt—with or without the damned watch.

The water was friggin' cold. *Freezing!*

When I hit a wall of ice, I almost lost consciousness. And I sank like a rock. The extreme cold made me gasp and the air in my lungs erupted in a burst of bubbles. I watched the last of my air race to the surface. Gulps of air lost. My muscles had instantly constricted and I got hit with uncontrollable shivers.

My body felt sluggish and too heavy to move. I floundered

in the deep water, flailing my arms and legs in a desperate attempt to pull White Bird to the surface. My lungs felt like they were about to burst. The more I struggled, the worse I hurt. He was too heavy or I wasn't strong enough. It didn't matter which. My body was working against me and my brain was shutting down. In minutes it would be too late to save either of us.

I don't know exactly when it was that I gave up, but when I did, I turned my head to look for him.

White Bird's body had rolled under mine. When I reached for him, I held on and we sank into the depths. I felt everything in me shut down and I was numb from the cold. To survive, my body had shifted any heat I had left to my chest. And when my thinking became muddled, I knew it was only a matter of time before my brain would stop, too. And being in a no-win struggle to live, thrashing around in sheer panic wasn't the way I wanted to spend my last minutes.

My mother's voice filled my head and I saw Grams smiling at me. It was my way of saying goodbye.

And with the last bit of awareness I had, I held on to White Bird as we spiraled into the deep. When I looked into his eyes one last time, he had never looked more beautiful than at that moment. He had a peaceful look on his sweet face and his long dark hair drifted in the current. I felt my heart slow to a crawl as we drifted down. Both of us were swallowed in billows of cobalt blue, as the shimmering light from the surface grew dim.

I kissed him for the last time. And when his arms wrapped around me, I felt whatever heat remained in my body slowly leave me. I closed my eyes and fell asleep in his arms. I didn't want to die, but I wasn't afraid.

Everything went dark and as my body went limp, White

Bird and I drifted apart. In the quiet of the deep, I heard my mother's voice again.

"Stay with me, Brenna. Honey?"

She sounded so real, I wanted to tell her how much I loved her, but my mouth wouldn't open.

"Brenna, can you hear me?" This time she yelled. And she shook my face.

When I opened my eyes, the stark white was back. And a bright light spun over my head in circles until it stopped. It took me a while to recognize that I was staring into a light fixture and I was lying on a floor, shivering. In the water, my body had been numb, but now I ached all over. And when a sudden rush of noise hit my ears, it scared me. I reached out my hands and someone grabbed hold.

It was Mom.

"Honey, are you all right?" She had tears in her eyes and she kissed my forehead, like a million-gazillion times. "Oh, my God. She's awake. She's gonna be okay, isn't she?"

When my mother spoke to someone else in the room, I gazed around to see the shadows of several others. Two faces emerged from the haze. Joe Sunne came into focus. He looked tired but damned good. Seeing him made me smile, I think. And Dr. Ridgeway had tubes in his ears and was checking my heart. I knew that I was back at the hospital, 'cause it smelled like one.

After I realized where I was, my heart lurched and I scrambled to sit up.

"White...Bird." I choked on his name. "Where is...he?"

I looked to my right and saw Dr. Ridgeway hunched over his body. Instead of being dressed in jeans, like I'd last seen him in the vision, White Bird was again dressed in pajamas and a robe, with slippers on his feet.

"What happened?" I sat up and ran a hand through my hair. It was dry. And my mind grappled with what I remembered, but how much of it had been real? "Is he going to be okay?"

When no one answered, I yelled, "White Bird?" and struggled to stand, but Mom held me in her arms. Her warmth felt good.

"He's awake, honey," she said as she grinned at me. And when she leaned closer, she whispered in my ear, "You did it. You brought him back. I don't know how, but you did."

I heard my long-lost—*very lost*—friend cough. And when Dr. Ridgeway helped him into his wheelchair, White Bird saw me for the first time. He was so totally exhausted that he could barely keep his eyes open, but his blank stare turned into a warm smile that was contagious.

"What took you so long?" was all he said.

I grinned back. And for a change, I had nothing to say.

In that moment, I believed he had sensed me the first time I had touched him. And he'd sent up the equivalent of a mental flare for help that he knew I'd "feel" when he came to me in my dreams. I also knew the vision that we'd both shared had really happened, at least to us.

"We need to examine him, but that won't take long." Dr. Ridgeway sucked all the joy from the room. "I'll come get you when we're done. And you'll have plenty of time to visit. How's that?"

The doc didn't wait for anyone to answer. He never did. He swept from the room, pushing White Bird on wheels. And I felt like someone had stolen my best friend.

No, wait, that's exactly what happened.

Mom helped me to my feet and pulled a chair under my butt so I could sit at the only table in the room. Behind me, she straddled the chair and hugged my neck. But when Joe plopped down across from me, I knew he had something more on his mind than a pat on the back and giving me a big "Atta girl." He had beads of sweat on his forehead and I swear to God, he looked older. Seriously older.

"Your job ain't over yet." He winked and slid a small notebook and pen across the table, things he had stashed in his sport coat. He had come prepared. "Write down everything. In order, if you can. And don't leave anything out."

My brain was fried, but thankfully I considered that fairly normal. I knew what Joe wanted. I still didn't know why making the list was such a big deal, but I got to work. Joe wasn't an easy guy to say no to.

And the sooner I got the list done, the sooner I'd see White Bird. I couldn't believe he was back from the virtually dead. And I didn't care how it happened. Soon we'd have real time together. And after the past two years of hell, that was as good as eating dessert first.

Red Cliffs Hospital—An Hour Later

This time it was me who paced the floor, wringing my hands, with Mom sitting patiently watching me. And Joe was looking over the notes I'd written. He'd promised to give me his insights and interpret whatever I saw. And since I hadn't held anything back, his job wouldn't be quick or easy.

I should have been more patient, especially after coming back from a virtual trip that seemed like it had lasted days, when it had only taken less time than Dr. Ridgeway was spending examining White Bird.

"What time is it, Mom?"

"Five minutes from the last time you asked." Normally she would have sounded annoyed, but Mom had this goofy smirk on her face. She looked really happy for a change, but I sure wasn't.

Ridgeway still had us waiting outside the locked door of the detention unit. After all that had happened, I felt like I was back at square one, wondering if any of what I remembered had actually taken place. Seeing White Bird awake and being able to talk to him would make things real for me.

"You think he's okay?" I didn't wait for anyone to answer. "What could be taking them so long?"

"Bren?"

When Mom called my name, I turned and she nudged her head behind me. Dr. Ridgeway had buzzed through the locked door, but he wasn't smiling.

"How is he, Doc? Can I see him?" I swallowed, hard.

"He's lucky. And it's a miracle how lucid he is." The doctor shook his head. "I don't know what happened in there. And if you have time, I'd like to talk to you about..."

"Yeah, I'm sure. But I'm a little fuzzy, you know. Maybe it'll come to me." I stepped closer and fixed my eyes on his. "You promised. Can I see him?"

"Yes, you can. Follow me." He turned to escort me, but when he saw Joe and Mom stand, he said, "He's a little weak. It would be best if only Brenna came with me. I hope you understand."

The doc sounded almost human. Almost.

Mom looked disappointed, but she shrugged and said, "Sure. We'll be here when you're done, honey."

And Joe only nodded.

Walking from the waiting area to White Bird's hospital room was a total blur. Ridgeway said stuff, but I didn't listen. Nothing became real until the doctor opened the door and I saw him lying in a hospital bed.

When he looked up at me, the room closed in. And stupid stuff went through my mind. Things like—

Why didn't I look in a mirror while I was friggin' waiting? My face was still battered and my lip was cut. What was I thinking? And I'd grown real breasts since he'd last seen me. Would he notice? And my damned hair was cut off. Would he like it? I dragged a hand through my hair and fidgeted with my clothes. I had changed ten times and I could've changed twenty more and it wouldn't have mattered. I'd never feel right about seeing him after all this time—especially after what I'd done.

But the biggest question in my arsenal was *could he ever forgive me?*

All of that swirled in my head, pulling a three-sixty like a flushing toilet. And the most genius thing I came up with to say was, "Hey."

"Brenna? It *is* you. I thought I dreamed you." His gentle voice was exactly as I remembered it. It always sent chills over my skin.

I walked closer to the bed. And to keep my hands busy, I twisted his bed linens. It was all I could do not to touch him.

"They cut your hair." I said. "It looks…good."

Good? It looked frickin' great. The boy could totally be bald and look amazing, but I felt heat rush to my face. The last thing I wanted to do was call his attention to hair. My hair was sort of a disaster.

"Did they?" He ran a hand through his short dark hair. "Yeah, guess so, but you're one to talk. You've got short hair, too."

"Oh, yeah. Long story, but it's growing on me, literally." I smiled as I touched the hair on the back of my neck.

A comfortable silence filled the room. And White Bird stared at me the way he used to. With any other boy, I would have turned bright red. But seeing him look at me felt…*right.* And when I stared back, he didn't look away.

"I'm not sure about what happened to me, but I'm sure that I've missed you, a lot."

"Yeah. And I've missed you, too."

He had the same soft brown eyes, colored with flecks of gold and green that reminded me of wheat blowing gently in the breeze. And with his skin darker than mine—the color of sweet caramel—I liked how we looked together. Like a two-scoop vanilla sundae with nuts on top…me being the nuts.

"You've grown up, Brenna." He smiled and reached for my cheek. I noticed his fingers shook, but I pretended not to see it. "And you look…beautiful. More…beautiful."

When his fingers touched my cheek, I reached for his hand and held it, with his warm skin pressed against my face. And I kissed his palm as a tear slid down my cheek. I wanted to talk with him forever, just the two of us. I had a new school in North Carolina that I wanted to tell him about. And he didn't know my grandmother had died and how sad that made me. And his sweat lodge…I wanted to tell him how proud I was of him, but all of that would have to wait.

I had to clear the air about what I'd done, mostly because I didn't feel worthy to talk to him unless I told him. And a guy like White Bird deserved to know the truth. He'd always been honest with me. If I'd learned anything in the past two years, it was to face my fear head-on. Ignoring shit didn't make it go away and demons only got stronger. I was tired of hiding. And if I didn't tell him, I'd be a hypocrite to pretend I was his friend.

"White Bird, I've got something to say. Promise me you'll listen."

"What's the matter, Bren? Are you crying?" He wiped a tear from my cheek with his thumb. "Talk to me. I'm listening."

The tears came harder now. And I choked on my sobs to get out what I needed to say.

"Two years ago, I was the one who turned you in to the sheriff."

"What?" He grimaced as he stared at me. And I saw his body stiffen, but he didn't pull away.

"You promised that you'd listen," I cried. "I didn't see anything except you kneeling over Heather's body. What was I supposed to think?"

I should have rehearsed what I would say to him. Words were spilling from my mouth like puke, each one more rank than the last. I was grasping at anything to say. And everything came out wrong.

"I should have believed in you. You were my friend."

"Were?" This time he pulled his hand away and crossed his arms. "You mean I'm not now? From what the doctor said, it's been two years, Brenna. Guess a lot of stuff has happened since then."

"Yeah, but Joe thinks you might've been a witness."

I told him about Joe's theory, that under the influence of peyote, he might have gotten separated from his spirit guide and lost his way in his quest. And that Joe believed he might have been a witness to what had happened to Heather.

"Joe thinks that? So what do you think, Brenna? Do you think I killed her?" He didn't wait for me to answer. "Guess so. You were the one who called the cops."

"But you don't know what's happened since I came back.

Lots of stuff. All you have to do is tell us what happened that night. And maybe all this will be over."

"Oh, is that all?" He raised his voice and pressed fingers to the side of his head. "I can't remember anything. And I've got a headache the size of Oklahoma. Now probably isn't the best time for us to be talking about this."

He was right, but I wasn't sure I'd get another chance, especially when the hospital door opened and Sheriff Logan walked in.

"Time for you to leave, Brenna. I'm placing Isaac Henry under arrest for the murder of Heather Madsen. And it's about time he gets his day in court." The sheriff pulled his handcuffs and grabbed White Bird by the wrist. "One of my deputies will be posted at his door until Dr. Ridgeway releases him."

After Sheriff Logan cuffed him to the bed, White Bird got really mad and he yelled terrible things. He didn't understand. And I'd run out of time to explain it, even if I knew how.

"Were you working with the sheriff, Brenna? Is that why you're here?" He yanked his arm and the handcuff clanged on the metal bed rail. "I thought we were…friends. Why are you doing this to me?"

When he wouldn't settle down, Dr. Ridgeway came back with an orderly and a nurse. Through a sea of white uniforms, I saw White Bird staring at me. He was mad—*really mad at me*—for the first time. The doctor ordered a nurse to give him a shot. It must have been strong, because he dropped like a rock and stopped struggling.

And all of this had been my fault.

I pressed my back to the wall of the hospital room and sank to my knees, crying. And when the sheriff knelt by me and put a hand on my shoulder, I pleaded, "Why are you doing this? Why couldn't you have waited?"

With a pained expression on his face, Sheriff Logan said, "Murder charges don't just go away. He's got to face up to what he's done. And Heather's parents need closure. You knew this would happen, didn't you?"

I choked back a sob and asked, "So what's going to happen to him now?"

"Two years have gone by since the murder. The District Attorney will probably want to try him as an adult now. Juvenile detention is out."

"What? But that's not fair." I grabbed his arm. "He was a kid when Heather died."

"She didn't die, Brenna. She was murdered," Sheriff Logan argued. "And for the record, what happened to that girl and her family, that's unfair. You better get your priorities straight."

The sheriff pulled me to my feet, but he was done talking. He sent a nurse to get Joe and my mom. And when they came, I collapsed into my mother's arms and cried for real this time. I walked from White Bird's hospital room, feeling totally beat up. But when I looked at Joe, he had something to say.

"I know you're sad, Brenna, but we don't have time for tears." He walked down the hospital corridor with Mom and me, his hands clasped behind his back. "We've got work to do."

I stopped in the hall and stared at him for a long moment, drilling through my memory of what he'd told me when he talked about dream symbols and what they meant. Joe had believed that White Bird might have been a witness to Heather's murder. And if that were so, then the answer might lie in the notes I'd written down.

And before I had entered the vision, Joe had tried to warn me when he said, *"White Bird is locked in his mind, but even if you reach him and show him the way out of his torment, he still won't be free."*

"You knew this would happen, didn't you, Joe?" I asked. "You tried to warn me."

The Euchee Shaman didn't answer. The look in his eyes was enough for me.

"Warn you about what?" But Mom was clueless. She looked at both Joe and me, waiting for one of us to answer her.

"I'll explain it to you later, Mom. But now, I think Joe and me have work to do."

With his squad car pulled over onto the shoulder of a road on the north side of Shawano, Will Tate had just finished issuing a warning to a speeder in an SUV. His spiraling red-and-blue lights had attracted gawkers and traffic around him had slowed to a crawl, even though the violator had already merged into the nearest lane. He had his vehicle door open and was finishing his warning citation when he got the return call from Jon Fischer at TimeOnMyHands.com. Fischer had called his cell phone and Will recognized the area code on his caller ID.

"Yeah, this is Deputy Tate. Thanks for returning my call so quickly."

"Always glad to cooperate with law enforcement." Fischer had a real thick accent—Brooklyn or New Jersey maybe—and he talked a little too fast. "I don't get calls like this every day, you know. To tell you the truth, this breaks up the job for me. What I do ain't exactly rocket science, if you know what I mean." The guy laughed, then got down to business. "You said you needed a name and shipping address for a specific transaction." The guy rattled off the etched number inside the watch.

"Just a minute. Let me confirm that number." Will had brought a digital photo of the watch and had it in a manila folder on his passenger seat. After he checked the number, he said, "Yeah that's the one. You got that name and address for me?"

Will grabbed a notepad to take down the information, but when Fischer read off Matt Logan's name and address, he stopped writing.

"What? Are you sure about that name?"

"Hey, buddy, I'm not exactly makin' this stuff up over here. You want the name, or what?"

"Yeah, read it to me again."

This time Will didn't write anything down. He already knew the name and address too well. After he ended the call, he stared out his windshield and watched his lightbar cut its red-and-blue beams through the dark. Sheriff Logan had seen the watch earlier and didn't make a big deal about it. He acted like he'd never seen it before. Will wanted to give him the benefit of the doubt, but how did the sheriff's watch end up at that sweat lodge campfire? That site had never been part of the original crime scene where Heather's body had been found.

And whoever took the watch from the evidence locker had done it without following procedure by signing for it. That made Will even more suspicious of a man he respected. Matt Logan had the experience and the opportunity to mess with the Madsen murder investigation.

And maybe he even had motive.

"Damn it, Matt. What the hell did you do?" He heaved a sigh, blocking out all the terrible thoughts he had in his head as reasons Matt might have been involved in Heather's killing. Each thought was uglier than the last, but he couldn't get his head wrapped around any of it. Though he had a few blind spots, Matt Logan was one of the finest men he knew. And he deserved a chance to explain his actions.

When Will contacted dispatch to locate the sheriff, they gave him Red Cliffs Hospital as his last known location. He shut off his emergency lights and headed for the hospital. He needed to talk with Logan, one-on-one. And this time, there'd be no pussyfootin' around who was doin' what with the Madsen case. As far as Will knew, the sheriff had tampered with evidence and who knew what else. He needed answers and pronto.

It took him a half hour or more to get to the hospital, but by the time he got there, the sheriff was gone. His cruiser wasn't in the parking lot and hospital staff told him Sheriff Logan had already left. The man worked long hours on a normal basis, but at this time of day, the sheriff could have called it quits and gone home. To make sure, Will called dispatch again, but this time he contacted the on-duty operator on his cell phone. He didn't want anyone listening in to his radio frequency.

"I'm still trying to locate the sheriff, Jolene. He's not at Red Cliffs. You got his twenty?"

"No, Will. I've got nothing. And that's not like him. You want me to check around?"

Jolene had been a dispatch operator since God had invented Oklahoma red dirt. And when she told him that the sheriff normally told her where he was and when he was off duty, Will knew something was up. Until today, Logan had taken pride in doing everything by the book. And lately he'd seemed distracted, especially after the Nashes had come back to town and the Madsen case had new evidence.

"No, ma'am. It's no big deal. It'll wait till morning," he said. "Thanks for your help."

"Anything for you, doll."

He could have waited until morning, like he'd told Jolene, but Will had no intention of doing that. He got back into his cruiser and headed out, looking for Matt Logan. And when he found him, he wasn't sure how it would go down, but he was determined to set things right. He suspected the sheriff had tampered with evidence—or worse.

And no one was above the law. *No one.*

chapter seventeen

"Your uncle is the sheriff, Derek. Buy a vowel and get a clue. After we renovated the Nash place last night, I don't think a surprise visit from him is a good thing. His timing sucks." Talking to Derek on her cell phone, Jade DeLuca couldn't believe he was so clueless. "This can't be good."

After she locked her bedroom door, Jade kicked off her shoes and flopped on her bed.

"I don't know. He acted all casual and stuff," Derek argued. "Maybe it's nothin'."

"And maybe you need to avoid him for a few days, just to be on the safe side." She raised her voice. Derek was too laid-back and it pissed her off.

"I can't. We've got a family deal this weekend. At my house. And Mom says he's comin'."

"Can't you tell your mom you made other plans? This isn't exactly complicated." She crammed a pillow under her head. Beef boy was giving her a headache. "And stay clear of that skank Brenna. No more following her."

"You act like that was my brilliant idea. You're the one who likes screwin' with people."

From the tension in his voice, she knew Derek wouldn't take her usual abuse.

"Okay, okay. Chill. *Gawd!*" She shut her eyes and breathed deep. "Maybe we both need to relax and kick back a little."

"What are you sayin'?"

"Chloe's got a new stash and I could seriously use a hit right now."

"What about her parents?"

"They're MIA. She said she'd have the house to herself tonight. You want to meet me there in twenty?"

"Yeah, sure. But you know weed makes me horny." His mood had changed.

Derek's idea of foreplay was talking dirty. And if she looked up the word *crude* on Wikipedia, his picture would be staring back. Playing along, Jade teased him back, using her sexy voice.

"Yeah, me, too."

She ended the call, not waiting to hear what he'd say. The guy was the original horn dawg. His boy toy was like 7-Eleven, open 24/7, three hundred sixty-five days a year. Absolutely everything made him horny, even the crack of dawn.

But Jade had another reason for getting the three of them together tonight. All of them had a hand in what happened to Heather, even precious little Chloe. And she wanted to remind them that they had as much to lose as she did.

Of course, only she knew that wasn't exactly true. Jade had much more at stake, but that choice tidbit would stay her little secret. It *had* to.

After Matt Logan had heard Will Tate's call to the dispatch operator over his radio, he'd cut off all communications and didn't tell Jolene where he was now. His deputy was looking for him and he had a bad feeling the call was about the watch that he'd taken from the evidence locker. He should have put the damned thing back. Taking evidence went against everything he'd stood for, but family was important, too. And his interference wasn't just about his nephew. If the kid did something wrong, he should pay for it like everyone else, but this was about more than protecting Derek.

He'd spent his whole life taking care of his little sister. And she didn't need the shit storm that would rain down on her if Derek had anything to do with Heather's death. Newspeople would have a field day at her expense, simply because she was related to the sheriff. He'd been called "the preacher" before and some folks might like to see him taken down a notch.

Now he was wedged in a corner of his own making and had no one to blame but himself. That's why he was parked down the street from his sister's house, waiting in the shadows. He was deciding his next step. He still had time to fix things, as long as he stayed clear of Will Tate. He could put that damned watch back without anyone being the wiser.

But he had to talk to Derek. He had to know the truth, man-to-man.

When Derek got into his truck and pulled out of his driveway, Matt knew what he had to do. He followed the boy from a safe distance so the kid wouldn't see him in his rearview mirror. When the time was right, he flashed his lights and pulled him over. He felt like a traitor, but his sister needed his help more than Derek would.

The boy rolled down his window and looked relieved to see his face, but that lasted only until Matt opened his mouth.

"Park it and give me the keys, Derek. *Now!*"

"What's wrong, Uncle Matt?"

"And you can drop the Uncle Matt. Tonight, I'm Sheriff Logan."

Having had a long career in law enforcement, Matt knew how to intimidate anyone. And this time, he'd be playing hardball with his nephew.

"You're coming with me. And don't you dare argue, son."

Joe came home with us and Mom made him dinner. Even before we got done eating, we were talking about what I'd written and what everything meant.

He told me that when I pictured White Bird at the start of my journey, that triggered the link between us. I listened to what he had to say. Seeing my vision through his eyes was like watching *The Matrix* a second time, seeing cool things I'd missed before.

He said that the sea of white at the beginning of my vision represented my spiritual nature and my willingness to accept mystical stuff. And the weird, lime-green Jell-O forest was my last refuge before I ventured into the charred trees and stinky blood flowers, the danger part.

When we got to the bear and the mutant animals, I noticed Mom went to do the dishes and she got really quiet. At first, she'd been interested in what I told Joe, but when I got into the creepy part, I knew it scared her.

I scared her.

I knew all of this vision tripping would be hard for her to believe. That's why I'd never brought up that I was a card-carrying member of the "I see dead people" club. Mom was rooted too firmly in reality. And my "gift," as Joe called it, was probably some other bizarre quirk that I'd gotten from my father's side of the family.

At some point, when both of us were ready to deal with the questions I had about my dad, I would ask Mom about him, but she looked tired. Eventually Mom went upstairs to take a long bath and left us to work. I thought if I looked at my jumbled notes that I'd see a pattern. I really wanted an "Aha" moment when everything would become crystal clear, but that didn't happen.

I had something else on my mind. And it had zapped my brain energy.

"I can tell, something is blocking you. What's the matter?" Joe had a weird way of talking, but he knew how to get to the point.

"He hates me, Joe. He thinks I was working with the sheriff, this whole time. What happened two years ago is old news to us, but to him it's a fresh wound."

"That boy is smart. He'll figure it out." Joe's easy way of talking felt like a hot cup of cocoa on a wintry day. "You're a good girl, Brenna." He nodded his head and winked. "He'll notice."

"Not if he's in jail for the rest of his life." I took a deep breath and shut my eyes, fighting off the sting of tears. "And all because of me."

I couldn't forget the look of real anger on White Bird's face when he thought I'd betrayed him to the sheriff.

"You forget. He played a part, too. You're taking way too much credit for how things went down." He shoved aside his notepad and leaned across the kitchen table. "Remember what I said about tests in your life?"

"Not…exactly."

I seriously wished I had remembered what he told me. Things that came from Joe always seemed important. Like White Bird, the man didn't waste words.

"Stop questioning the tests that are put in your path. You're given only what you can handle. And those tests—making mistakes and figuring stuff out—that's what makes you stronger." He locked his eyes on mine. "Quit looking back, Brenna. The only thing you can change is what's ahead of you."

"Yeah, I guess so. But I wanted for us to be..." Even as close as I felt with Joe at this very moment, I still didn't want to share my feelings for White Bird. They were too personal and I hadn't even talked to him about how I felt.

"You love him. I get that, but there are no guarantees in life. Open your heart and see what fills it," Joe said. "Help him because it's the right thing to do, not because you want him to feel the same way you do."

"But I didn't do any of this because..."

Joe didn't let me finish. He put a finger to my mouth and got me to shut up, a trick Mom would have loved to learn.

"You don't have to explain." He narrowed his eyes. "From what you told me about your vision, both of you are here because you did a selfless thing. You risked your life to save his. That's what brought you back."

I hadn't thought about how or why we made it back until now. What Joe said gave me goose bumps.

"You're strong, you have good instincts when it comes to people and you have a big heart," he said. "And if that boy can't see it, then he doesn't deserve to be your friend."

I took in what he said and let it simmer in my brain. Joe was the first man that I could see as the father I never really had. A part of me was sad that once we got Grams's house sold, we'd go back to North Carolina. I'd miss Joe...and one very special person. But if Mom hadn't dragged my butt here, I never would have met him—or seen White Bird again.

I guess Joe's Zen way of thinking was rubbing off on me.

"So I never heard. What kind of bet did you make with Dr. Ridgeway?" I asked.

"I bet him a dollar," Joe said with a straight face.

"Oh, big spender." I laughed. "You sort of had an edge. Why didn't you use it?"

"That would've been too easy. By him betting on that boy, it told me how desperate he was to make things happen, when in actuality there was no amount of money that would have made him take that bet under normal circumstances. He knew he had nothing to lose by letting us try to reach White Bird." Joe smiled. "That doctor may not have believed in superstition before, but now he's not so sure. I kind of like that."

"Yeah, me, too." But after I thought about what he said, I scrunched my face. "So you only bet a buck on me? That wasn't exactly a big show of faith."

Joe shrugged. "What can I say? You're a rookie."

We got back to work. And I'd never done so much talking. Joe said that if I kept yammering, I'd find the answer on my own, that he was only a listener. Searching for the answer in my brain was as lame as playing *Where's Waldo.*

"I thought Derek was coming right over. Where is he?" Chloe peeked through the drapes in her living room one more time.

Jade was getting more edgy, just watching her. And she didn't like it.

"He'll be here. Relax." She sprawled on a sofa and kept her voice calm, even though that wasn't how she felt.

After talking to Derek about his uncle, Jade had a bad feeling. Ever since Brenna came back to town, things had gone to shit. Now the sheriff might be snooping around. She wasn't worried about the vandalism. The only ones who could point a finger at her had done the deed. If they talked, they'd be in as much trouble as she was. Messing with Brenna and her mom had been intended as a punishment as well as a distraction. She figured Brenna's mother might step in and stop her daughter from sticking her nose where it didn't belong.

But maybe she'd figured wrong about the Nashes. Until now, Derek had been her safety net, but things had been different since Brenna came back.

"You trashed her grandmother's house, didn't you? You and Derek and his asshole friends," Chloe mumbled as she stared out the window. She didn't wait to hear what Jade would say. "You shouldn't have done that. That was mean."

Jade gritted her teeth. Mousy Chloe, the loser, was growing a backbone.

"Oh, shut up! You're pathetic," she yelled and pushed off the couch. "And you don't know what you're talking about. I had nothing to do with that."

"Yeah, right." Chloe laughed. "You're always innocent."

"And you're predictable. You're a damned follower, Chloe. You always have been."

"You remind me of Heather. You're even beginning to look like her." Chloe turned with a strange smile on her face. "Maybe you're possessed. She was too nasty to die and she's taken over your body. You ever think about that?"

"Don't say that. Now who's being mean?" Jade acted hurt. "And quit talking about Heather. She's dead."

Chloe had been a fellow lab rat when they'd both been subject to Heather's whims and moods and social experiments. But now that she'd stepped into Heather's shoes, Jade saw that Chloe was seriously weak and flawed. When this was over, she would cut her loose and recruit someone new, someone more worthy. Nothing of Heather's old circle would remain. *Nothing!*

"Come to think of it, wasn't it your idea to spy on that cute Indian boy?" Chloe reminded her. "You were a little Heather in the making, even back then, weren't you?"

The bitch wasn't letting it go. And her trip down memory lane was a little twisted.

"I said shut up, Chloe!"

"You should have left Isaac Henry alone. He wasn't hurting anyone. But you had to show Heather that you were worthy, didn't you?" Chloe pushed and got in her face. "So what if Brenna liked him. Why did you have to mess with her, too? She hadn't done anything to you. She wasn't a threat to any of us."

"Us? You're not one of us. You never were." Jade lashed out with anything that would sting, but Chloe was on a roll. She wasn't listening.

"You heard someone sold him peyote. And you told Heather he'd be naked in that sweat lodge he was building. You knew she had the hots for him." Chloe glared. "Hell, she had the hots for *any* guy someone else wanted."

"So *that's* it." Jade laughed. "I always wondered if you knew."

"What are you talking about?" Chloe's eyes got watery. "Knew about what?"

"You found out that Heather screwed your precious Lucas, didn't you?"

"What?" Chloe grimaced and walked away, but Jade followed. "Don't…say that."

"As I recall, she said he was a really good lay, too, but you wouldn't know about that, would you? He doesn't even know you exist." Jade went on the offensive to get control and hit Chloe where she'd hurt the most.

"That's not true." Chloe shook her head and kept her nose to the wall. She was too much of a coward to turn around. "And Lucas wouldn't have done that. He was too good for her."

"No, you knew about them. That's why you can't look me in the eye."

When the blonde didn't say anything, Jade knew she was right. It was hard for her to understand a girl like Chloe, except that if the girl admitted to knowing Heather had screwed Lucas, she'd have to admit that Lucas had "betrayed" her, too, her twisted version of betrayal, that is. And that was something Chloe would never do.

"You are in serious denial." Jade softened her tone, all part of the Chloe game. "The minute she found out how you felt about Lucas, that put a target on his sweet ass. As far as Heather was concerned, he had 'Fair Game' written on his forehead. Didn't you get that? She did that to me, too. You remember Ethan?"

Talking about Ethan brought back bad memories. Jade still hated Heather for what she did. Any chance she'd had with Ethan had been ruined. And Heather had done the same with Chloe, who had gotten real quiet, the way she always did when she didn't like what she heard. The blonde stuck a finger in her mouth and chewed a nail.

"That's why we have to stick together, Chloe." Jade closed the gap between them and rubbed her hands on the girl's shoulders, pretending to be sympathetic. "Heather did that to both of us. That's why I hate talking about her."

Chloe turned around and hugged her. The move took Jade

by surprise. She rolled her eyes and hugged her back until the girl quit crying.

"Why don't you light up? That'll chill you out. You'll feel better."

Grass had become a crutch for Chloe. And Jade knew how to use it. The girl nodded and slumped on the couch to light up a joint. When the smell of marijuana filled the room, Jade waited until Chloe got real mellow before she grabbed her purse.

"I've gotta pee. And I'm calling Derek again." Jade made a show of grabbing her cell phone and heading for the bathroom, but when she was down the hall, she went up the back stairs near the kitchen. She wanted a closer look at Chloe's secret drawer—and that damned journal.

She'd never thought about it before, but what if that idiot Chloe had stuff in her diary about the night Heather died. The girl was stupid like that.

And Jade had too much at stake not to find out what Chloe had written.

Without saying a word, Matt Logan drove his nephew out to the trailhead that led to the old bridge over Cry Baby Creek. Derek didn't say anything, especially after he saw where they were going. Matt parked the cruiser and turned off his headlights.

"Get out." He glared at his nephew.

The boy did as he was told. He looked scared, but he kept his mouth shut. An innocent kid would have protested real loud by now. Matt kept his face stern, but inside he ached for his sister—and for Derek.

He took the kid to the bridge, where Heather's body had

been found. It was pitch black, except for the bluish haze of the moon. But even in the dark, Matt knew Derek was crying.

"This is where Heather died, Derek. I'm telling you this, but I think you already know."

Derek kept his head down. He didn't bother to hide his sobs now. The grating chirp of crickets and the darkness closed in on both of them—and the truth could no longer be denied.

"Did you kill that girl, Derek?"

"What? Why'd you say that? *No!*" When his nephew raised his voice, the crickets stopped.

Matt had finally gotten a reaction from the kid.

"They found your watch at the crime scene. You know, the one I bought you. They're gonna trace it back to me. And too many people know I gave that damned thing to you. You'll be linked to the murder. You're a damned suspect now, Derek."

His nephew had plenty of opportunity to deny that his watch had been found at a crime scene, but when he didn't, Matt knew he'd been right. And Will Tate might already know it, too.

"But I didn't do anything. Not really."

The minute the kid said, "Not really," he knew he'd said the wrong thing. He got real quiet.

"Don't you get it? You're about to be hauled in as a suspect in a murder. Your momma is gonna freak out. And the media and this whole damned town will tar and feather me, so I can't protect you." Matt had his hands on his hips, yelling at the boy, who couldn't look him in the eye. "You've gotta tell me everything, so we can figure out what to do before all this goes down. This is your last chance to make things right."

When Derek hesitated, Matt didn't hold anything back.

"Didn't that poor girl mean anything to you? She died right

here, drowning in her own blood." He grabbed the kid by his arm and hauled him to the spot where Heather took her last breath. "Someone stabbed her to death and I gotta know everything about that night. For your mother's sake, do the right thing now, boy, before it's out of our hands. You owe your mother that much."

Derek finally broke down. He didn't admit to killing Heather. He didn't go that far, but he did tell his uncle about the others. He had gone with Heather, Jade and Chloe to track Isaac Henry into the woods to his sweat lodge. They had heard the Indian had bought peyote for some ritual he was doing. The whole thing had been Jade's idea. At first, they only intended to scare the kid and mess with him by stealing his peyote, but when Heather took over, things got nasty and out of control.

They had attacked the Indian kid while he was under the influence. He was stronger than Derek figured and they'd scuffled by the fire pit. That's where Derek lost his watch, although he'd never been sure. He had his hands full with Isaac Henry, who was beating the crap out of him. And afterward they all split up and ran.

"What happened to Heather?" Matt demanded. He grabbed Derek's arm and shook him. "Who was with Heather, damn it?"

"I don't know. Ask Brenna. She was the one that called you, right? She saw that Indian kill Heather, didn't she?"

Not exactly, Matt thought. With what Derek told him, he had more pieces to the puzzle, but something was still missing. He needed everyone who was there that night to tell what they saw.

"Where's Jade and Chloe?"

"They're at Chloe's house. I was gonna meet them when

you pulled me over." Derek wiped his face. "What's gonna happen now, Uncle Matt?"

It hadn't been an accident that Derek now called him uncle. The kid was already playing on his sympathies, but it was too little too late.

"We're going to the Seavers' place. And I'm taking all three of you in for questioning," he said. "We're getting to the bottom of this. Now get going." He grabbed Derek by the shoulder and hauled him back up the trail.

Matt had a pretty good idea what would happen now. Soon it would be out of his hands and he'd have no say. But getting at the truth was the right thing to do—for all of them. And when his nephew's back was turned, he made the sign of the cross and prayed for Heather.

The girl had deserved better.

Jade crept down the dark hallway to Chloe's bedroom. She hadn't flipped the lights on. She was afraid Chloe would notice. When she got to the room, Jade turned the knob and slowly closed the door so she wouldn't make a sound. Once she got inside, she grabbed a jacket Chloe had hanging over a chair and stuffed it at the base of the door. She didn't want light shining through, a dead giveaway that she was snooping.

Jade flicked on a lamp and a pale glow washed over the room. It was bright enough for her to see. She knelt at the base of the armoire and felt in the back for the little key. When she found it, she unlocked the drawer and looked over Chloe's prized possessions.

Everything was exactly as she had seen it before. Lucas Quinn's number one fan had been stalking him for years. Jade smiled as she knelt in front of the glitter-filled drawer. A stalker's tribute to a boy Chloe would never have. But Jade's smile faded fast when she didn't see the journal.

What the hell? She fumbled through the bags of hair, old ticket stubs and sparkling pictures of Lucas's smiling face. Jade was losing it. She knew that stupid Chloe had written everything down in her damned journal. That idiot was the weak link. And dumb, lovesick Chloe would tell. She should have taken the journal the first time—and burned the damned thing, sight unseen. Now it might be too late. Chloe would ruin everything.

Jade was so obsessed with rummaging through the drawer that she didn't hear the bedroom door open.

"Is this what you're looking for?"

Jade yelped at the sound of a voice behind her. When she turned, she saw Chloe holding the journal in her hand. Lucas's smiling face was on the cover that was trimmed in absurd lace. The blonde cocked her head and blinked her blue eyes. Her pink glossed lips curved into a faint smile.

Jade thought about denying she'd been looking for the damned thing, but that was before Chloe made it easy. Before Jade could say anything, Chloe held out her diary and walked it over to her.

"I would've let you read it if you'd asked me. I've got nothing to hide."

Jade reached for the journal with trembling fingers. Her heart was still racing and her breathing was shallow and fast. She didn't want Chloe to see how scared she'd been after she got caught.

"I was just curious what you wrote about the night Heather died. That's all." Jade grabbed the diary and flipped through the pages, looking for the date she'd never forget. She didn't hear Chloe inch closer.

"How did you know I kept a journal...especially in *that* drawer?"

She realized too late that Chloe had figured out that she'd been in her secret drawer before. The bitch had set her up.

"You shouldn't have looked in there," Chloe whispered in her ear.

It was the last thing Jade heard. She never even got a chance to look up. A jolt of pain shot through her skull and dark splatter hit the armoire. *Again and again.* When she hit the carpet, she felt her body spasm and she couldn't move. She wanted to scream, but she couldn't do that, either.

Chloe leaned over her and whispered, "Now look what you made me do."

That's all Jade remembered before everything went black.

chapter eighteen

With the rest of Grams's house dark after Mom had gone to bed, Joe and I worked at the kitchen table under a soft light, surrounded by shadows. It was late and I was exhausted, but I forced myself to work. Joe had been pleased to hear that a grizzly bear had been my guide for part of the journey. White Bird had claimed the bear clan as his, so maybe the bear had chosen him, too.

But the mutant menagerie of animals in my vision was what had interested Joe the most.

Since he had a theory that White Bird had been a potential witness to Heather's murder—and not the killer—Joe thought that his mind might have projected the images in my vision as a way of communicating with me. White Bird might have been trying to tell me what he'd seen.

"Do you think he'd remember what happened now?" I asked. "I mean, he's not zoned out anymore. Why can't he just tell the sheriff what he saw?"

"He was under the influence of peyote. He wouldn't make

a reliable witness anyway." Joe shook his head. "The symbols you described might have been buried deep in his mind or maybe they came from you and your experiences. You gotta remember that he's been trapped in his vision for two years. If his experience was anything like mine, he'll have holes in his memory that he'll never get back," he explained. "Visions don't work like a video. They're only suggestions to be interpreted."

I got what he meant. I couldn't go to the cops and report a giant spider attack without taking a serious Breathalyzer test or being checked for Mad Cow. What I saw had been some form of communication, from White Bird or from my subconscious. So we peeled back the layers of my vision and focused on the images that were most dangerous to me—the horse, the jackal and the spider that was too big for me to squash.

Joe told me that the stallion in a dream or vision symbolized power and male sexuality. And the fact that the horse was breathing fire and glowed red was also a sign of aggression or danger or blood.

"The horse was definitely aggressive. It barged in like it had the right. A real..." I stopped before I said it.

"A real what?" Joe asked. "Say the first thing that comes to your mind."

"A real bully, was what I was going to say." When I nodded, he didn't need to make his point. He knew I got it.

"What else?" he prompted.

"The jackal I saw in my vision had gray eyes. It reminded me of someone."

He nodded and smiled. "The jackal is a scavenger," he said. "It eats other animals to live. In Egypt, Anubis was the jackal god. He was the guardian to the underworld. But no matter how well the Egyptians sealed their tombs, those damned jackals always found their way in for takeout."

"Thanks for the history lesson, but I have a hard enough time sleeping." I grinned. "So tell me about that damned spider. If Jade is the jackal, which I totally get, seeing the way she feeds on other people. And Derek is that stud stallion. Who is the spider? I'm having trouble with that one."

"The spider weaves a pretty web of illusion that's a trap for its prey," he said, but when I still didn't come up with anything, he asked, "Any other distinguishing marks on that spider? If the jackal had gray eyes, maybe you're leaving something out about the bug."

I ran a hand through my hair and nodded.

"Yeah, you're right. The spider had red on its back. It looked like a splatter of paint, but I remembered flashing back to that field of red flowers, 'cause they stank like blood. And come to think of it, that spider had green eyes, too."

When I looked up, I saw movement in the shadows behind Joe. At first, I thought Mom had come back downstairs, but when the room got chillier, I knew it wasn't my mother creeping around in the dark.

It was Heather.

She drifted through the gloom, weaving in and out of the dark like she was playing a macabre game of hide-and-seek. Joe didn't react to the dead girl in the room. Guess he didn't see or sense her.

"You know who it is, don't you?" he said, like he had read my mind. He was getting vibes off me, not the spirit that had joined us.

"Yeah…and I'm looking at her, right now." I looked past Joe and glared at Heather.

After Joe glanced over his shoulder and didn't seem to know

where to look, he turned back around and said, "Guess I need 3-D glasses. Now you know what to get me for Christmas. Tell me about her."

Heather had been the clacking spider that almost killed me. I stared her straight in those green eyes of hers, and I knew it had been her in my vision. And from the expression on her face, she wasn't denying it. Although ghosts didn't talk, they also didn't have reason to lie.

"You little..." When I glared at her, a sad smile nudged her lips and she shrugged.

Guess that was her way of saying sorry. Heather was as nasty dead as she was alive. Some things never change.

"The spider was Heather," I said. "But if White Bird didn't kill her, does that mean Jade or Derek did it?" I was asking Joe, but I kept my eyes on Heather.

"Don't jump to conclusions. We may not have all the moving parts to this thing."

I could tell by Heather's reaction that Joe was right. She had turned her attention to the stash of DVDs we hadn't packed yet. But when we had talked about Jade and Derek, I got nothing from her. If one or both of them had killed her, I thought she would've responded. It made no sense that she ignored us. I was missing something, but I was too fried to think anymore.

"You look tired," Joe said.

I smiled at him. He had read my mind and always seemed a step ahead. Hanging with this guy was like wearing my favorite jeans, the kind that stretched when I ate too much and never felt too tight or made my butt look too big. We were so in sync that it was seriously crazy.

"Yeah, guess I am. We can hit this tomorrow." I didn't

even have to ask if he'd be up for another day at this. I knew he would be. Joe was rock steady.

Heather had cleared out. At least for now. I felt her presence in the room, even though she didn't show me where she was. Sometimes the dead got off on playing head games with the living. And that would have gone double for somebody cruel like Heather.

I walked Joe to the door and gave him a hug under the porch light. I don't think hugging came naturally for him. And it never had for me, either. But today, I needed one from him and it felt right, like we'd done it a million times. And would do it a million more times, in the lives that stretched ahead of us.

Since I'd met White Bird and Joe, I'd become a firm believer that anything was possible.

"Hey, Joe..."

After he'd headed for his truck, I called out to him and he turned back.

"You were the thunder. And the owl, right?" I grinned. Joe had been watching over me in my vision. And a part of me always knew he'd be there.

But Joe never really answered me. He only gave me his lazy smile and said, "People like you and me, we may share a vision, but it's never the same one. Each journey is personal and filtered through our experiences." He winked. "Like I said, you're strong, Brenna. You'll figure this out. It'll hit you when you least expect it."

I watched Joe drive away as I sat on the porch under the gazillion winks of light in the night sky. I didn't feel like playing hide-and-seek with Heather. Sometimes the dead cheated, because they could. But when I thought about Jade and Derek and Heather, my mind automatically pictured someone else in that pitiful bunch.

Chloe Seaver.

She'd been the puppet everyone played. If Jade and Derek had been with Heather the night she was killed, where had Chloe been?

"That's it."

I rushed off the porch and headed inside, without a sideways glance to see if Heather was still hanging out. If anyone knew what had happened that night, Chloe would. I had to talk to her. She was always the quiet one, the one who had been manipulated by the popular crowd, but she'd also been a friend once. Maybe I could appeal to the nice girl that had been buried underneath the caustic influence of Heather and Jade. She went along with those two, but she never seemed to buy in completely.

I went to my bedroom to grab my new cell phone before I headed to the garage to get my bike. If White Bird's vision was real, then Jade and Derek were there the night Heather died. But what if they weren't the only ones?

Maybe Chloe had been there, too.

When I got to Chloe's house, the place had no lights on, except for a few security fixtures on the lawn. Those were probably on timers and would make it harder to avoid being seen. But with all the windows dark, the Seavers were probably asleep, including Chloe. Her bedroom was dark, too, or maybe she had her drapes shut.

When we used to be friends as kids, I not only knew where her room was, I knew how she got in and out at night without her parents knowing.

"Let's hope some things stayed the same," I whispered. "Otherwise I'll be SOL."

I ditched my bike in some bushes and crept around to the side of the house. I didn't want her parents to see me. At this hour, they'd call the cops first and ask questions later.

I stayed close to the shrub line and dodged from shadow to shadow until I made it to the trellis and tested it before I climbed. When it took my weight, I scaled the sturdy lattice to Chloe's window and tapped on the glass.

"Chloe," I whispered. "It's me. Brenna."

I waited for her to flick on the lights and pull the drapes open, but she never did.

"Chloe." I tried again, but nothing happened. This time I wedged my finger under the window and it slid open an inch.

For a split second, I thought about staying put and not going in. But when I imagined White Bird going to prison, I had to do something, even if it meant Chloe would scream and call her parents.

"Screw it." I opened the window and crawled in.

Chloe's room was dark. It took a while for my night vision to kick in, but when I saw her under the blankets on her bed, I crawled toward her on all fours.

"Chloe? Don't scream, okay?" I whispered again. "It's me. Brenna."

I listened for her breathing, but didn't hear anything. She hadn't moved or made a sound. I crawled closer. And when I went past her dresser, my hands knocked into stuff she had on the floor. I had to be more careful. I ran my fingers ahead of me, feeling as I went along. She had plastic bags all over the floor, maybe an arts and craft project. I shoved everything aside to get at her bed.

When I was close enough, I got to my knees and clamped a hand over her mouth.

"Don't scream." I raised my voice, enough for her to hear. "It's only me."

My fingers felt something wet and sticky. And when I smelled something metallic, I yanked my hand back and gasped.

"Chloe?" Without thinking, I got to my feet and reached for the lamp on her nightstand. When I flipped on the switch, the light flooded the room and I squinted, holding up my hand to shield my eyes. When I looked down, I screamed and nearly jumped out of my skin. It wasn't Chloe in that bed.

I was staring into the bloody face of Jade DeLuca.

"Holy shit!" I screamed again. *"Shit, shit, shit!"* I didn't care if anyone heard me now.

Jade had her hands tied on the bedposts. And her face was so covered in blood that I barely recognized her.

"Jade?" I choked when I called out her name. And I swear to God, she wasn't breathing.

I looked down at my hands and they were covered in blood. This couldn't be happening. Not again. I wiped my hands down my clothes and stared at Jade. Her red hair glistened with blood. That was scary enough, but she had something strange stuck to the top of her head. Long strands of brown hair hung down her neck, longer than the length of her own hair.

It looked like she wore a weird hair extension, something from an old Halloween costume. And the top part of the hair-piece wasn't pinned down. I leaned closer and lifted it with my fingers. The strand of hair had brown shriveled gunk holding it together. And it stank real bad. I dropped it quick.

"Jade? Wake up…" I tried touching her, but she didn't move.

When I backed away from the bed, I kicked something with my foot. It was an empty plastic bag with a label on it that read *4 LUCAS* in caps. And Chloe's armoire was open with stuff tossed all over the carpet. What was going on?

And where was Chloe? Why hadn't her parents come running when I screamed? With every question, my stomach twisted into a knot and my body shook all over. I wanted to run, but when I turned to haul ass out the window, I stopped.

Chloe stood at the bedroom door, with a hand behind her back. Her dark smoky eyes were ringed in red, making her look crazed. And in the dim light, her skin was a ghostly white. She looked dead.

"What do you think of the new Heather?" She smiled down at Jade, proud of her handiwork. And her voice was childlike and unemotional, like nothing was wrong.

"What did you do, Chloe? That's not Heather. It's Jade. Is she dead?" I inched closer to the window, my only way out with Chloe blocking the bedroom door.

"I don't know, but she may as well be Heather, don't you think?" When I didn't answer, she stepped into the room. "I saved that piece of hair. Couldn't get rid of it. I didn't know it would come in so handy."

"Saved it from what?"

"That was Heather's hair. She always loved how long and shiny it was. She bragged about it all the time. I got sick of hearing it, but you know how she was, right?" Chloe smiled and came closer to me. "So I took it from her. I did it for Lucas. I *had* to. She would have ruined him if I had let it go on."

Suddenly I remembered what Deputy Tate had said at the sweat lodge. And I knew what Chloe had been talking about. Jade was wearing Heather's scalp. The brown goop was Heather's dead skin with dried blood on it. Chloe had murdered Heather and scalped her with the knife.

I gagged and almost puked. I had touched it. And imagining the hatred Chloe had to have in her to mutilate a body like that was even harder to understand. Heather's dead face flashed through my mind like a vicious strobe light. The blood. Her glazed dead eyes covered with a film of white. All of it came back in a rush. I took a deep breath and kept my eyes on the girl who had killed Heather and set up White Bird to take the fall.

"Chloe, where are…your parents?" My voice was shaky.

"Gone. They're always gone." She pursed her lips and gave a fake pout.

When she came closer, I moved, too. My heart was pounding so hard, I felt light-headed.

"I've been waiting for Derek downstairs," she said. "Guess he's not coming. Too bad. I had a murder-suicide story all planned for him and Heather 2.0. But I'm glad you're here now, Brenna. You'll do nicely. Perfect, in fact. I'll take care of Derek another time…if I have to."

When she pulled the hand out from behind her back, Chloe had a butcher knife. And I gasped.

"Don't do this, Chloe." I raised my hand. "You don't have to do this."

"But I do now, don't you see?" The blonde smiled, but her face twisted into a grimace. "I swear, it was only gonna be the one time. I *had* to kill her. She forced me into it. Heather was gonna ruin Lucas."

"Lucas?" I remembered him and had seen stuff about him on Jade's Facebook page, but I wanted to keep her talking.

"Yeah, Lucas Quinn. You remember him, right?" She

heaved a sigh. "And I would've gotten away with what I did, too. All I needed to do was…nothing. And I would've been all right."

"But why did you hurt Jade?"

"I didn't want to, but she found all my secrets. And she saw the part of Heather I couldn't get rid of. That's why she's wearing it." Chloe looked at Jade on the bed and laughed. "And for the record, I really wouldn't have dragged you into it, but you only have yourself to blame." She shook her head and stepped closer. "You wouldn't let it go. Why couldn't you just let it go?"

I tensed my body, ready to move. Chloe was getting way too close. I clenched my fists, ready to punch her, but when the jarring ring of the phone caught us both off guard, Chloe was the first to move.

She lunged at me with the knife. And I dodged out of the way, but not before she cut me.

The sting of the blade sliced my belly and sent a shock wave of chills through me. I grabbed her hand and wrestled her for the weapon, pulling her to the floor. We rolled over the carpet. And I couldn't stop thinking about Heather and how she died. And I pictured the same thing happening to me. Chloe had pounded a knife into her, more than a dozen times.

Please, God. Don't let that happen to me.

When I got Chloe's back against the armoire, I had her pinned under me. I whacked her wrist on an open drawer until she dropped the knife. With a cry of pain, she cradled her arm and rolled onto her side. I didn't wait to see what she'd do next.

I stumbled off the carpet and charged for the open window, with adrenaline surging through me. I thought I could make it. And I didn't give a shit about how I'd land below. But when I got stuck halfway out the window, I felt Chloe's hands on my legs.

"Help me!" I screamed, grappling for the cell phone in my pocket. "Someone help me."

I got my fingers on my phone, but when I pulled it from my pocket, it fell out of my hands as we fought. My phone fell to the ground, into the shadows. I had been so damned close. I struggled against her grip and strained to let my weight be too much for her. All I needed was a little time. Down the street, dogs barked and a neighbor's light came on. I yelled again and again.

But when Chloe yanked me back inside, I knew by the time help arrived, it would be too late. Whatever was about to happen would be over.

Parked outside the Seaver house, Matt Logan sat behind the wheel of his police cruiser with the cell phone to his ear. He had one ear plugged so he could hear if someone picked up the phone. His dispatch radio was crackling with activity from Jolene. Six rings and no one at the Seaver place had picked up. At this time of night, that meant only one thing.

No one was home.

"I thought you said Chloe and Jade would be here. No one's answering." He looked into his rearview mirror. Derek had his head turned, staring at the dark house.

"I swear, Jade called me and told me to meet her here, because Chloe's parents would be gone." His nephew looked at him through the reflection. "They're there. They've gotta be."

"You better not be lying to me, boy."

"I'm not. I swear to God."

"You leave God out of this. You're in enough trouble." Matt looked over his shoulder at Derek, sitting behind the metal mesh of his back seat. "When I bring those girls out here, I don't want to hear a peep out of any of you. And I'll be watching."

Matt left Derek locked up in his patrol car and headed for the front door. Under a security light, he punched the doorbell several times and waited. When no one answered, he dropped his chin and shook his head. If the girls thought he'd go away if they didn't come to the door, they were dead wrong.

But when he heard a girl's scream coming from the rear of the house, he pounded the door with his fist.

"Chloe? Open up. *Now!*" He yelled. "This is Sheriff Logan. I know you and Jade are in there."

When he heard another scream, the hair at the back of his neck stood straight up. Matt knew he had no time to lose. Using his shoulder mic, he called for backup Code 3. Following procedure, they'd arrive using sirens. He had just unzipped his fly and soon everyone would know his business. But that didn't matter now.

Someone inside had yelled for help. And he prayed he wouldn't be too late.

Chloe had a good grip on my legs. I wouldn't ditch her now. When she grabbed my hips and hoisted me back inside, the doorbell rang and she cried out. I knew she was scared, but not half as afraid as me. At the sound of the bell, I shifted my weight and shoved back on her.

We both fell to the floor.

"Help me! Please," I screamed and felt the heat rush to my face as I fought her off. Someone was at the front door. It was my only chance.

I thought about how Mom always said I was a fighter. And I pictured Joe as a little kid, struggling to survive his vision quest after being bitten by a rattlesnake. But most of all, I thought about how strong White Bird had been to survive his two-year ordeal, alone.

Borrowing from his strength, I balled my fist and punched Chloe in her stupid little bird face. *Once. Twice.* The release felt good. I socked those smoky black eyes and gave her something to cry about. And when she screamed for me to stop, I didn't. *I couldn't.* She'd taken so much from me.

Chloe had killed Heather. And she'd stolen White Bird's life, and mine. I'd hurt my mother because of her. And Grams had died thinking I was a real loser. My rage took over. I knew it was wrong, but I didn't care.

The sheriff had to pull me off her. I saw uniforms fill the room and everything faded into a blur. Others stood over me and I didn't care. All I saw was Chloe.

Twisted, sick little Chloe.

"Stop it!" Matt Logan yelled. "Get off her."

Brenna Nash was out of control and covered in blood. She had Chloe Seaver on the carpet, punching the hell out of her. And Jade DeLuca was another bloody mess on the bed. She looked dead.

"What did you do?" he demanded.

One of his deputies had Brenna by the shoulders. He'd subdued her, but Matt saw that she was in no position to talk. She had a wild look in her eye. And he had no idea what to make of all this.

"Sheriff, you gotta see this."

Matt turned to see what his deputy was talking about.

"This looks like a real scalp, sheriff. I think this came off

Heather Madsen." Deputy Sanford grimaced and lifted a bloody strand of hair off Jade, using his pen to lift it.

"What the hell did you do, Brenna?"

He'd been wrong about the Nash girl. At the hospital, he'd felt sorry for her. He had the feeling she'd gotten caught up in something she couldn't handle. Now it looked as if he'd been all wrong. And he would have arrested her on the spot for assaulting both these girls, if he hadn't heard the garbled voice coming from the bed.

Jade DeLuca was alive.

"No. Not...B-Brenna." Jade choked on every word. And she struggled to sit up, but couldn't. The battered girl pointed a trembling finger. And she pointed it at Chloe Seaver. "She did it. Chloe killed...H-Heather. And almost...me, too."

"That's not true," the Seaver girl ranted. "Jade and Derek. They were the ones who killed Heather. *They did it!* They're ganging up on me, like they always do. Just ask anyone. They'll tell you."

Matt had no clue what had happened, but given the fact that Heather's scalp had been in Chloe's possession in her room, that evidence was as hard to refute as a smoking gun. And given the finger pointing between Jade and Chloe, he had a feeling that he owed a serious apology to Brenna Nash and her mother. He had a lot to figure out and from the looks of things, it would be a long night.

"Get an ambulance for Jade. And arrest this one for assault, for starters, until we sort this out." He pointed at Chloe, who was still screaming and giving him a serious headache.

When Brenna stood, she almost collapsed. He grabbed her in time and held on to the thin, trembling girl. When he wrapped his arms around her, she didn't pull away. The girl was sobbing.

"Shhh. You're okay. You're safe now, Brenna. It's over. It's really over this time." He held her tight and whispered in her ear. "Come on. I'm taking you home. I've got something to say to you and your mom."

An apology to the Nashes would be hard enough. But if what Jade said was true, and Chloe had killed Heather Madsen, then what would he say to Isaac Henry?

chapter nineteen

Ever since he'd said them, the sheriff's words kept playing in my head. *"It's over. It's really over this time."* I thought if I heard them enough, especially coming from him, I would believe it was true.

Guess I still needed time. And wounds that had cut so deep would never go away without a trace. I had to accept that.

After the sheriff had driven me home and explained things to Mom, it was my turn. She wanted my version of the truth. And after I got done with that and she'd patched me up, there wasn't much nighttime left, but I made good use of my sack time. I had slept hard and I didn't remember dreaming—until I heard a lawn mower outside my bedroom window.

That's when I knew I was definitely dreaming. When I looked out my window, I saw Derek Bast and his buddies hard at work.

"Well, I'll be damned." I shook my head.

I got dressed real fast, as fast as I could with a fresh bandage on my stomach from where Chloe had clipped me with that butcher knife. Thinking about that gave me chills. So I raced downstairs looking for Mom. She was in the kitchen, drinking coffee and reading the newspaper.

"They're calling you heroic, honey." Mom grinned and raised her coffee mug.

"Oh, my God. I definitely must be dreaming." I shook my head. "A friggin' nightmare."

Me, in the damned papers again. Two years ago the local papers were nothing but a rumor mill. Today I was heroic. *Jeez!* I didn't need any of it. I wanted the whole thing to blow over. Mom didn't look like she minded the story getting out, given the way she was glomming onto every word in that small-town paper. But me? I could use some serious downtime.

"And tell me that's not Derek Bast and his buddies out there, fixing Grams's house?" I scrunched my face, not doing a very good job of hiding a smirk.

"Sheriff Logan dropped him off. And Derek called the rest of those boys. Guess you could call it advance community service." She smiled as she ran her fingers through my hair. "I get to keep them until everything is done. And Derek is paying for everything. How's that?"

"It's a start." I poured some orange juice. "Did the sheriff say…anything else?"

From the look on Mom's face, she figured out what I was really asking. She skipped to the chase, the way mothers do sometimes.

"He said that he expected White Bird to be released from Red Cliffs today. You need the car…for anything? It's got all new tires, just waiting for some miles." Mom was playing it sly, too.

"Maybe. I'll let you know."

I knew Mom wanted me to talk to her, about how I felt and about all the things rolling loose in my head, but I couldn't do it. I had a lot to think about and I had to do it alone. I suddenly felt like writing. And I thought I knew how to finally finish the poem that had been kicking in my head.

But as strongly as I felt about getting my thoughts down on paper, only one thing could challenge my creative juices. White Bird had been angry with me, for what I'd done and said. Showing up at Red Cliffs like nothing had happened didn't feel right. But I knew today would be a long day of waiting, of hoping—and maybe a little letting go.

I made a PB&J on toast and headed upstairs where I wouldn't look pathetic waiting for the phone to ring. Pathetic I could do alone.

Shawano Sheriff's Office—Midmorning

Sheriff Matt Logan had gotten a phone call from Dr. Sam Ridgeway that Isaac Henry was in the process of getting released after the criminal charges had been dropped. That was a good time to visit the boy and sign for his release. Matt was heading out when Deputy Will Tate knocked on his office door. With Tate being on duty last night, he'd heard the news and only got a short briefing at the end of his shift. He was told what they had at the time.

"Come in, Will. Have a seat."

Will had two mugs of coffee and he handed one to Matt.

"You look wasted." Will took a gulp and settled into a chair.

Matt definitely was exhausted. It had been a long night.

"Before I fill you in, I need to tell you that I took that watch out of evidence. I recognized it as a gift I'd given my nephew. I had no intention of destroying it. I only wanted to confront Derek so we could figure out what to do if he'd been involved." Matt found it hard to stare his young deputy in the eye. "The watch is back in the evidence locker now. And I put my name and signature to that log. I can't believe I was so stupid."

"You were protecting your family," Will said quietly.

"That doesn't matter. It was wrong." He shook his head. "I'm giving a hard look at resigning. I've been at this job too long."

"You made a mistake, but you're a good cop. You won't do it again," Will argued. "Don't let this be the legacy folks will remember. Make it right. And start with these kids. Tell me what happened."

They sat in silence for a long while. Matt didn't feel like talking. He had a lot to think about, but he owed Tate an answer. His deputy had kept after the investigation. If he hadn't pushed, who knows where things might have ended up?

"Derek finally did the right thing. He confessed what had happened the night Heather was murdered. He confirmed that Jade DeLuca had convinced Heather to stalk that Indian kid into the hills to harass him." Matt felt himself get angry at what his nephew had done.

"When they got there, the kid was drugged out. Some vision quest thing," he continued. "His condition made it easy for them to give him hell, but Isaac Henry had enough fire in him to fight them off. They ran away from the kid, like the cowards they all were. And they had to split up. Derek couldn't tell me much after that, but Jade filled in the gaps when she was able to talk."

"Is she gonna be okay?"

"Yeah. She came away with a cracked skull and a concussion,

but it could have been a lot worse. All things considered, that girl was damned lucky," Matt told his deputy. "If it hadn't been for Brenna Nash, Jade would have died at the hands of Chloe Seaver."

"No shit." Will shook his head.

"And it seems Jade had a secret of her own about that night. She'd left Heather to die." Matt set down his mug on the desk. "After they'd run away, Heather had taken a bad tumble. She'd twisted her ankle. And with the Henry kid on their tail, Jade thought only about her damned self. She ran and left Heather behind, all crippled up. No one else knew about that. And Jade had been determined to keep it that way."

After she left Heather, covering her own ass, Jade believed Isaac Henry had killed the girl. She had no idea that Chloe was still out there and stalking Heather in the dark. The Madsen girl might still be alive today if Jade hadn't left her behind. If they'd stuck together, Chloe might not have had the chance to isolate Heather.

Matt would've felt sorry for Jade having lived the past two years with the guilt that she'd left Heather to be killed. Fortunately for Jade, it turned out that wasn't much of a burden.

"You should be the one who tells the Nash girl all this," he told Will. "Normally we don't talk about an active case with civilians, but she and her mom have a right to know."

"Yeah, guess so." Will stood and headed for the door. "I'm on it."

"And thanks, Will. For everything."

His deputy only grinned as he closed the door behind him, leaving Matt alone with his thoughts.

He was sick at what almost happened to Isaac Henry. The kid had looked guilty. How could he have been so wrong?

He had real soul-searching to do. And a good first move was a visit to Red Cliffs Hospital.

There was a young man he had to see before he got released.

A Half Hour Later

"Brenna." I heard Mom's voice from downstairs. "You have a visitor."

When I looked out my window, down to the driveway, I saw a patrol car and my heart lurched. What did the sheriff want now? Sheriff Logan had apologized to me and Mom, but I still couldn't shake the feeling that he didn't like me much and never would. I took a deep breath and headed downstairs.

When I hit the first landing, I was relieved to see Deputy Will Tate at the door. I couldn't help it. I smiled.

"Hey, Deputy Tate, what's up?" I sounded casual, but whenever cops showed up at my door these days, I figured something bad was about to happen. Guess I had to get over that sometime soon. Maybe.

"You got that look in your eye, Brenna, like you're expecting the other shoe to drop." The deputy grinned and showed off his dimples. "Relax. This is only a courtesy call. The sheriff wanted me to fill you in on the case, at least what we know now. You deserve to know."

Mom invited Will to sit in our living room. Seeing a cop in my house felt unnatural. But then again, *unnatural* was a pretty broad term in my world. Over a cup of coffee, Will told us about the case. When he was done, Mom had questions.

"So are murder charges pending on Chloe Seaver now?" Mom asked the deputy. "I just can't believe it. Chloe Seaver."

Chloe had surprised me, too, but after seeing the crazed look on her face and hearing what she said last night, guess it all fit now.

"Chloe had the perfect opportunity to kill Heather Madsen and blame it on someone else," Will told us. "No one saw her do it, except a drugged-out kid who was too far gone to stop it."

"But why did she do it? I don't get it," Mom said.

"Heather died because she'd slept with a boy Chloe had her eyes on, Lucas Quinn. We found a drawer full of evidence that Chloe had been stalking this Quinn kid. And she'd kept a diary. We're going through it now, but it's all there."

"Unbelievable." Mom shook her head.

"So what about the two knives?" I asked. "If White Bird had Joe's knife, where'd the other one come from…the murder weapon?"

"We still need confirmation on that, Brenna. Chloe's parents are flying back from some trip they were on. But when they get here, I'll bet money her daddy is missing a hunting knife. If that's so, then we're looking at premeditated murder."

"That's harsh, real harsh."

"Yep. Chloe had set up your friend, Isaac Henry, to take the fall for what she'd done when she scalped Heather. And she made sure he had Heather's blood on him, and even wrapped his hand around the murder weapon to get his prints on it. She bragged about that in her journal. In his condition, no one would have believed that Indian kid, even if he'd been able to talk. She would've gotten away with murder if it hadn't been for you."

I might have been the one at Chloe's house last night, but I really believe White Bird's visions put me on the right track.

He'd been a witness after all. And thanks to Joe's help, I was able to figure out his dream symbols.

"And as it turned out, even Derek owed you," Will added. "Sheriff Logan made sure his nephew knew about that." To my mom, he said, "Chloe had been waiting for Derek last night. She'd planned to kill both him and Jade, making the killings look like a murder-suicide. Chloe Seaver was one messed-up girl who wanted the Quinn boy all to herself. The whole ugly mess would've come out in a trial, but I doubt the case will ever go to court. Chloe's at Red Cliffs, under Dr. Ridgeway's care."

I hated that any of this had happened, but it had. Everything would take time to figure out, but Sheriff Logan had plenty of real proof this time.

"With Jade and Derek talking, we've got eyewitness testimony, Heather's missing scalp and even Chloe's diary to make sure we have the right kid in custody this time." Will looked me in the eye. "Bottom line is, it's all over. And we have you to thank for getting it right."

Mom reached over and grabbed my hand, giving it a squeeze. She had tears in her eyes. Guess I did, too.

Red Cliffs Hospital

When Matt Logan saw Isaac Henry, the kid was dressed and pacing the floor of his hospital room, staring out the window into the sunlight. After he'd knocked on the door, the boy turned with a look of eagerness on his face, but that changed when he saw who was standing in the doorway.

"Hey, Isaac. I came by to see if you needed anything, but I hear Joe Sunne brought you some clothes."

"Yeah, he did."

The Euchee Shaman had bought the kid clothes that would

fit. Isaac was older now. And he was a tall kid, taller than Matt had remembered him.

"Listen, I won't stay long. I know you probably don't want to see me."

The kid didn't bother to correct him.

"I owe you an apology." Matt had planned to say more, but the Henry kid interrupted.

"For what? Doin' your job?" The boy stopped his pacing and stuffed his hands in his jeans.

"It's just that I was dead wrong about you. I was so sure I had the right guy."

"Did me being an Indian make a difference?" Isaac asked the question without anger in his voice. It was a simple question, one Matt should have been able to answer without hesitating, but when he couldn't do that, both of them knew the answer.

"Then I won't apologize for doin' my job, but I still have plenty to regret. And I don't know how to make it right."

He'd admitted something to the boy that he hadn't said to anyone. Doubt was hard to live with, especially when he'd always thought his job was to set a good example for the town. He had no idea how to change, enough to make a real difference.

But in his quiet way, Isaac Henry gave him something to think about.

"A journey takes time." The boy shrugged and looked him square in the eye. "And I guess the lessons we learn best, they come from the journey, not the destination."

Matt narrowed his eyes at the boy and let what he said sink in.

"Can't argue with that, son."

Outskirts of Shawano

Earlier when I had told Mom that I wanted to see Joe Sunne, she didn't argue and she didn't even ask why. She'd handed me her car keys and kissed me goodbye. It had been her way of telling me that she trusted me. And that she understood there'd be things in my life that would be mine.

It was a start. And I *totally* kissed her back.

It had taken me twenty minutes to drive to Joe's place. And without hesitating this time when I drove through his gate, I jostled over the ruts and potholes of Joe's dirt road and parked the Subaru in front of his house. Like I remembered him from our first meeting, he sat on his cluttered porch as if he'd been expecting me.

"Hey, Joe." I waved when I got out and joined him, propping my feet on his railing, right next to his dusty boots.

"I heard you figured it out." He twitched his lip and gave me a sideways glance.

"Yeah, but I wasn't…cool about it. Almost getting killed is not cool." I nodded my head and pursed my lips. I found humor where I could. Otherwise I'd be too tempted to cry. And I'd done enough of that to last a lifetime. I was ready for a change.

I told Joe how I had mistaken the little bird in my vision—the one that almost had gotten trampled by the stallion—as a blast from my past. I thought White Bird had sent the image as a message for me not to be afraid. But when I thought about it some more, I remembered that he'd always told me Chloe reminded him of our wounded little bird with the busted wing, the one he'd healed at the creek. Like that bird, Chloe thrashed around, all wounded, and hadn't realized what she was doing to herself. And forget about her knowing what was good for her. The girl was clueless. Anyway, White Bird had always felt sorry for her and so had I.

And my little blind spot—of not recognizing Chloe in that bird vision—had nearly cost me my life.

"You would have figured it out," Joe said with confidence, until he added, "...eventually."

The guy could have been a stand-up comic, I swear to God.

We sat in silence and watched the afternoon sun stretch its shadow fingers into his scrub oaks, cedar trees and over his stone medicine wheel. I thought I looked relaxed, but my damned knee gave me away. I had a nervous shake and Joe never missed much.

"You haven't asked about him. Why not?" he asked.

"He hasn't called me or tried to get in touch after the sheriff had him released from Red Cliffs. Shawano's not that big that he couldn't find me if he really wanted to." I shrugged and swallowed the lump in my throat, not looking Joe in the eye on purpose. "The next step is up to him."

"Smart girl."

I acted tough, but inside I wasn't. I felt like a melty Rolo center, real mushy. And I was nowhere near as smart as Joe gave me credit for. The truth was that if White Bird didn't want to see me that would hurt way too bad. Why would I go looking for that kind of pain? Seeing his eyes filled with anger or hate or indifference would kill me. So I figured leaving the next step to him was the only way to protect my heart.

"I thought you should know." Joe turned and looked me in the eye. "Paperwork is in the works for new foster parents for White Bird. If things work out, it'll be permanent."

"Oh. My. God." My jaw dropped. "So tell me about 'em."

"I shouldn't say. I don't want to jinx it," he said with a straight face.

"Jinx it? I can't believe you just said that. Who would have thought you were superstitious?"

When I saw the lip twitch again, I knew I was breaking him down.

"They're good people. And they're Euchee."

Knowing the couple was Euchee meant that White Bird would get the tribe and the family he had always wanted. That was plenty of good news, but I had to hear more.

"Well, what else? You're killin' me."

"Ask me what clan."

I didn't have to. I already knew. And when I grinned, he did, too. In my mind, I pictured that bear like he'd been in my vision with his big hairy butt sitting at the crossroads between mediocrity and the next big adventure. And I even knew which road I'd take—which road I would *always* take, from here on.

"And if the boy still has an interest in becoming a healer, I might take on an apprentice. Who knows? Anything's possible, right?"

"So I'm told. Thanks, Joe."

I stood and kissed his cheek, hugging his neck. And when a soft creak of wood caught my attention, I looked up to see the face of Joe's dead wife staring down at me from the window where I had first seen her. Only this time she had a sad smile. The dead never really looked happy, but she gave it her best shot and I appreciated the effort.

I smiled back and settled into my chair, drifting into a comfortable silence with Joe. For real, this time.

I had the feeling Joe could use some female attention to shave off the rough edges of being a guy. He'd get used to having me in his life. I planned to make a habit of pestering him, whether we stayed in Shawano or not. After all, Joe and I had crossed paths for a reason. And I grew on people, like a wart.

But before the sun went down, I had one more trip to make—and a stop along the way. It was something I had to do. And I had a strong feeling this trip couldn't wait.

Pioneer Cemetery—Dusk

On my way back into town from Joe's house, I stopped by a flower shop and picked out something that would be fitting. I wanted to say goodbye to Heather Madsen. When she was alive, we never had much in common. And with her being dead, that hadn't changed. But since I was pretty certain I'd never see her again, I needed closure.

With so many flowers to choose from, I got totally confused, but the nice lady behind the florist counter saw me looking at the beautiful white lilies behind the chilled glass.

"I've always loved lilies, especially the white ones," she had said. "The lily is the sign for transformation, through life, death or rebirth."

I smiled at her and said, "In that case, I'll take two."

She had me at the word *sign*.

I asked her not to wrap them, that they would find a home soon enough. And after I parked at Pioneer Cemetery, I knew exactly where to go. The evening was picture-perfect. A gentle wind had kept things cool. And the sun had exploded glowing fire along the horizon, mixed with the cool blue of the coming night sky. I walked toward Heather's grave and found myself smiling at every stone angel. They were like old friends. But when I looked down the row of headstones, I saw someone was standing at Heather's grave.

White Bird was there.

For some stupid reason, I ducked behind the mausoleum for the Tucker family and peeked around the corner to watch him. I didn't think the Tuckers would mind. I wasn't ready for White Bird to see me. And I didn't want to intrude, but the God's honest truth was that I really wanted a chance to take him all in. He was the most beautiful boy I had ever seen. He still was. And I loved looking at him.

Dressed in new jeans, a light blue dress shirt and a red patterned tie, he stood at Heather's grave with his eyes closed. Although I didn't hear him, his lips were moving like he was praying. And in the faint breeze, Mother Nature was running her fingers through his dark hair like I wanted to. He looked tall and strong, the way he used to, but somewhere along the way, without me, he'd stepped into the shoes of a man.

And a part of me ached for those missing years.

When he was done praying, White Bird placed flowers on Heather's grave. And when he looked like he was ready to leave, I couldn't hide anymore. I'd learned to trust the coincidence of life's special moments. So when I stepped out from where I was hiding, I pulled my shoulders back, held my head up and took a deep breath.

It didn't take long for him to see me. He looked over his shoulder like he knew I would be there.

"Hey, Brenna."

The sound of his voice on the evening breeze sent chills down my arms.

"I heard you got released." I forced a smile. "I'm glad. I'm really happy for you."

When his expression softened, he smiled. He probably felt the awkwardness between us and he knew exactly how to melt it away. He did the one perfect thing that would make that happen.

He raised his hand to my face and touched a finger to my cheek. In one simple gesture, he'd put hot fudge on my vanilla sundae.

"I've missed you," he said. "We've got a lot of catching up to do."

I felt the sting of tears, but this time, I was happier than I'd ever been. And I always wanted to remember the moment when I knew my heart belonged to him.

"Yeah, we sure do." I smiled and after a moment, I looked down at Heather's grave. "It was nice of you to bring her flowers."

He stared down at her headstone.

"I don't remember much about that night, but I think she was really afraid. I still get flashes, you know?" He clenched his jaw. "I wish I could have helped her."

"Yeah, me, too."

He gave me a moment to put my lily on Heather's grave and I said my goodbye. I wasn't sure if the dead learned stuff, but I really hoped that dying had taught her something that would do her some good.

When I was done, I saw White Bird still had flowers in his hand.

"What are those for?" I asked.

"They're for your grandmother. You want to come with me?"

Okay, this time I totally cried. I nodded with tears running down my face and when I saw the sympathetic look in his eyes, I lost it. My choked sobs became laughter. I was being such a girl. White Bird chuckled, too, and when he pulled me to him, I heard the rumble of laughter in his chest and it made my ear tickle.

"Don't cry. I hate when you cry." He quit laughing and lifted my chin with his finger.

He kissed me as we stood between the rows of headstones and I never felt so alive. I tasted his lips and breathed in the warm scent of his skin with his arms wrapped around me.

After we pulled apart, I said, "Grams is gonna love you." And that made him grin.

We held hands as I took a very special young man to visit my grandmother. He was someone who had always accepted me for who I really was and who had taught me what it meant to forgive and to love.

As we walked to her grave, I pointed out my favorite markers and told him all the stories I had made up about the people buried here. Sharing my love for this cemetery with him felt like we'd both come home. And like the little shelter he'd built by the creek, this place had always been a refuge for me.

In the arms of stone angels, in the peaceful stillness of a cemetery, I had never been afraid. I thought it had been the stone angels that had given me strength, but I'd been wrong. It had taken a humble yet powerful Shaman from the enduring Euchee tribe to put a label on it and tell me about my "gift." The strength had always been inside me. I just needed to embrace it. Embrace *me,* for a change.

I'll always be grateful to Joe "Spirit Walker" Sunne and White Bird for opening my eyes to a whole other world that stretched farther than my mind, my heart and my eyes would ever see. Thanks to them, I felt like I fit in to something greater. And they helped me finish a poem that would stay with me forever.

Because finally and completely, I belonged.

I had a part in the universe and had staked out my place in the night sky with a destiny to follow. And my gift came with a responsibility that I couldn't ignore anymore. I vowed to leave my mark—even if I wasn't quite sure how I would do that yet. That would be *my* journey.

But White Bird had given me the greatest gift of all, when he taught me how to love.

acknowledgments

The inspiration for this book came from the love of reading that I share with my niece, Dana. She had just graduated high school and we became fast conspirators on the idea of a dark, edgy YA novel. Once we got together over the July Fourth weekend in 2009, while I was between book projects, we brainstormed the cast of characters and put faces to names. Dana helped me breathe life into this story. And she opened my eyes to see her in a different light, too. Just spending time with her was a gift. (Thanks, Dana, you little sweetie!)

And when it came time to flex my plot muscles, a librarian friend of mine and fellow Okie, Susan Johnson at the Sapulpa Library outside Tulsa, was there to help. Being in charge of the Native American Collection at her library, Susan had wanted me to set a book in Oklahoma with a Native American influence. And after a timely email to me, while an inkling of this book had started to gel, she made suggestions that triggered my thoughts on calling attention to the Euchee tribe that eventually gave birth to White Bird, my fictitious Native boy. Susan answered my many questions and sent helpful links and resources for me to read as I researched this novel. And after she read my first draft, she was excited enough to share it with her mother. That meant a lot to me. (Thanks so much for your generosity, Susan. You are truly amazing. The library and its patrons are lucky to have you.)

But when I was explaining the fictional teen boy in the story to Susan over the phone, she said, "I know that boy." I didn't have a name for my character at the time, but when Susan told me about her young friend, White Bird, I loved his name and asked him if I could use it for this book. He graciously said yes and even helped me research how to make a proper sweat lodge. After the real White Bird sent me a photo of his cute self, he became the real-life inspiration for one of my main characters. (Thanks, White Bird. You are a cool kid that anyone would be lucky to know.) I've since moved my home from Oklahoma to Texas, back to my old hometown, but my heart is still in Oklahoma with the many friends I made while I lived there. And because of Susan and the real White Bird, this book will always be a reminder of my Okie family.

To my new Harlequin family, I was born under a lucky star to get Mary-Theresa Hussey as my editor. She shared her amazing insights into this book and its characters, making it feel like a true collaboration—and she made it fun. That's a real gift. And since it takes a village to package a book and get it out there, thanks to everyone on the Harlequin team who left their mark on my stone angel.

To my angel in the trenches, my agent Meredith Bernstein, I want to say how grateful I am that you're in my life. And to the long-suffering folks that have put up with my quirky idiosyncrasies for a lifetime, I want to thank my family for their never-ending support and sense of humor—my parents, Kathryn and Ignacio, and my sibs Ed, Ignacio, Debbie and Denise.

And saving someone very special for last, I want to recognize the incredible support I get from my husband, John. He's my sounding board, my troubleshooter and my wingman, but most of all he's the cornerstone for every hero I will ever write.

"*THE IRON KING* IN MY FAVORITE YA BOOK OF 2010!"
—WickedLilPixie.com

"A MASTERFUL OPENING TO AN EPIC FANTASY SERIES."
—VampireBookClub.net

"A REAL PLEASURE TO READ. I RECOMMEND *(THE IRON KING)* TO TEEN AND ADULT READERS ALIKE."
—FantasyLiterature.com

www.EnterTheFaeryWorld.com

HTIRONFEY3BKTR1